# MURDER IN SCHWYZ

A THIRD-CULTURE KID MYSTERY

# MURDER IN SCHWYZ

# D-L NELSON

**FIVE STAR**
*A part of Gale, Cengage Learning*

GALE
CENGAGE Learning·

Farmington Hills, Mich • San Francisco • New York • Waterville, Maine
Meriden, Conn • Mason, Ohio • Chicago

GALE
CENGAGE Learning®

**LIBRARY OF CONGRESS CATALOGING-IN-PUBLICATION DATA**

Names: Nelson, D. L., 1942– author.
Title: Murder in Schwyz / D–L Nelson.
Description: First edition. | Waterville, Maine : Five Star Publishing, 2016. |
  Series: A Third-culture kid mystery
Identifiers: LCCN 2016007116 (print) | LCCN 2016011732 (ebook) | ISBN
  9781432832230 (hardcover) | ISBN 1432832239 (hardcover) | ISBN
  9781432832070 (ebook) | ISBN 1432832077 (ebook) | ISBN 9781432834869
  (ebook) | ISBN 143283486X
Subjects: LCSH: Murder--Investigation--Fiction. | BISAC: FICTION / Mystery &
  Detective / General. | GSAFD: Suspense fiction. | Mystery fiction.
Classification: LCC PS3614.E4455 M898 2016 (print) | LCC PS3614.E4455
  (ebook) | DDC 813/.6—dc23
LC record available at http://lccn.loc.gov/2016007116

First Edition. First Printing: September 2016
Find us on Facebook– https://www.facebook.com/FiveStarCengage
Visit our website– http://www.gale.cengage.com/fivestar/
Contact Five Star™ Publishing at FiveStar@cengage.com

Printed in the United States of America
1 2 3 4 5 6 7 20 19 18 17 16

To Barbara, a role model and friend for decades
1936–2014

# ACKNOWLEDGMENTS

As always, to Julia of the twenty pages for her editing and for her friendship. To my second reader, Rick Adams for asking "why?" To Christianne Lindemann for introducing me to Einsiedeln and being a friend. To Christian Berlan for the tour of the La Cure Gourmande cookie factory (www.la-cure -gourmande.com/) in Sète, France, as well as the boxes of cookies you gave us. Anyone who runs across one of their stores should go in and forget about your diet. To my grumpy and wonderful editor Gordon Aalborg, thank you and someday I'll explain about those chapter heads. To readers who are not aware of the banking problems of ex-pats, the financial and citizenship dilemmas described in the following story are very, very real and are causing havoc with the lives of U.S. citizens who live and work abroad.

# CHAPTER 1

*Day 1, Monday*

Annie Young-Perret dreamed of cookies and warring families, seeds planted by her agent about the assignment she would begin in the morning.

"You'll need the diplomatic skills of a Bishop Tutu, Nelson Mandela, and Mary Robinson all put together," Sharon had warned.

As Annie shook herself into wakefulness, she saw that the skylight above the bed was covered in white. For a minute she wasn't too sure where she was, but she knew it wasn't her own bed in Argelès-sur-mer, France. There was no skylight in her bedroom there, and snow happened maybe once a decade—and definitely not in October, climate change notwithstanding.

Her husband, Roger Perret, lay beside her, not snoring, but breathing heavily.

Their daughter, Sophie, now five months old, was in the travel cot at the bottom of the bed. She, too, was still asleep. Sophie was a baby who woke without crying. As she grew older, she'd poke her head up over the bumper guard and wait a reasonable amount of time before alerting her mother or father that food and a clean diaper should be considered in the immediate future.

For a moment Annie couldn't remember where she was. Then it came to her. She was in Einsiedeln, Switzerland, where she was about to start a new assignment as a translator of documents for Leckere Keks GMBH, commonly known as LK. She and her family were also house- and German-shepherd-sitting for her agent, Sharon Friedman, who had secured her this one-month assignment, although the final timing was fluid, depending on when she finished the project.

Sharon was on a month-long tour of Thailand, having told Annie that it had been two years since she had a vacation, and if she didn't get some time off she'd go "freaking mad."

Annie had worked as a freelancer with Sharon's computer consulting agency, ITAid, for years as a tech writer and translator using her Dutch, English, French, and German. It was her favorite agency because they'd always treated her fairly. Finding work as a tech writer or translator had always been easy for her because she was multilingual, thanks to a childhood of bouncing around Europe as her father had changed countries with each new job. Sharon had become a friend as well as an agent, and so the assignment and house-sitting combination was a boon to both of them.

As always, Roger had been a bit annoyed that she once again would be traveling from their Southern French home, but the reaction was mainly habit: this time he could travel with her rather than relying on communication by email and Skype, which had been the norm for the duration of her earlier stays away. He was newly retired as police chief, a situation forced by his recent heart attack.

His own daughter, Gaëlle, had just started university at Sup-Agro in Montpellier the month before. That she wanted to be a farmer was something Roger didn't understand but blamed on her boyfriend, whom he didn't like, despite Annie's having tried to convince him that the boy was perfect for Gaëlle. That the young couple was living together in Montpellier bothered him almost as much as the career choice. Still, with Gaëlle being away at school it left him free to accompany Annie rather than stay home and complain about whatever his first daughter was doing. He could complain in Einsiedeln as well.

They had arrived last night a half hour before dark.

Roger had to admit that the lake, which was a few minutes' walk from the house, and the nearby mountains were incredibly picturesque. Annie had always thought that if the western part of Switzerland was drop-dead beautiful, the eastern part—with its mountains, valleys and lakes—was paradise. She had friends, who had grown up in its valleys, tell her that they felt imprisoned by the mountains, but Annie felt when she was in any of the valleys that she could soar up the sides and continue heavenward. Thus, a chance to spend some time in Schwyz, one of the three original cantons forming the country, was an opportunity not to be missed.

Once Roger had agreed, they'd bundled baby Sophie and their German shepherd, Hannibal, into the car and had driven from Southern France, stopping in Geneva to have Annie's parents oooh and aaah over their only granddaughter.

Sharon had left a full refrigerator and a list of things to see and do in the area, including ski places and instructions on how to deal with Curie, her female German shepherd. Annie was happy that the Young-Perret's German shepherd, Hannibal, had come with them. The two dogs had circled each other, sniffed butts, and decided that not only could they coexist, they might enjoy each other's company.

Roger turned over in bed, opened his eyes, then sat up fast, staring at the skylight. "My God, it's snow! It's only October, for God's sake."

"We're in the Alps." Annie thought it a bit early in the season too, but she'd spent enough time in Switzerland, although in the milder climate of Geneva, to know that Mark Twain's saying about New England weather—if you don't like it, wait a minute—applied to Switzerland as a whole.

She knew average snowfall in November could run up to a foot in this part of the country, but Roger was right: this was early. Still, she had packed warm clothes for them all just in case.

Annie went downstairs to let the dogs out. Hannibal, who had never seen snow, put one paw out and pulled it back, but his desire to follow Curie was greater than his doubts. Instead of immediately asking to come back, the two animals began rolling in the snow and tossing it in the air with their noses.

Annie prepared Sophie's oatmeal and bottle then brewed a pot of tea for herself and her husband.

Today would be the first day on the new assignment and she was more nervous than normal before starting a job, based on Sharon's repeated warning that the two owners of the family-owned firm were at war. "I don't use the word loosely," Sharon had said at least three times. "The atmosphere is toxic because the brother, Fritz Bircher, wants to sell the business to an international company. His sister is dead set against it."

Annie thought of the lucrative paycheck and accepted the assignment despite the warnings. She'd worked in toxic company environments before, and she wouldn't be there that long. She could put up with almost anything short-term.

Sharon had explained that the sister, Petra Ritzman, had plans to expand the cookie-making business without going public. It was Petra who wanted Annie to write in German, and translate into French and English, a history of the company since its founding in the 1800s to the present.

Petra's goal, Sharon had said, was to create a mystique about the company and market the cookies as the champagne or foie gras of cookies throughout Europe then into the States, although no specific marketing plans had been created as yet.

Brother Fritz's desire to sell the company to an international conglomerate was far more advanced, despite Petra's plans to stop him.

A Skype interview conducted before she came for the job had left Annie with the idea that she could be friends with Petra, but at the same time she didn't want to be automatically biased against Fritz based on the rumors from Sharon. In principle, Annie thought small companies were better than large ones to work for, having done many assignments for both types. Still, she was feeling jumpier than most of her first days anywhere.

Roger interrupted her worrying as he walked downstairs carrying Sophie. Annie pulled the bottle out of the warm water and handed it to her husband. Sophie reached up and put her hands on it while Roger cuddled her.

"Nervous?" he asked.

"The first day anywhere is strange," Annie said. "Once I learn where the toilet and tea kettle are, it will be a bit better."

They looked out the window at the snow and the dogs playing as Sophie sucked on her bottle. Roger removed it from her mouth and began spooning in the oatmeal that Annie had put in front of him.

"Are you worried about the roads?" Roger asked. "I can drive you."

Annie had never liked driving and had never had a car of her own, preferring to walk or take public transportation. On a good day, the cookie factory, which was less than a mile, would make a wonderful walk. "Not really necessary. What I'm more worried about is the dynamic between the brother and sister."

"You'll be fine," Roger said.

Annie wasn't as sure.

# CHAPTER 2

*Day 1, Monday*

As a last attempt to get his wife to change her mind about a ride to the cookie factory, Roger said, "You could be killed."

Annie put on her boots and shook her head. Before his heart attack he'd only worried about her when she was doing something that he deemed "stupid," such as getting involved directly or indirectly in murder investigations—as had happened too many times before.

Since his heart attack he was convinced that she'd fall, get sick, or have some other unknown and dire thing happen to her. Annie chalked up the new attitude to his being afraid not only about losing her but also, that if she died, he'd have to raise Sophie himself. Although he'd done a good job being a single father to his daughter, Gaëlle, Annie knew that worry about his own health made him more concerned about the future than he had ever been before he'd collapsed and had been rushed to the hospital and gone through a bypass.

Sophie watched her parents from her chair. A bit of red frizz was appearing on her little bald head, a preview that she would have the same hair color as her mother. However, there wasn't enough to determine if it would fall in uncontrollable ringlets the way Annie's did.

The dogs, still damp from their romp in the snow, lay in front of the wood-burning stove where Roger had started a fire.

Outside, the lake was almost invisible through the snow curtain.

"There are sidewalks. I'll be careful." This was so strange for Annie. On her other assignments before Sophie was born, her life became one hundred percent her own, unlike when she was in Argelès. This assignment, the first since the birth of her daughter, made her import her Argelès life with her rather than escape from it. She wasn't sure she didn't prefer her freedom as long as it was temporary.

Not that she would have made Sophie go away. From the second they had laid the baby on her chest, skin to skin, and her daughter had found her way to a nipple, much like a newborn calf seeking the mother cow's teat, Annie had never known such overwhelming love. Every cell in her body adored her daughter.

"A car can skid into you," Roger said as Annie zipped up her windbreaker.

"And they can skid into me if I'm driving, too."

"But you'll have metal around you."

Annie pulled on her gloves and kissed her husband on the cheek. "It's not that far. I'll text you when I get there so you won't worry all day."

Outside, she reveled in the snow hitting her cheeks. She was definitely a winter person, loving snuggling into heavy clothes and having her cheeks turn red from the wind. Roger, after years of living in Paris, reveled in the warmer climate of Southern France. However, Annie couldn't imagine being based anywhere else once she'd found the seacoast town.

For years she'd felt as if she hadn't belonged anywhere as her parents moved from Massachusetts to the Netherlands, then to Germany, and finally to Switzerland. She had adjusted each time, but always felt that she was an outsider looking in. Only when she learned that there was a term for children raised outside their parents' country—they were called "third-culture kids"—and that the sense of not belonging was normal, did she begin to think of her childhood as enriching rather than something about which to complain.

The sidewalks had been swept clean at least once. As she approached the center of Einsiedeln she gave a deep sigh at the beauty of a large beige-gray stone Abbey in the falling snow. Across the street was the *Rathaus* with its dark wood half timbers against the white stucco. Despite it being only late October she felt she was walking through a Christmas card. A few notes from "Silent Night" wafted through her mind until she banished them.

The cookie factory was on the other side of the small town center in an old but well-kept white, ornately decorated typical Germanic-style building. The smell of baking cookies that floated from the building into the crisp air reminded Annie of coming home from school on afternoons when her mother her mother would be pulling chocolate chip or gingerbread cookies from the oven. Not that it was a daily occurrence by any means, but the times it happened remained in her database filed under great memories.

Annie's mother, Susan Young, was an artist. Although she couldn't, technically, be employed in the countries where she was the accompanying spouse, she used the time to perfect her art, and over the years she had had reasonable success selling her paintings, sculptures, and jewelry. But periodically she'd go on a domestic craze. Annie was still waiting for a similar craze to hit her. So far it hadn't happened.

Since Sophie had been born, Annie spent much more time thinking about her mother's life than she ever had before, and with a greater appreciation for the sacrifices her mother had made as she was yanked from place to place. With each announcement of her father's latest move, she'd sigh, "Not again," get out the packing crates, say good-bye to the friends she'd made, learn yet another language, and begin the task of putting down new roots.

The relatively quick adjustment to new situations, Annie had recently decided, was one reason she could take varied assignments in different places. She'd developed a settling-in routine, be it for two weeks or two months. It also allowed her to go back to Roger and her village, for she now thought of Argelès as her village.

Inside the factory, Annie found the executive suite: "executive" was perhaps too elevated a word for the corridor, which had closed wooden doors on each side and resembled the hallway of a 1930s American school building.

A receptionist sat at the entrance to the hall. The wood for her plebian, old-fashioned desk was oak which hadn't been a tree for at least a century, a stark contrast to the modern computer on one side. The floors of the executive corridor were polished parquet: the ancient walls were painted a soft yellow, lifting the place from dreary into almost warm.

The receptionist pointed Annie down the corridor with its five shut doors. The titles of those who occupied the offices behind the first three doors were engraved on the milk-colored opaque glass in black letters: Accounting, Marketing, IT— certainly not a huge management staff.

Two final doors bore the names Fritz Bircher and Petra Ritzman, and each was labeled with their common title, "Codirector."

Between the two final doors were portraits of the different family members who had run the factory since its founding. On the left were photographs of the factory, cookies, machinery, and recipes. The latter surprised Annie. She wondered if revealing recipes wouldn't give the competition a chance to steal any company secrets. When she looked closer, she saw that the recipes had ingredient quantities for a family, not for mass production.

Annie opened the door with Petra Ritzman's name to see a secretary with another old-fashioned desk and another modern computer. One window looked out on the back of the grounds of the Abbey under its blanket of snow.

The secretary was an older woman, probably in her late forties, although Annie long ago had learned not to judge age. A fifty-year-old woman could look like she was in her late thirties and vice versa.

It wasn't the secretary, though, that caught Annie's attention. It was the hollering behind the door: a man and a woman's voices almost drowned out the soft classical music playing on a radio sitting on the secretary's desk. The secretary turned up the volume, which, if it were to hide the argument, did little to muffle the yelling.

Annie could not understand one word that they were saying. She'd long ago learned that Swiss German was not like the German *Schwäbish* dialect she'd learned when she lived in Stuttgart. Even that was closer to the *Hochdeutsch* than what she was hearing coming from the office.

She shouldn't have been surprised. Each Swiss valley had a different dialect, so people in the Canton of Schwyz spoke very differently from those in the Canton of Bern.

The door opened. A man stomped past her and the secretary, slamming the door behind him. He moved so fast Annie would not have been able to tell his age or what he looked like had she been called on to identify him in a police lineup.

A woman followed: she was not much over five feet, had dark hair, and was dressed in creased black slacks with a black turtleneck sweater that set off her black geometric-cut hair. Around her neck she wore a red-fringed scarf. Large red hoops dangled from her ears.

Her trajectory had seemed to be to follow the man, until she saw Annie. "You must be Frau Young-Perret. I'm Frau Ritzman." Her English carried a British accent.

Annie stood and held out her hand.

Frau Ritzman's handshake was strong but not overbearing.

"Guilty," Annie said.

"Sorry for the unpleasant introduction to the company. That was my brother and codirector. This is probably not the best time to introduce you."

"Family-run businesses have their own dynamics," Annie said.

"Frau Küper will get you something warm to drink. What would you like: *Kaffee, Tee, oder heiße Schokolade?*"

Annie managed to catch that she used the formal *sie* not the informal *du* with the secretary. Annie adjusted her earlier thoughts made during the Skype interview about possible friendship. She now assumed at no point would she and this woman ever be on even a first-name basis, much less using *du.*

Annie selected the hot chocolate, which was brought in a porcelain pot decorated with violets on a wooden tray with two square matching cups and saucers. A plate with assorted cookies covered with a linen white napkin was to one side of the tray.

The secretary poured the hot chocolate and left the women sitting in Petra Ritzman's office. It too had utilitarian oak furniture from another century, maybe even a couple of centuries back, but the computer equipment was right up to date. The walls were painted a light green, and heavy curtains on the two windows were a forest green. Gold leaf marked the moldings on the doors. A bookcase was filled with books and folders. Photos on the second from the top shelf were of three children at various stages of development. Annie assumed they were Petra Ritzman's children, but she didn't feel comfortable asking.

The hot chocolate was some of the best that Annie had ever tasted and she'd drunk a lot, which she told Frau Ritzman.

"We are very fussy about what chocolate we buy. This is part of a new line of hot chocolate we want to start offering both in gift packs with cookies and on its own. What do you think of the cookies?"

Annie bit into one, still warm and gingery. "Delicious." Annie knew of the LK brand although it was carried more in the German-speaking part of Switzerland than the French-speaking cantons. The quality was far higher than many of the brands produced by the big companies. In the French section LK cookies were served in the higher-class hotels along with coffee.

"You're not just saying that?"

"I speak my mind."

When Frau Ritzman smiled, Annie noticed she had dimples. "Where am I to work and exactly what do you want me to do?"

Unlike previous assignments there had been no in-person interview. Sharon had sold Frau Ritzman on samples of the tech writing Annie had done for other companies as well as the two books Annie had written—one was about a survivor of a Nazi concentration camp and the other about an eighth-century English saint. There had also been three recommendations from former clients.

Her agent had said that Frau Ritzman made fast decisions. Annie's start date had been postponed first because of Sophie's birth and then secondly because Ritzman had asked for a delay—for a reason Annie didn't know, but it hadn't mattered to her because the later start date worked well with her own plans.

"First let me give you a tour of the bakery. I like calling it a bakery—not a factory nor a plant. Finish your cookies and chocolate first."

# CHAPTER 3
# 1879

## THOMAS BIRCHER'S OATMEAL MOLASSES BREAD

**Ingredients:**
4 cups boiling milk
2 cups rolled oats
2 tablespoons lard
2/3 cup molasses
1 tablespoon salt
1 cake compressed yeast
1/2 cup lukewarm water
9–10 cups flour sifted

**Directions:**
Preheat oven to 350°F/176°C.

Pour boiling milk over the rolled oats and lard, cover, and let stand an hour.

Add molasses, salt, and yeast cake (dissolved in lukewarm water).

Add flour, gradually.

Let rise until double, cut down, and shape into loaves. Let rise again.

Press into buttered bread tins.

Let rise again.

Bake 40–50 minutes.

Makes four loaves.

Thomas Bircher would only admit to himself that he really didn't like his son.

He sat at his desk in his study, which also served as his office, located just off the entrance of his two-story, six-bedroom house. The location was perfect, just outside the town square of Einsiedeln. In front of him was his cash box, divided into sections for the bronze *Rappen* and the silver francs of different denominations, the payments from his clients for whom he wrote wills and contracts and to whom he gave legal advice.

He wished someone could give him advice on how he could deal with the boy, the youngest of his four children. He'd wanted a son from the beginning to follow him into his practice.

When Lina was born twenty years ago, he had not been all that disappointed. After all, his wife had come from a family where there were many children of both sexes. Lina was now a wife and had just given birth to her first child, another girl. What was wrong with these women that they couldn't produce sons? All the other lawyers he knew had wives that spit out sons almost annually.

Nora, born a year after Lina, was about to be married. Then Vreni came a year after that. Three years went by without any more babies because his wife's health would not support another pregnancy. Finally, finally, finally Hans-Rudi was born. He then had hoped for more sons, but only miscarriages followed until they had given up.

A knock at the door caused Thomas to start. "Enter."

The maid brought in his lunch tray and sat it on the round table to the left of his desk where he sat with clients. He felt that his large wooden desk with its carved deer and trees was too much of a barrier when people needed to talk with him about personal affairs. At the small table he could reach over and touch a hand in sympathy when necessary, yet it was large enough to hold whatever paperwork needed to be examined.

Thomas made it a point to never join the family at lunch. They ate breakfast and dinner together. That was enough. Had his office been outside the home he would not have come home for the noon meal, so why should he interrupt his schedule just because he was a few steps from the dinner table?

His children knew never to disturb him, but the maid had permission to knock to bring his lunch or a client who arrived unexpectedly. However, almost all his clients made appointments in advance. The few that didn't, he made wait—on general principles, even if he were not in the middle of something complicated. It established a sense of his importance as well as his largess by making time for the person doing the interrupting.

Thomas insisted that there be a firm routine in his life, his work, and in his household.

"Do you want me to light the lamp?" the maid asked. Maria had been with the family for over five years. She was good at her job, but Thomas knew she was thinking of marriage, which would mean she'd have babies and quit her post.

The cook had been with them nineteen years. She was a widow, who had claimed that she never intended to remarry, when he had interviewed her. That he would not have to take the time to find yet another cook anywhere in the near or distant future was the primary reason he had hired her. Luckily she was not only a good cook, but also one who wasted nothing. More than once he'd been in the kitchen as she was turning cake batter into a pan and the bowl when she finished looked as if it had been washed. In the beginning he had her discuss menus with him, making sure that all the leftovers were used. Only when he was certain that she was being as economical with his supplies as was possible did he turn the cook's supervision over to his wife.

What was bothering him now was the amount of time Hans-Rudi spent in the kitchen, especially when Maria was baking. Once he'd found the boy helping mix batter for something or other. He had put a stop to that behavior immediately.

"Please," he told the maid as he cleared the table of mail and the few papers that he had yet to file. At one point he had tried having secretaries, but no one was as organized as he wanted them to be.

The November day had become grayer with the promise of snow hanging heavily in the air. He was glad that he'd gone out this morning for his routine half-hour walk so that he could stay in his office for the rest of the day. Not commuting, even to the village center, was a time-saver. He checked to see if the snow had started by looking though the two floor-to-ceiling windows hidden behind sheer curtains and flanked with heavy, almost black-blue drapes.

Thomas did not want people to see in from the street. His clients deserved privacy, although he had no control should some passerby notice a person coming or leaving his front door. At one point he had debated having a side entrance put in, but then people still might be glimpsed going down the path, and he felt that it wasn't right to have his clients go to the back like tradesmen did.

His wife accused him of wanting to live like a mole in his office. He would never admit how accurate she was, especially in the winter. If he started work early and ended late, he might never see the sun except for that short walk he took every day at three in the afternoon. Even moles peeked out of their burrows once a day.

In late spring, early summer, and early fall, it was different—the days were longer, and he would take his walk after dinner but before sunset, his reward for finishing his tasks.

The lunch on the tray was hidden by a white, starched, and pressed linen napkin. Whisking it away, Thomas saw beet soup in a blue porcelain bowl. On a nearby plate was a slice of heavy cereal bread. He wondered where the cereal had come from. Over the past decade cheap cereals from Eastern Europe had flooded the local market, hurting local farmers.

He'd helped those with farms outside of Einsiedeln to create a dairy cooperative that sold cheese locally to replace the loss of income when they could no longer sell their cereals. Thomas had made many trips with locals to look at chocolate markets. The bonbons were beginning to be a good export, but so far the farmers couldn't imagine how that would be worth their time, since the cocoa had to be imported.

Outside the office he heard steps running down the stairs. He debated getting up to yell at Hans-Rudi, the only person to ever run in the house.

The boy was a total disaster. His tutor said that he had no interest in German, French, Latin, history, mathematics, or geography—in other words, nothing. As for sports, the boy was beyond clumsy, which could not be attributed only to his rapid recent growth. Thomas remembered at Hans-Rudi's age how he was always tripping over his own feet, but Hans-Rudi never been able to do anything gracefully.

The beet soup was excellent, just the right combination of beets, meat, and onions. Thomas heard the front door slam. Damn that boy, why couldn't he just shut the door like normal people?

Standing up from where he was sitting, Thomas peered through the drapes. A few snowflakes had started. His son crossed the street and entered the *Bäckerei*. Thomas looked at his pocket watch: 12:17. The *Bäckerei* closed at noon and reopened at three, giving the bakers a chance to have their own lunch before starting the next round of baking for housewives shopping for the evening meal.

Why wasn't Hans-Rudi eating lunch with his mother, Vreni, and Nora? No discipline, that one. Thomas wondered why Hans-Rudi couldn't be like the sons of his friends, boys who worked hard and went on to study medicine or law at the University of Zurich, something Hans-Rudi would be incapable of doing.

He found it strange that the forty-six-year-old university had been founded by the state and not the church, but already it was winning a reputation for its academics—not that it made any difference to his family.

If his disappointment in his son's lack of educational progress was great, he was at least grateful that he wasn't his friend Herbert whose daughter was studying medicine at the university. Imagine a woman doctor. Thomas shuddered. Who would ever trust her? He couldn't imagine himself exposing his body, no matter how sick he was, to a strange woman.

His son had not come out of the *Bäckerei*. What on earth could the lad be doing? He hoped he wasn't bothering the baker, who was a good client.

Hans-Rudi Bircher had flour halfway up his arms as Kurt Schelling, the baker, watched. "Do you feel the difference in the mixture?"

The dough's texture had changed from a sticky, soft mass to something almost elastic. Hans-Rudi nodded as Herr Schelling reached into the bowl, pulled out a small piece, and tasted it— indicating with his hand motion that Hans-Rudi should do the same. "Taste the yeast?"

The dough was smaller than the usual amount that Schelling

made, but if the boy were to learn, he needed to start with the basics. "I wish you would let me talk to your father about becoming my apprentice."

Hans-Rudi figured that the idea of a Bircher being a baker would take away any chance of his father ever having a good thought about him. Bircher men became lawyers, doctors, and an occasional architect or priest but never, ever, someone who worked with their hands. Those people were clients, not friends, not family members, not even neighbors, because although the clients earned their living at these trades, none of them would earn the money needed to pay for one of the large houses on his street.

Ever since he was a little boy, when his mother or the cook went into the *Bäckerei,* Hans-Rudi had loved the idea of baking. The smells of yeast and hot sugar were better than the violet-smelling perfume that his father gave his mother for Christmas. She only wore it when they went out for some special event.

Frau Schelling appeared at the doorway that led to the upstairs where the baker, his wife, and three children lived. "I've fried up some dough and we'll put honey and butter on it for lunch," she said.

Hans-Rudi shaped the bread into four loaves, put them in the pans, and covered them with a linen cloth. He followed the baker and his wife upstairs.

Somehow, he was determined to find a way to be a baker. He couldn't imagine doing anything else.

Maybe Herr Schelling would take him on as an apprentice and let him live in his attic, where the last apprentice had lived before moving to Bern, where he'd set up his own *Bäckerei.*

His own *Bäckerei:* that was and would be his dream today and tomorrow.

# CHAPTER 4

*Day 1, Monday*

The factory tour intrigued Annie. It was set up like no other factory she had ever seen. Except for the ultramodern equipment and the almost surgery-like white coats, booties, and shower caps worn by the employees, it felt like she'd stepped back into the nineteenth century.

"You'll notice that there are no long production lines," Petra said as they came off the third floor. As on the first and second floors, all the equipment had been set up in small production units.

"I've divided my employees into teams. They decide what they do and are responsible for all levels from creating the recipes through sales and delivery. Of course, they have the marketing manager at their disposal to help them. They can switch around roles, although I've discovered those who do sales tend to stay selling, but even then we insist that they spend some time in production so they don't make promises they are unable to keep. Bonuses are based on how well the entire floor does."

"Does that mean they all have the same salary?"

"Yes and no." Petra Ritzman avoided the subject. "They get a chance to create new recipes, but I told you that." Petra picked up a cookie still warm from the upright oven, which looked more like a many-shelved armoire. She broke it in two and gave one half to Annie.

She led Annie to the elevator, an old-fashioned wire cage, to take her to the sixth floor of the building—more an attic, with shelves and shelves of books, ledgers, photographs, journals, file cabinets, and newspaper clippings in large scrapbooks. At that point, Annie wasn't sure what all else was there. She could see outside through the floor-to-ceiling windows that the snow was still falling.

From all that was around and the age of the material, cobwebs and dust should have been blanketing the room. It was spotless.

Frau Ritzman inhaled and spoke so fast that Annie had to struggle to keep up with the dialect. She wondered why the woman had switched back to German, but if the client were more comfortable in her mother tongue, so be it. "I've had it cleaned and have set up this desk and laptop for you to use. There's a phone, so if you need anything let me know. My extension is two. Oh, and there's a list of emails and other information you'll need in the top right hand drawer of your desk."

"*Danke.*"

"*Bitte.* We put out an announcement of who you were and what you'd be doing so you won't have to explain over and over. Now, I really have to get back to my office."

Frau Ritzman vanished, and "vanished" was the correct word. It was almost like one of those old episodes from the sixties TV show *Bewitched,* where the good witch Samantha twitched her nose and was gone. Annie had been about to ask several questions about expectations, deadlines, but Frau Ritzman must have used a stairway that Annie had not noticed before. For the brother and sister, leaving fast must be a family talent, she thought to herself.

For a few minutes she wasn't sure where to start, although she knew exactly what was expected of her. Then she decided she needed to look more into what was there, and to do that she would begin at the right of the room and work her way around. Once she had identified what information was available, she could decide what to present as a project plan. What she didn't want was to produce a book only to be told that it in no way bore any relationship to what Frau Ritzman wanted.

First she needed to check out computer access: she opened the drawer where she found an envelope with an old-fashioned seal and the company logo pressed into the wax. Her name was on the front in hand lettering done by a person with exquisite penmanship.

When she broke the seal, she saw a password on a sheet of paper along with a message that she'd been set up with her own intercompany email in case she needed to contact any employee or use the Internet as part of her research.

The laptop was a Swiss keyboard—fine—she could adjust to the QWERTZ after the French keyboard AZERTY she'd been using at home. It would only take her a couple of hours to adjust. At one place she worked she went from the QWERTZ and AZERTY to the American QWERTY several times a day. She must remember that she needed to hit the cap key for numbers: some of the letters were in different places and the punctuation remained. At least she had the accents and umlauts which she would need.

Her name had been programmed in, with a place for the password. Despite her assurance of being able to adjust to the different keyboard, she mistyped her password the first time she tried to log on.

When she went into Word, a list of documents appeared on her screen. One was titled "Directions for Annie Young-Perret in the Preparation of the History of LK 1890s to the Present." Annie already knew she was to begin with Hans-Rudi Bircher, the founder. The book had to be interesting, Frau Ritzman had stressed over and over in the interview. It should read more like a saga than a history book. The same goal was emphasized in the document.

Annie skimmed the instructions. The first one said that the cabinet between the windows contained the journals of the different people who headed the company and their wives. Also in the cabinet were the financial records and minutes from meetings. An asterisk added this note: "Frau Ritzman also kept a journal until she took over as codirector, but her brother, Fritz Bircher, had written nothing at all."

The personal information from the journals, the instructions read, needed to be balanced with business information from the ledgers. At that Annie shuddered. If there were a disease called Number Aversion Syndrome, she would have been diagnosed with it.

She walked to the window and looked down. She could see the parking lot. A man she thought was Petra Ritzman's brother stomped to the only luxury car in the parking lot, which was otherwise filled with sturdy and less flashy cars. He skidded out of the parking lot and turned onto the street much too fast.

She hoped that the brother-sister feud would not hamper her project, but it was more likely that she might be caught up in it.

Leaving the window, she started dipping into the different materials to plan her methods. In one file cabinet she found a wooden box with the initials AB burned into the word in a Gothic style of lettering. She opened it up to find recipe cards for cookies in a handwriting that was delicate and very clear.

# CHAPTER 5

At noon, Annie headed for the cafeteria. Frau Ritzman had told her that whenever she needed a break, she should take it, including her lunch when she was hungry. "Research and writing isn't like working on an assembly line," the woman had said.

Annie did not have to point out that she was being given a weekly consulting fee, not an hourly rate. Her contract stipulated that within one month she would deliver the German version. She would then have a fixed rate to give the French and English. It was her choice on how much she could get done in the month she would be in Einsiedeln.

The pay was going to be good. Unlike many well-defined projects, she would discover what would work best as she went along.

An employee information booklet told Annie that about two hundred people worked on the production line. Not all were full-time. Many mothers left for a two-hour lunch break when their children came home from school, or they job-shared. However, in a town of just under fifteen thousand people, an employer of two hundred was substantial, she thought as she delved into the first documents about Hans-Rudi Bircher, born 1862 and founder of the firm. There was a hodgepodge of letters by his parents, a birth announcement, school report cards, and scraps of paper. There were even old food-shopping lists.

For a moment Annie thought of all the technical manuals she'd written about hitting this or that key, inserting a part A

33

into a part B. This was her reward: ferreting out lives from bits and pieces. Only when her stomach told her she was hungry did she realize that three hours had passed.

The basement cafeteria featured a salad bar and a serving station with three hot dishes: salmon and vegetables, spaghetti Bolognese and *Rösti*, the Swiss version of hash browns topped with an egg.

Annie saw the prices were lower than an equivalent *Tagesmenu* at a restaurant. Baskets of broken or less-than-perfect cookies were offered free along with other to-pay-for desserts.

The physical ambiance was that of a ski lodge, with wide wooden board walls and tables seating either four or eight, with red-checkered tablecloths. The same checked material was used for the curtains that were small and high up. Annie noticed some legs walking by and she guessed that the windows were looking out on the parking lot, but her sense of direction was not good enough for her to have bet on it.

She took her tray with the spaghetti and went to an empty table. Just as she was grating cheese with the miniature grater that the cashier had given her, a voice behind her said in English, "May I join you? Eating alone isn't much fun, and being the new kid on the corner isn't much fun either."

Although she wanted to be alone to think about all she'd discovered this morning and what words she would write to describe how Hans-Rudi was a disappointment to his lawyer father, she was so surprised by the accent where the *r*'s sounded like *h*'s that she nodded.

The man was about her age and had wavy brown hair, brown eyes, and a grin. "Brett Windsor." He put down his tray and stuck out his hand. "Welcome to the wonderful world of Cookieland."

He had a double order of the *rösti*, a heaping plate of salad, at least ten half cookies of various types, and a cup of coffee.

The tray was invisible under the food. Annie wanted to ask if he had a tapeworm, because if that was how he ate regularly, he was so thin it was unfair to all chubby people anywhere in the world. "Is that a Boston accent?"

"Raised in Waltham part of my life," Brett said.

"And I lived in Stow until I was eight."

"We were neighbors." Brett had a smile that seemed to have limits, but Annie couldn't quite figure out why she thought that.

"May I ask what you're doing here?" Annie had been so trained by one of her Brit friends to ask if she could ask, as a matter of politeness, that it had become automatic.

"My dad worked in Maynard for Digital."

"So did mine."

"He was also assigned to the Zurich office for a number of years when I was a teenager." He began to eat—that is, shovel his meal into his mouth. She noticed that he used American table manners and kept his left hand in his lap and used only his right hand for his fork.

He took a swig of coffee. "I know what you're doing here, but do you want to know what I'm doing here?"

She nodded.

"I'm head of marketing. We—the 'we' being myself and a couple of others—work with the teams who come up with ideas but haven't got the skills to execute them."

"Like?"

"Graphic artist, copywriter. I want to get a social media expert on staff, but so far no one is buying. Maybe you can push the idea, since you're on Dame Petra's team."

"Interesting."

"What is? Everyone is responsible for everything and they decide the work roster each week. I'd say no one ever leaves the company because the freedom they have to define their own work, but, in general, the Swiss tend not to change jobs like we Americans do. Then again, it is hard to find a company that pays better in the area as well." He shoveled more food. "It will be a shock to everyone if Little Brother Fritz wins the battle."

"What battle?" Although she knew about the differences of opinion between brother and sister, pretending she didn't might gain her more information. She doubted that Petra Ritzman would want it in the family history, which despite the talk about honesty must have certain puff-piece elements.

"Let's say the political battle between the siblings for control. If this were the Middle Ages, you'd have a sister and brother getting knights to go to war."

"But it's modern times."

"True," Brett said. "The hatred is the same. Instead of wearing armor and going after each other with swords and spears, they fight with stock and lawyers."

"Less bloodshed." Annie loved analogies.

"For the moment, but if Petra thought she could win, you'd see her lifted on horseback and she'd come flying across the battlefield." He wiped his mouth. "Bringing it into today's terms, Little Brother came into the business officially about five years ago, unofficially longer, by which time Big Sister had totally changed the plant around to her system. He'd gone to business school, Harvard, kicking and screaming at the time because he's lazy or least he was through most of his childhood. Maybe there was some kind of Damascus Road conversion there, because suddenly he's all into numbers, maximum production, etcetera. He's definitely into money and show."

Annie thought about the what-might-have-been-a-Ferrari that looked out of place with all the more utilitarian cars in the parking lot.

"Now he wants to sell. Some venture vulture wants to buy the company, although no one knows for certain which one."

"And Big Sis doesn't want to sell." Annie didn't feel all that comfortable calling Frau Ritzman "Big Sis," considering she was at least six inches taller than the codirector, but she wanted to match Brett's tone.

More food went into Brett's mouth. After he swallowed, he said, "You got it in one. She feels that the company makes a good profit, and that the factory benefits its workers and its customers. She's making enough. She lives in the old family mansion. Her idea of expansion is to get a luxury product throughout Europe instead of just in the cantons, but to do it as private company."

"A Rolex of cookies."

Brett had to cover his mouth so he wouldn't spit out food when he laughed. This time he pointed his finger at her when he nodded.

"You should be a copywriter. The workers also own a percentage of the company. We, and I include myself, haven't been told enough about it . . . anyway, it's going to get a lot worse fast."

Annie wasn't sure if he was obnoxious or just very un-Swiss in his behavior. "Why?"

"The annual general meeting is in a few weeks. That will be when more shit hits the fan. Both of them are plotting how to beat the other."

With luck, I'll be long gone with the pay in my pocket, Annie thought. "How long have you worked here?"

"About five years. I was brought on board to try to help create new brands working with the different teams. My wife grew up here, but we met at Boston University where she was doing an exchange. I was sent back to the States for college. I'd lost my C permit by then. She wanted to come home. Couldn't imagine living in the good ole US of A. *Voilà*—it all came together."

That he'd thrown in a French term amused Annie but not

enough to ask about his other languages. She was more interested in the human behavior behind the creation and selling of products. "And the new brands?"

"We've done some of that, as I've said, but nothing has stuck. One of the problems with working with group consensus is getting that consensus. And Petra keeps changing her mind, as well." He waved his fork in the air as he talked after swallowing a large amount of potato. "I try to train the workers in marketing, but most of them don't think that way, silk purses, pig's ears, and all that . . ." More eating. "Not that they aren't good people. Salt of the earth as they say. But how much imagination does salt have?"

Annie wasn't sure how to answer Mr. Master of Run-On Sentences. She ate the last mouthful of her pasta.

"Here, have a cookie." Brett held out what looked like half a flower. "Take it. I know what your project is, and you won't be able to do it if you don't know what the product tastes like. In any case, with the warfare going on between brother and sister, who knows what will happen."

Annie never needed an excuse to eat a cookie. She took it, but she was wondering if maybe she should have said no to the project. Nah . . . this kind of project should be fun. All she had to do was *not* to get involved in office politics.

# CHAPTER 6
# 1910

## CARAWAY COOKIES

**Ingredients:**
1 cup butter
2 cups sugar
2 eggs beaten slightly
1 cup sour cream
1 teaspoon soda
1/2 teaspoon salt
About 4 cups flour or enough to roll as soft as possible
3/4 teaspoon caraway seeds

**Directions:**
Preheat oven to 375°F/190°C.

Mix sugar and butter, add eggs and cream and salt.

Sift flour and soda and add gradually.

Add caraway seeds and chill.

Roll to 1/8-inch thickness and cut into squares.

Bake for about 8 minutes.

Makes 8 dozen.

Annabel Bircher first thought when the clerk from the bakery had stood in the doorway, looking at the ground as he told her of the sudden death of her father-in-law, Hans-Rudi, it was almost a lucky event. Well not lucky for him, by any means, but for her. She chastised herself almost at the same moment for such thoughts, for she truly liked her in-laws, sometimes more than she liked her own husband.

The clerk had said that Hans-Rudi had been trying one of those newfangled machines that mixed the dough for his bread, for his latest experiment using chestnut flour that he had had ground by the local mill, when he pressed his arm to his chest and keeled over.

"I thought it better if you told Frau Bircher . . . death announced by an employee . . . in case of shock . . . needs a family member . . ."

Annabel had put on her hat and coat and rushed to her mother-in-law's. Dieter's parents lived two doors away.

Time moved at a slower pace over the next few hours. Herr Doctor arrived, holding his hat in his hand and saying it must have been a massive heart attack.

A heart attack at forty-six—almost forty-seven. He had been one month short of his birthday.

Annabel still thought that at least for her the death was lucky, because she'd just spent a fortune on a new suit. The jacket came down to her hips and mink trimmed the sleeves. There were times she felt she had to live up to her husband's and father's image of her as an irresponsible woman, but the ensuing tension from her spending sprees was often not worth the beauty of whatever she'd bought.

She chided herself while she waited for her husband to rush back from the International Socialist Conference in Bern. Between the conference and the funeral expenses, she hoped her husband would never realize what she'd spent. He would be more upset that his last words with his father had been screamed, words that could never be taken back, no matter how sincere they were.

Her father-in-law had been furious at his son for going to the conference. Dieter's argument that there would be representatives from at least twenty countries and probably more had not impressed Hans-Rudi at all. "There's enough work to do with the business," was her father-in-law's mantra. And that's all the man was, she thought, a baker not a human. His interests were focused on how he could improve his bread and how he could get the hotels, hospitals, and grocers in the area to buy his products in bulk.

About the only one who could ever catch his attention was Annabel herself, and that was because she would listen to his stories about the price of flour, the problem with an employee, the way he would convince a person to buy more and more.

"I don't understand how you can stand to listen to the old bore," her husband would say to her when they walked the few steps down the street to their own home after some command appearance at her in-laws'.

Annabel didn't know how to answer that. So much of her life was boring. Yes, she loved buying clothes and looking pretty, but her days had little to fill them. A governess took care of Valentina, her five-year-old daughter, enforcing rules that Annabel would love to see her rebel against. None of this could she share with Dieter, who would claim she was ungrateful. She could hear the words, "Most women would give anything to be in your place." She wasn't most women.

Her friends would visit or she would visit them, and they would drink coffee and talk about their children or whoever wasn't there, often repeating the same old stories from the last visit.

She loved to read, but Dieter thought that too much reading might hurt her eyes, so she found herself hiding books and sneaking in her reading time when she retired each afternoon to take a nap. She had also kept a journal from the time she was a teenager, trying not to make it all negative with her frustrations.

When she married "a wonderful match"—as her mother, her mother's friends, and all her friends had told her—she thought life would be more interesting. Dieter was handsome and from a very successful family.

Dieter would now be forced to take over the business entirely. Annabel wasn't sure how she felt about that. With her husband's interest in politics, she could guarantee that he would be in Bern and Zurich regularly. Since he was dead, her father-in-law would no longer be stepping in with disgust to stop her husband's ever-increasing interests in national politics and socialism.

What would happen to the business was her concern. She did not believe that Dieter was capable of leading it, based on what her father-in-law had told her about the operation and his frustration with his son's lack of interest.

Death would also end the arguments between father and son. Hans-Rudi felt that what happened locally was the only thing that anyone could influence. To prove his point, he was always pointing out how many people worked for him.

Most of the discussions—if you could call voices so loud that the china in the cabinet to the right of the dining room table shook discussions—happened at the obligatory Sunday dinner at her in-laws'. When father and son started in, Annabel and her mother-in-law, Mathilde, would find that they needed to do something else: look at a new piece of cloth, make sure the cook didn't need help, work on the jigsaw puzzle in the library—anything to escape.

More than one time, Dieter had interrupted Annabel's time with her mother-in-law, whose company Annabel really enjoyed, to demand that they return to their own home that minute because he couldn't pass another minute in the house of such a narrow-minded individual.

Annabel had long ago given up on pointing out that Hans-Rudi gave Dieter a very generous salary for working at the bakery. Had she been in charge she would have terminated Dieter's employment for lack of presence, lack of results.

With Dieter in charge, would the business fare as well? No, of course it wouldn't. If the business went downhill, how would they survive financially?

Annabel had not objected when her father and mother and Dieter's parents had more or less arranged their marriage. He was good-looking, funny, and overall as a husband fairly considerate in comparison to the tales some of her friends told about their partners. He only objected when she splurged on clothes. He had also been older.

Her mother had assured her an older husband was wiser. Annabel later discovered that Dieter's parents had given up hope that he would ever settle down, and they were pushing the match to give him an interest other than politics.

She dutifully had produced her first child and now they were hoping to conceive a son. Had Dieter been home more often, probably the chances of a pregnancy would have been in their favor. Between his absences and the nanny caring for Valentina, Annabel was left with more free time on her hands than she wanted. Boredom was a huge problem, yet she lacked patience with those who complained about being bored. Somehow she thought it marked a lack of imagination and she tried different projects to alleviate her boredom: charity to orphans, painting (she had no talent), writing poetry (slightly better than her painting), playing the piano (scales were tedious). Even shopping wasn't all that interesting, but it took her out of the house to Zurich and sometimes even to Paris.

She never understood why Dieter didn't find the bakery more interesting. Sometimes when she would talk to her father-in-law—or more accurately, listen to him when he was discussing new equipment or types of breads either in ingredients or shapes—she would ask questions that started with "Have you thought of . . . ?" She'd been chuffed when he'd adapted a few of her ideas, such as adding raisins, or trying a new loaf wrapping with a drawing of a child eating a piece of bread. Or sometimes, when he mentioned a negotiation, she asked if he'd tried this or that? She didn't know where those concepts came from, but they made sense as she understood the situations Hans-Rudi had described.

She also found it fascinating to observe how he tried to find new customers.

Even though they had a cook, Annabel liked baking, especially cookies. She experimented with different combinations of flavors, adding spices like cinnamon or nutmeg. At one time she wanted to suggest to her father-in-law that he add cookies, but something held her back.

Her ideas were flukes that he appreciated, but they were still flukes. Her greatest use to him was being his audience. Had she reminded him that he'd found some of her ideas useful, she was sure he would claim that they were his.

Annabel sat in the Abbey listening to the choir sing at her father-in-law's funeral. The Abbey, with its high white ceilings and plethora of angels and gold leaf, should have inspired her to think religious thoughts or at least induce a certain sense of reverence. Instead it left her with an overwhelming sense of sadness. She'd written pages and pages about it in her diary.

She was in the first row with her mother-in-law, her husband, and five-year-old Valentina, a grieving family. The smell of alcohol emitting from her husband's skin was still strong. Always fond of drink, he had gone into a binge after his father's death. Only his mother's throwing him in a bath with the help of the servants and locking him in the bedroom allowed him to be sober enough to be presentable at the Mass.

Valentina was sitting with her hands in her muff. She had a handkerchief that she'd brought "to dry my eyes if I cry too hard for *Opa*." Sometimes Annabel couldn't think of her daughter without adding the word "prissy." As young as she was, the requirement to finish an unwanted vegetable could be turned into a major drama.

Annabel felt like vomiting. She suspected that she was pregnant, because of her queasy stomach and the desire to sleep all day. That was how she'd been with Valentina. She'd planned to check with the doctor, but her father-in-law's death had delayed her contacting him.

From the sounds of footsteps behind, Annabel was sure that the Abbey was filled. She suspected every resident of Einsiedeln as well as clients from surrounding villages were in the church to pay well-deserved respects to her father-in-law. He'd been a good employer.


"We should sell the business," Dieter said.

Valentina had been sent upstairs with her governess. The mourning family had uttered their last thank you to all those who had come to pay their respects. The maid had cleared away the food that no one really touched.

"We can't," Annabel's mother-in-law said. Mathilde was as strong in her ways as Hans-Rudi had been in his. "It's your duty, Dieter, to take over."

"I hate the business. Flour makes me itch." He issued the statement as if he were flirting with the women.

His mother smiled. Dieter's strength was to charm. Her mother-in-law's weakness was to fall for it. Annabel knew that was why he was considered to be successful.

"We need the money to maintain our lives," Mathilde said.

"Why can't we hire a manager then?" Dieter asked.

Annabel had been thinking ever since her father-in-law had dropped dead that she would like to run the business. Women of their class didn't do that. "I want to be the manager."

"Ridiculous," Dieter said. "It would take up too much time from your . . ."

"From my what?"

"Your trips to Zurich or Paris to buy more clothes than you need. And don't forget the baby."

"Did you ever think that if I had something more important to do, I wouldn't go to Zurich and Paris?"

"Your daughter," Dieter said.

"The governess does very well; Valentina needs far less of me than before." She resisted adding, "our daughter, not just mine."

"When the new baby comes, you'll have more to do."

"And the governess will handle it all."

"It isn't proper for a woman—much less a pregnant woman—to work. People will think I can't support my family."

Mathilde had not said much as the two bickered. She looked from one to the other. Then she clapped her hands. "Enough! What do you know about running a bakery business?"

"Hans-Rudi used to have lunch with me once a week." She'd treasured those lunches despite her father-in-law's attitude. She knew one of his goals was to get her on his side. "Tell your husband he should . . ." was said at least several times during any meal. There were other statements that Hans-Rudi made. He never guessed that those talks were like a university course in how to run a bakery . . . if such things existed, which they did not.

Once he'd delivered his spiel on how Annabel should force a major change in Dieter, he would issue statement after statement of his own beliefs. "A good wife can convince her husband of anything . . . Politicians are all corrupt . . . The bakery provides you all with a fine life . . . There's nothing better than the thrill of finding a new client."

One time, Annabel had said, "There are times I think you think of me as a messenger boy." She had long ago learned that the way to deal with difficult topics when chatting with Hans-Rudi was to speak softly, cock her head and smile in such a way that the importance of what she said was carried in content, while her demeanor was that of a delicate member of the fairer sex, a term Hans-Rudi used to describe every woman he'd ever met.

"He came every Wednesday." Annabel had her mother-in-law's attention. "Sometimes Valentina would eat with us. However, afterward he and I would talk. He'd tell me about some of the problems, we'd discuss his ideas for expansion, how to keep the employees at their most productive, where the factory fit into the town."

Mathilde nodded. "He told me about those lunches. He said that it gave him time with his granddaughter."

"I never knew that," Dieter said.

"I'd have told you if you'd asked."

"What were his plans?" Mathilde asked.

Annabel spent the next half hour explaining the ideas for increasing the size of the baking area to allow for the manufacture of cookies. That had been her idea originally, and her father-in-law had his doubts, but Annabel had shown him with numbers how it might work, giving him possible worst, good, and best results. He hadn't totally decided to do it, but if she could get Mathilde on her side, maybe, just maybe there'd be a chance.

"The men will never take orders from a woman," Dieter said.

"You could give the orders in the beginning, and little by little we can let them see that it is me, not you."

"She has a point, Dieter. If the factory is running well, their jobs are secure, they won't question or care. I don't want to hurt your feelings, my son, but I suspect Annabel might be better at this than you would be."

"Mother."

"Think about it. Your heart isn't in it. I suspect Annabel's will be. I think we should try it for now."

# CHAPTER 7

*Day 1, Monday*

The snow had reduced itself to a few flakes drifting intermittently to earth as Annie started the walk to her temporary home, where her husband and daughter were waiting for her. She'd debated calling Roger for a ride, but the idea of having him bundle Sophie into a snowsuit and put her in a cold car during the hour she should be getting her try-and-make-her-sleepy bath didn't seem worth it.

The fifteen-minute walk in the icy air would clear her head. The room where she'd been working confirmed what she'd been taught all her life . . . heat rises. She'd found herself pulling off her sweater, opening the top button of her blouse, and rolling up the sleeves. At one point she'd opened the window, but the snow had blown in and the wind had sent papers flying. She'd wasted almost a half hour trying to get everything back in order.

The employee parking lot was now half full. A second smaller shift was made up mainly of two-parent working families where one parent went to work as soon as the other came home.

The sidewalks and the roads had been cleared.

As she passed the butcher shop, she debated going in and picking up the last four sausages she saw in a tray displayed in the window, but she knew Roger would have dinner well on its way.

Having a househusband had many advantages: therefore, she went out of her way to praise whatever he did in case he was ever tempted to go out on strike. She did credit that his having raised his daughter, Gaëlle, alone for several years was what had made him somewhat more competent than she—as a longtime single woman—in the domestic arts.

The same luxury car that had peeled from the parking lot that morning pulled up next to her and a voice said in English, "Get in."

Annie thought she identified Fritz Bircher as he opened the car door. Having only seen him rush by earlier that morning, she relied on the photos she'd discovered as part of her research.

Annie never paid any intention to car makes and models, noticing if one was red, blue, big, small, but this one reeked expensive with its oak dashboard and leather seats. "Sleek" was another word she'd have used to describe it. "I haven't far to go."

"Get in anyway. I want to talk to you."

His tone annoyed her. Technically, he was her boss, since both he and Petra Ritzman had signed her contract. She got into the car. It had that new car smell she'd learn to recognize whenever one of her friends had a new vehicle and was eager to show it off by giving her a ride.

"I'm taking you for a drink."

"My husband and daughter are expecting me."

He handed her his cell. "Call them."

"A please would be most appreciated."

He frowned.

"I am a writer you hired, not your slave to order about."

"Please. There's a *Gasthaus* just down this street." He turned the corner and pulled into a parking place. "Call them. Your family."

She didn't move.

"Please."

Annie picked up the phone.

"Is everything all right?" Roger asked.

"More or less. I'm at . . ." She looked at the name of the *Gasthaus* and told Roger where she was and whom she was with. "I won't be much more than a half hour."

Inside, one wall was covered with a fieldstone fireplace that had a huge log snuffling and crackling. Other logs were piled to one side. Only one couple sat drinking beer and eating hot potato salad and sausages. Annie felt she'd been dropped into a Swiss-German stereotype.

A man with a full head of gray hair greeted them. "Dinner, Herr Bircher?"

"Just a drink."

When they were seated, Bircher ordered two beers.

Annie changed it to a hot chocolate. Had he chosen a hot chocolate she'd have ordered tea. If he'd ordered tea, she'd have asked for coffee. As much as she hated power games, she knew how to play them.

They were silent once the gray-haired waiter left. Annie refused to be the first to speak, power game number two.

When their drinks were delivered, Bircher sat back in his seat and fingered his glass.

Power game number three coming up, Annie thought. Instead of mirroring his body language, she folded her hands on the table and sat very straight. "Why all this?" she asked. Power game number four: take control of the agenda.

"You're direct."

"I worked hard today. I want to get home. I'm still within walking distance, so please, tell me what you want."

He laughed without mirth. "I can see you're truly American. No beating around the trees."

Bushes, Annie corrected mentally. She stirred the whipped

cream into the dark liquid and, praying it wasn't too hot, drank almost half. She looked at her watch. "I will be happy to talk as long as you want tomorrow at the office, but now I plan to finish my hot chocolate and leave."

"What does my sister really want you to do?"

"You signed my contract, too. I'm writing a history of the company."

He picked up a coaster from the several that were in a holder on the table along with salt and pepper shakers. Printed on each of them was a drawing and the name of the *Gasthaus*. He then took a second and a third and started building a tower with two touching to form a pyramid, a third placed on top. He repeated the sequence until it was five coasters high, and finally it collapsed.

Annie finished her hot chocolate and stood. "Herr Bircher, I'll see you tomorrow. Thank you for the chocolate."

# CHAPTER 8

*Day 2, Tuesday*

Sophie was not happy when she woke up that morning. Normally when Annie went into the baby's room, Sophie's head poked up over the bumper guard as she rewarded her mother's presence with a big smile. This morning she was fussy.

Roger stood behind Annie. "I can change her. You get ready for work."

"In a minute." Scooping up her daughter, Annie walked around the room, but the fussiness continued. Annie did not understand how much she could love such a small amount of protoplasm, one that limited her once-valued freedom, but she did.

She opened the baby's mouth. Her bottom gum was red. When Annie touched it, Sophie whimpered. Probably teething, Annie thought, feeling a maternal pride in being able to identify the problem, combined with sadness for her daughter's discomfort. She'd read that it was usually six months for the first tooth, but the book had also said it could vary either way.

That she could do little to prevent Sophie's pain made her feel helpless, and she could imagine how helpless she'd feel when sometime in the future a child hurt her daughter's feelings in kindergarten, she didn't get a part in a play she wanted, or a boy she liked didn't ask her to a dance. She knew Sophie would have to learn to slay her own dragons: Annie silently promised to try to give her the necessary armor and swords to do so.

Roger took the baby from her and nodded toward the bathroom. By the time Annie had showered, Roger was spooning cereal into Sophie's mouth, the dogs were outside in the garden, and toast and coffee were at the place that had become hers.

"She's teething, which is why she's fussy," Roger said. "And there's a bit of diaper rash like Gaëlle used to get every time she was pushing through a tooth."

Annie felt a bit more confident in her own opinion now that it had been seconded by someone who'd already been a parent.

The sound of a police siren—*do-ee, do-ee*—caused both of them to frown. They could not see the street from the kitchen window, so they went to the door to look at the road that led to the lake.

"Strange," Roger said. "I thought this was a quiet neighborhood."

Annie glanced at her watch. She was running enough behind schedule: she decided to take the car for the short drive to work.

"I can bring it back at lunch," she said.

"I don't think I'll need it, but if I do, I'll ring you." Roger blew her a kiss as she went out the door.

A strange feeling came over Annie as she entered the plant: She chalked it up to her imagination. The receptionist wasn't at her desk. The cafeteria was empty, but it was before the morning coffee break, so she poured herself a cup of tea and headed up to the attic and began work.

Last night before falling asleep, she'd tried to think of the best way to organize the materials in the time she had to do the project.

A knock at the door interrupted her, and Brett Windsor walked in. "Good morning, fellow American." He carried two cups of coffee.

Annie didn't want to tell him she didn't feel like an American nor anything else at this point in her life.

"Did you hear the news?"

"What news?"

"The police found Fritz Bircher's car in the lake about a half hour ago. He's missing."

# CHAPTER 9
# 1925

## ANNABEL'S SPICE COOKIES

**Ingredients:**
1/4 cup brown sugar
1/4 cup unsalted butter or margarine
1 egg slightly beaten
1/8 teaspoon pure vanilla extract
1 teaspoon ground ginger
1/4 teaspoon allspice
1/4 teaspoon cinnamon
1/4 teaspoon ground cloves
1 cup flour
1 tablespoon flour

**Directions:**
Preheat oven to 350°F/176°C.

Beat sugar and butter in bowl until the butter is creamed.

Beat in egg and vanilla.

Sift 1 cup flour and spices.

Add the flour and spices to the sugar and butter and blend well.

Lightly grease a baking sheet and sprinkle with 1 tablespoon flour, shaking off any excess.

Drop small amounts of cookie dough onto sheet at 2-inch intervals.

Bake for 6–7 minutes.

Annabel pulled on her gloves after fastening her hat with a hat-pin. She was late, but Dieter had insisted she pack for him. He would be in Bern for the next few days. The Swiss socialists were meeting with the leaders of the four-year-old Irish Republic, who were also socialists. He'd been fascinated with the formation of Ireland even more than he had been with the development of communism in Russia.

Dieter was, Annabel thought, fascinated with anything and everything as long as it had nothing to do with the company that kept a roof over their heads. More than that, it was she, Annabel Bircher, who kept the business going as well as the roof in good shape at the bakery, at this house and at her mother-in-law's house.

Her mother-in-law was just beginning to show her age, giving in to afternoon naps and moving stiffly.

Dieter was still able to work ten-hour days if it had to do with the Socialist Party. He looked younger, much younger than he was, but lately he'd been complaining about stomachaches. She'd instructed the cook to only make mild food: potatoes, rice, fish without butter, and well-cooked vegetables.

Although she'd asked him to stay to meet with the new Canadian flour salesman, he'd replied that he didn't give a damn about ruby or garnet wheat or whatever it was called. She could make the decision on whether to do business with them or not.

It wasn't that Annabel felt Dieter would pay much attention to anything about the meeting, but she'd learned since she'd gone to work that people would talk to Dieter. Many times she felt as if she'd swallowed an invisibility pill, the way her presence was ignored.

At first she felt angry. Then she realized it gave her an advantage because she could observe not just what they said, but what they didn't say and how they moved. She developed an instinct for who was lying and who was sincere. Sometimes she'd write a note during one of those meetings and slip it to Dieter to ask this or that question. At first he resisted, until the aftermath of a screaming match that might have rattled windows in faraway Zurich.

They'd been negotiating new mixing equipment. She told him to ask about the guarantee.

He forgot.

The contracts were signed without any liability on the part of the seller. When the mixer, promised to produce over one thousand loaves of bread a day, broke down within a month, there was no recourse.

Annabel resisted saying, "I told you so," although she felt the words almost choking her. Only when her mother-in-law, Mathilde, had berated her son for not asking for the guarantee, when Annabel had clearly wanted one, did he start accepting her notes and doing what she wanted.

Sometimes.

Annabel was late for her meeting with Olaf Stevenson after Dieter had left the house complaining that it had taken her much too long to pack his suitcase and if he missed the train it would be her fault.

For all his socialist ideals, her husband had bought a 25/30 Crossley from England and had hired a driver. When she'd chided him, he pointed out that they had given yet one more person a paycheck. She held her tongue when he took the train, leaving the car in their stable-converted garage.

It did work to her advantage.

He had refused to learn to drive, but Annabel had the chauffeur teach her, although Dieter still didn't know that she'd become a very competent driver. She wasn't sure when would be the best time to tell him. It was only a matter of time before someone would say, "I saw your wife driving your car the other day."

She'd plotted her reply—"Johann had a headache"—although the chauffeur not feeling well didn't explain her expertise behind the wheel.

Dieter did not like her to have skills he didn't. He would never admit that she was a better manager than he was. When he wasn't around, she could get the workers to do what she wanted them to by cajoling rather than threatening them. He voiced his dissatisfaction by complaining, "You walk into a room, and the employees fall at your feet, salivating."

With Annabel going behind him and putting her arms around him and dropping a kiss on his balding head, his resentment seemed to vanish. "I bet if we only had female workers and you walked into the room, the same thing would happen."

"Probably," he said.

Annabel didn't believe what she'd said at all. She knew she was good at making sure that the factory's interest and the worker's interest matched whenever possible. It had annoyed him even more when she was able to negotiate contracts with the Swiss Federation of Trade Unions. No amount of hugging and cajoling reduced his unhappiness that she had succeeded where he'd failed.

Her socialist principles, she suspected, were reality, while Dieter existed in a theoretical world. Socialism only went as far as his own pocket.

She never understood why he preferred what he considered an addle-pated wife, interested only in spending money, more than he liked an efficient one who brought wealth into the family, freeing him to do his politicking.

Since Johann was driving Dieter to the train station, and since Annabel didn't want to ride in the car with him and listen to his carping, she walked to the bakery. Dieter insisted on calling it "the bakery," although they now occupied a building four times the size of the original site of the company and she'd expanded the workforce by another fifty-two people since her father-in-law had died. They had won contracts with hotels, restaurants, and small food stores for regular orders, giving them a predictable cash flow, all because of her ideas.

A year ago they had signed a contract with Gottlieb Duttweiler, who had a fleet of trucks that went from village to village selling basics. He'd been convinced to add their bread, not a huge order, but she'd had a feeling that the man's business would develop. Dieter predicted that the man would be ruined by the cost of the trucks and to make sure payment was in advance. Instead, Annabel convinced Duttweiler to add her cookies and cakes to his line. Duttweiler was fast becoming one their biggest customers.

Dieter now complained that it was dangerous to rely on one big client. Without admitting it, Annabel agreed and encouraged her sales staff to find as many small customers as possible in case Duttweiler replaced them with someone else—although whom she had no idea. There was no other business of their size and quality in their canton nor in the canton of Zurich.

Annabel's main concern was expanding too fast. Even if her ideas tumbled over each other, she would research each step individually before implementing any of them. As for debt, she would never take a new bank loan before the previous one was paid off, and better it be paid off ahead of the repayment schedule.

She shoved any marital discontentment to one side as she

walked to the office at a pace that made others complain they couldn't keep up with her. How much better the shorter skirts were than when she had to have her ankles entangled with cloth. Despite being occupied with the business, she still enjoyed being in fashion.

The spring sky was a brilliant blue: daffodils and lilacs filled her neighbors' front gardens, but her mind was on the meeting facing her. Dieter thought she was crazy to be considering importing wheat flour from Canada, but local producers were switching to other crops, and the Eastern countries that had produced wonderful wheat flour, often less expensively than the locals despite import tax, had not fully recovered from the Great War to the point that they could meet the company's needs at prices Annabel wanted to pay.

The grandfather clock in the entry of the building was showing 10:08, making her twenty-three minutes late. She had no idea what the Canadian attitude toward promptness was, but for the Swiss she was being very, very rude to keep the man waiting. It gave her a disadvantage.

Herr Bauer, her secretary and Dieter's, had seated Olaf Stevenson in the waiting room. Herr Bauer was one of the battles with her husband that Annabel had forfeited. That man didn't like taking orders from a woman. Whenever Dieter was in the office and Annabel asked Bauer do anything, he would check with Dieter first.

When Dieter was away, Annabel would preface all the requests with, "My husband would like you to . . ." even when Dieter had no idea at all about what she was doing. Still, he had accommodated the salesman with the proper ritual, which the couple expended on any person waiting to see either of them whether it was a client, vendor, or employee.

As Annabel entered the waiting room, Olaf Stevenson placed a cup, which she knew contained hot chocolate, on the side table next to his chair and stood.

He was tall, well over six feet, much taller by at least several inches than the average Swiss man. Annabel at five eight was taller than or the same height as most of the men she knew. Dieter was only slightly taller than when she was in shoes with a one-inch heel.

For a moment she stood still, absorbing his appearance: blond, well-cut hair, blue-blue eyes, and chiseled cheeks. He stuck out his hand.

She removed her string gloves and took his hand noting how warm it was. "My apologies for keeping you waiting." Taking a deep breath to steady herself, she said, "I've set aside the day for you, although I'm sure we won't need all that time." She wished they would, then chided herself for reacting like a teenage girl who had just been smiled at by a teenage boy.

Once seated in the office she shared with Dieter, Olaf started talking about hard winter wheat of various strains. "They have a much higher gluten content, which is why they are good for yeast breads." He reached into his case and brought out charts and tables.

Annabel didn't say that she had already researched wheat types and qualities. She knew that she preferred the softer wheats for the cookies that the factory produced. She let him talk, taking in his face. Stop it, she told herself. Grow up. You're a married woman—with children.

"I bore people with my love of wheat," Olaf said. "My father was a wheat farmer in Saskatchewan. I went to an agricultural college and did my thesis on the history of wheat."

No one Annabel knew, even her husband with his interest in politics, had a passion, a real passion, for anything. Oh, they might say they liked playing the piano or enjoyed reading, but she read passion in Olaf's eyes. For a moment she wished she were a stalk of wheat.

Stop it, she told herself again. A woman in my place does not drool over a salesman.

She wondered how old he was. He wore no wedding ring, but many men didn't. What the Canadian customs on wedding rings were she had no idea.

To Olaf she said aloud, "I'm sorry, did you say the cultivation of wheat goes back to eighty-five hundred B.C.?"

"I did, but not the type we grow now. I'm sure you don't want to know the development of each type."

Yes I do, if it will keep you talking, she thought, but said, "I do find it fascinating, but it's more important that I know how it will affect my product and the price."

"Did you notice the large case I had? I left it outside the door next to your secretary's desk."

Annabel shook her head. She'd noticed his eyes, his skin, his hair, and even how well his suit sculpted his body, but not the case.

"I've brought samples. It may be presumptuous of me, but perhaps you could use the winter wheat for some sample loaves and the softer wheat for your cookies. There's enough to try combinations as well."

He pulled out more charts with drawings of the different types of wheat next to drawings for what they were best suited.

Annabel forced herself back into buyer's mode. "About a year ago I installed a test kitchen, more for trying new cookie recipes than anything else. Bring your case and I'll have the staff go to work."

Although she felt shaky being in his presence, she stood and led him to the test kitchen, the same kitchen that Dieter had considered a complete waste of money. It had three stoves—gas, wood, and electric—all of which were the types of stoves that would be found in any well-equipped family kitchen. They were far less expensive than the industrial ovens used in the factory.

The smell of lemon and baked sugar dominated the room. On one of the steel tabletops, a tray of thin wafers was cooling. Frau Renate Krause, who also worked in the factory when she wasn't baking new product ideas, was the chief and only tester. Her workload depended on whether anyone from the janitor to Annabel had an idea for a new product.

Dieter had never understood what sense it made to get ideas from the lower echelons. Sometimes Annabel wanted to ask him how he could be a socialist when he had such contempt for ordinary workers, but she didn't. Peace was better than confrontation unless that confrontation would bring about the changes she might want. "Select your battles" had become her mantra.

"What are you doing today?" Annabel asked Frau Krause after a polite greeting and a question about her son who was lame.

"Two different recipes. Maria Buch thought up these spice cookies. And I've tried this new recipe I made up for lemon wafers." She handed a cookie so thin it was almost transparent to Annabel, who bit into it and then took a second to give to Stevenson, who ate it and asked for a second one. Then they both tested the spice cookies.

Looking at Frau Krause, Annabel said, "Ask Frau Buch to come to my office so I can thank her." She had three ways of giving thanks: verbal, money, a day off. All three would leave Dieter sputtering.

When had he become such a complete grouch?

It had been gradual, she supposed. The more she accomplished in the business, the more he complained.

"What about costs?" Stevenson asked. "Lemons can be expensive."

He knows about more than wheat, she thought. "I don't know of any other bakery in the area that offers lemon cookies, which means we can charge a bit more, especially if we promote them."

She had added an advertising department, made up of only one very clever woman, again over Dieter's protests.

Together the woman and she regularly visited every bakery within a fifty-mile radius. She thought of her four luxury hotel clients that might like an unusual cookie. "Make up about two thousand. We'll test them on the staff and in the shop." She made a note to meet with the sales clerks for promotional ideas. Her walk-in customers were not always adventurous and she'd learned that samples helped them to decide if they liked a product or not.

"If you're willing, we could try breads as well as cookies." Stevenson was looking around the kitchen. "I'm sorry that I don't speak German. Does Frau Krause speak English?"

Annabel wondered why he didn't ask Frau Krause himself, but she relayed how he wanted her to try the wheat with her regular recipes and also with several he produced from his case. "The winter wheat may need more liquid and baking time," she translated.

Frau Krause held up her hands and wiggled her fingers, "I feel when the dough is right. Good baking is an art."

When Annabel translated, Stevenson smiled. "Please tell her, we are kindred spirits." This in turn caused Frau Krause to smile after Annabel relayed his message.

"The samples won't be ready until about two," Frau Krause said.

"Herr Stevenson, if you don't have another appointment, perhaps you would like to see the Abbey and I'll have lunch made. It could be ready by the time we are back here." *Please,* she thought. Although she had hundreds of small tasks she'd planned for the day, because every Wednesday was her odds-and-ends day, they would have to wait.

"What a wonderful idea," he said.

# CHAPTER 10

*Day 4, Thursday*

When Annie returned to the house well after eight that night, Roger was walking up and down with Sophie in his arms. The moment he stopped, she whimpered.

Cold rose off Annie's coat. Although she'd driven home, the ride was so short that the car hadn't had the chance to warm up. Rather than hang anything up, she dropped her coat and hat on the nearest chair and reached for her daughter. Sophie's immediate reaction was to let out a howl.

"It's not you. She's been unhappy all day," Roger said. "All I've been able to do for dinner is to make up a couple packages of soup."

As long as she didn't have to fix her own dinner, Annie was not about to complain. She continued walking the baby while Roger put two bowls on the divider between the kitchen and living area, which doubled as a place to eat.

It took well over an hour before Sophie gave up and fell asleep long enough for Annie to place the child in the crib. Only then did Roger dish the soup into the bowls. It was a beef and vegetable soup, and no matter that they usually made all their soup from scratch, it smelled wonderful to Annie, who had worked through lunch, only going to the cafeteria for an apple, pastry, and tea around three after all the lunch menus had been stopped.

As soon as they were seated and Annie had taken her first three tablespoons, the doorbell rang. Both jumped to answer it before a second ring might wake Sophie.

A policeman stood there. He held out his badge, which read "Rolf Bauer, Korporal" and showed that he was from the cantonal crime division. "Frau and Herr . . ."

"Perret," Annie said. It still seemed strange to use only Roger's last name. More often she still thought of herself as Annie Young, or at best Young-Perret, but she was sure that the policeman wouldn't care.

The policeman looked at a paper, which Annie could see was a list of residents on the street. "It says here that the . . ."

"We are house-sitting for our friends. They're on holiday."

What the policeman said next, Annie had trouble understanding. His local accent was a form of *Schweizerdeutsche*. As a little girl, Annie had thought someone learned a foreign language and that was it. Learning German in Germany had disabused her of that notion quickly. She'd picked up the *Schwäbisch* of the Stuttgart area, which sounded as different from High German as someone raised in the deep South of the United States sounded from a native Bostonian, if not more so. And although she'd lived in the Francophone part of Switzerland, she also discovered that the different Swiss-German dialects could be almost as incomprehensible to one another as they were to a francophone.

The policeman spoke a dialect that required Annie to ask him to repeat and repeat again until she understood that he was asking about Herr Bircher's car. She then explained to Roger in French.

"Probably checking everyone on the street," he said in French. The policeman showed no understanding of what the couple said, despite most Swiss being able to speak at least two if not three of their national languages along with English at some level.

The next two exchanges were a blur of sounds. The policeman had as much trouble understanding Annie's *Schwäbisch* accent as she was having with him. *"Sprechen Sie English?"* she asked.

*"Ein bischen.* A little," he said.

Annie guessed he was probably in his early thirties, tall for a Swiss, close to six feet. He had dark hair, dark eyes, and could have passed for an Italian actor. She invited him into the living room and offered him a cup of coffee, thinking he might be cold. He sat but refused the coffee.

"How can I help you?" she asked as he unbuttoned his coat. Roger had started a fire in the ceramic stove heating the room to a point that made sweaters unnecessary. Then the policeman took off his hat and was turning it around in his hands. "We want to know if you heard anything Monday night: a car racing down the road, for example."

"It would be hard for a car to race down this road—it's too short," Roger said in English, which Annie repeated in German. "When you turn from the main road, there are only eight houses, four on each side before the lake, and they are fairly close together."

Annie didn't translate that. She resisted telling Roger that the policeman probably knew that, unless he had serious eyesight problems. And she also wondered what had taken the police so long to get around to questioning people.

The policeman nodded. "Still, we were hoping someone heard something, anything at all. Were you here last night?"

Annie continued translating between the two men.

"All night. I was here all day," Roger said. "I didn't hear anything."

"Have they found Herr Bircher?" Annie asked in German,

ignoring Roger's frown. She wasn't sure why, because she knew he didn't understand what the *Korporal* was saying.

"How did you know it was Herr Bircher?"

"I'm on temporary assignment at the LK factory. Everyone was talking about it at work."

As the policeman pulled out his notebook, Annie wondered why he hadn't done so earlier.

"What can you tell me about Herr Bircher?"

"Not much, this is my second day on the job."

"Then what were people saying?"

"That his car went into the lake. He wasn't in it. He hadn't come into work this morning. The area where I work is located away from the employees."

"Why is that?"

"My assignment is to write a history of the company. They've buried me in the archives."

The policeman stared at her more closely. "I heard he had a drink with a curly-haired redhead last night. Was that you?"

"He offered me a ride, we stopped for a drink. I had hot chocolate and wanted to get home to my husband and baby."

"What did you talk about?"

"My assignment, that's all."

Korporal Rolf Bauer seemed to be fumbling for his next question. He took in a deep breath. "What do the people at the factory think of him?"

"I don't know. Two days . . . just two days on the job." Annie wondered why he didn't understand that two days didn't give her much time to learn about a person or a place. "I'll be there a month at most. On short assignments, I usually don't have time to mingle with the staff. I go in, work solidly through the day, and leave."

When he asked her why, she explained how she took contract

work as a technical writer, a historian, and a translator.

Korporal Bauer snapped his notebook shut and pulled out a card with his name, phone number, and email on it. "If you think of anything let me know."

"Maybe Herr Bircher will appear soon," Annie said.

"We doubt it."

"I'm an ex−police chief," Roger spoke very slowly in English. "Do you think there's foul play? After all, a car in a lake, an expensive car . . ."

"How did you know it was expensive?" Bauer asked Roger in his dialect, leaving Annie to translate, although she realized that the *Korporal* understood more English than he let on. She was glad that she and Roger had followed their rule: never assume that people can't understand what you're saying when speaking a different language from them.

"My wife told me. She's the least interested in cars than anyone I know, and she said what a beauty it was. I gathered from that it had to be expensive." This time he spoke very slowly and clearly.

"It was. A real shame. No one drives a car like that into water on their own and then walks away, much less from water that cold." The *Korporal*'s English accent was difficult to understand.

"He'd probably have frozen to death," Roger said.

"And he wouldn't have rolled up the windows after he got out of the car," the policeman said.

"And he couldn't have opened the door if the windows were closed. Too much pressure," Roger said. "Any thoughts of suicide?"

"No note left," Bauer said. "Or if he did, no one has found one."

Annie smiled to herself. Roger was getting information police-man to policeman despite any language difficulties. One of his staff in Argelès had told her he could get answers when people

70

didn't know they were being asked questions. She'd seen him use the technique on Gaëlle, although over the years, his daughter had caught on to the trick.

"I'm sure that, as any businessman, he has some enemies," Roger said.

Bauer turned to Annie. "I know you've said that you've only been working there"—he consulted his notebook—"*two* days."

She nodded.

"There are rumors around Einsiedeln that his sister wants to develop the factory and brand and that Herr Bircher wants to sell it. Do you know anything about it?"

Annie thought of the argument that the brother and sister had been having her first few minutes on the job. "I never knew a management that was in total agreement on the future of a company," she said. "In a family business, the dynamic can be a bit different."

"How so?"

"In a multinational a vice president would not be angry with another vice president, because he had been the favored child or at least perceived to be the favored child. There's no dynamic of memories of one being taken fishing by a parent and the other child ignored, carried into the workplace," Annie said.

"Was that the case with the Birchers?" the *Korporal* asked.

Annie shrugged. "No idea."

"What my wife is saying is that your job will probably be harder because of the family management of the company, and then again there may be absolutely no connection between the family and the disappearance. I don't envy you." Roger spoke in English so slowly that Annie almost wanted to pull the next word out of his mouth.

Korporal Bauer stood. "My brother and I still fight over my father taking one of us and not the other to a certain big football game. The subject comes up every time we're together for a holiday." He tapped the card that Roger hadn't put away. "In case you need to get in touch with me if you think of anything." He shook their hands.

"Sometimes I miss my work," Roger said. "Although I always hated that someone was missing or killed, I loved unraveling a case."

"I know what you mean." Bauer made his way to the door.

When he was gone Annie put the soup into the microwave. As soon as they sat down Sophie let out a holler.

# CHAPTER 11

*Day 8, Monday*

When Annie arrived at her work area in the factory attic after the weekend, the first thing she saw was Brett Windsor sitting in her chair with his feet on her desk and a blue folder open in his hands. A cup of steaming coffee was to one side.

After putting down her tea and unwrapping her scarf, she asked, "May I ask what you're doing?" She wanted to scream, "Get the hell out of my work!" but resisted. Hostility generates more hostility. She knew she could revert to hostility if necessary, but it was hard to go from hostile to nice if she were wrong and the bastard had a right to be up here going through company files.

Windsor jumped and put down the file. "I got started before you got in."

"Started on what?" Annie took off her coat and hung it on the hook on the door.

Brett had turned around and was facing her. "I was hoping the early files would give me some marketing ideas for the new line. Create a mystique, a story."

"That is if the company isn't sold."

"With Ferrari Fritz gone, I doubt it will be." He swiveled around and drank from his coffee.

"Ferrari Fritz?"

"He's one of those idiots that wants top brand names in

everything including cars and clothing. Loves logos. Doesn't he know that he's just giving them free advertising?"

Annie had to agree with Windsor on that. She had never seen the sense in being a billboard for any clothing or shoe company. In fact she carefully removed any logos from anything she bought if it were possible to do so.

"I'm not against brands for identification," Brett said. "I just hate the idea that wearing this or that makes someone feel superior."

Annie started to agree, but Brett didn't let her get a word in.

"Petra has some really good ideas on building this brand. She wants to keep jobs here. In fact by keeping them here, she can enhance the brand image . . . Swiss made and all that."

When Windsor pulled a briefcase from under the table, it was the first time Annie had noticed it. He retrieved several sketches that were for packaging.

Two were typical Swiss scenes of cows, mountains, and chalets. One was for a metal box with paper inserts for information on ingredients, but not just the usual listings. Instead there were drawings with a hen and eggs, a wheat field, and a lemon interspersed much like a children's story. The lettering matched and was reinforced with the beginning words, "Once upon a time." The first O was done in an ornate red letter with the design of a vine interlaced, something a monk preparing a medieval manuscript would have been proud of.

"I've printed them out. This artist works online, but Petra reacts better to paper—not that she isn't up-to-date on computers." He moved his coffee cup to the other table. "She will want to have whatever we decide framed." He held the artwork out at arm's length. "This is just one concept. In fact, I don't like it all that much. And Petra usually wants more than one idea."

Brett walked over to an armoire that Annie still had not tapped for information. Inside were picture frame after frame, all facing the back of the armoire. When Annie turned them around she saw they were advertising campaigns and copies of cookie boxes going back through the ages.

"She's talked about creating a gallery and using it for publicity when she does her new brand launch. She's after me to get the Swiss business program on TSR1 to do a segment for the francophone part of the country."

"Any luck?"

"Not yet. I suppose I'm lucky she doesn't want a major segment on Bloomberg or MSNBC. Of the new stuff, what do you like?" he asked.

She flipped through them all. "Hard to decide."

"I never show Petra more than two designs or her decision-making abilities freeze harder than a glacier, although with global warming that may not be such a good analysis." He took the drawings from Annie and put them back in his briefcase. "But I can't show her just one either."

"Will you use social media?"

"Of course we'll work with Twitter, Facebook, etcetera, to do a social media campaign, but that also is a little harder for Petra to grasp."

"Are you that close to rolling out the new cookies to market?"

"The sale of the company slowed everything down."

Annie merely nodded.

Windsor smiled. "Listen, even though I'm jealous they brought you on to do this assignment, because I'd have loved to spend my time prowling through these old files and have nothing else to do but write 'the Bircher family story,' I like you."

Annie didn't know what to say to that. She wasn't sure she liked Brett, nor was she sure she didn't like him. He had an energy within . . . yes that was how she would describe him . . . a person who had an energy within, which showed up in how he ate, how he talked.

"Let's have lunch across the street today. I'll fill you in more," he said.

When he left the room, it was almost like he took half the air with him.


Although Annie hated to take extra time for lunch, she was curious enough to want to know what Brett Windsor knew about the family. The masses of documents she still had to go through in the restricted amount of time made the word "daunting" do calisthenics in her brain.

The financial records, in tight columns, were almost beyond her understanding: her favorite saying when confronted with anything to do with numbers was, "I'm a wordsmith, not a mathematician." She'd given up on those, but there were enough letters, invoices, reports, and journals to get an idea behind the fiscal records of the company. She was grateful that it wasn't the financial that Frau Ritzman wanted emphasized. "Make it read like a novel," she'd said again when Annie passed her in the corridor on her way to join Brett for lunch, "or at least like an interesting history text, if such things exist."

At noon Annie faced the biting cold and walked the block to where Windsor had told her to meet him. The building, across from the huge beige Abbey, could have been out of any German fairy tale book with its half timbers. Halfway between the top of the doorway and the windows of the second story was a metal sign in an elaborate circle. Inside the circle was a steaming pot on a wood stove.

Annie thought she should start photographing all these traditional signs and create a coffee table book, but filed it away with the million other ideas that flashed through her mind. Each would take weeks, months, or years and she knew she only had one life.

Inside, the restaurant lived up to its stereotype with yet more red-checkered tablecloths and half curtains on the windows, wooden paneling, and wonderful smells. Annie wondered if any local restaurant would ever try a different décor.

Windsor was already there and waved his arms like a referee signaling a penalty. When she joined him, he pulled out her wooden chair with a heart carved in the center.

"I thought you might not be coming."

"I do have to eat. You did tweak my interest."

He raised an eyebrow.

The waiter brought their menus: bound, brown, large leather books with the word "menu" in gold lettering. Annie turned the pages and decided on the daily menu: salad, *spätzle,* green beans, chocolate cake, and coffee. Windsor did the same. Both ordered the local beer.

Their salads arrived almost immediately. As Windsor picked up his fork, Annie worried that eating would slow his talking. It didn't. "The problems with the two Birchers go back to child-hood."

"How do you know?"

"My wife. She grew up with Petra. They were in the same school, same class. I wouldn't say they were best friends, but they did spend a lot of time together with a group of other girls, most of whom are still in Einsiedeln."

"I guess that qualifies you, not that I'm trying to."

Windsor flashed a fleeting smile, and Annie realized that he was one of those people who smiled so fast it was possible to miss it if one blinked.

"It was just the two kids," he said. "Fritz was around ten years younger."

"Was." He used the past tense. Did he think he was already dead? Annie's own thoughts tended in that direction. The man had no reason to disappear when a sale was so close . . . or maybe it wasn't.

"Petra was the older and the first and almost a miracle baby because Frau Bircher, her mother, had had a series of miscarriages. Her husband was so desperate for an heir he made Henry VIII look like he didn't care about having a son."

Annie smiled at the analogy. The man had a sense of history at least.

"Anyway, although Herr Bircher wanted a son, he made do by almost turning Petra into one. He took her into the factory and she loved it. But when Fritz was born, Petra became a has-been. She did everything to get her father's attention: top grades, working on new cookie recipes. She studied business on her own during high school."

Annie picked at her salad. "Poor girl."

"Her father didn't want her to go to a business school, a battle that he won. When he died, she fought with the trustees to get control, convincing them even though she was only nineteen or so and had only a year of university, where she took liberal arts courses. She presented them with business plans, and they said that she could hold the business for when Fritz was ready. They were named codirectors, he in name and her in reality. It was thought she'd quit when he was ready to take over, although why they thought that, I'll never know."

"Only he was never ready?"

"You got it in one. He was a PIT."

"PIT?"

"Playboy in Training." This time Windsor's smile lasted a little longer.

He expects me to be amused. I'll smile, Annie thought.

"He did get the business training. When he was ready to take over from Petra, she didn't want to go. The board saw what a great job she'd done and they continued to keep them as cos. From then on, there was a fight about every decision. Petra has tried to shield the employees. Fritzie Boy doesn't give a damn about any of them, the town, anything but himself. So that's where they stand."

Hmm, Annie thought. Back to present tense when referring to Fritz. Maybe the past tense reference to him was misspoken.

The waiter cleared their salads and replaced the salad dishes with the *spätzle*. Annie glanced at her watch. Right before she left for lunch, she had discovered a new series of letters that she wanted to work on and she could barely wait to tackle them.

"Saturday night my wife and I are giving a small party. There are several other mixed couples, American and locals. Would you like to come?"

"I'll have to check with my husband. We do have a baby daughter and I don't know any babysitters."

"Bring her. We have a crib left over from when our girls were small."

As they walked back after the meal, Annie felt groggy from too much food and the beer. The cold helped slap her alert, but not as much as when the receptionist said to Brett Windsor, "They found Herr Bircher. Dead. He was shot dead."

# CHAPTER 12
# 1932

## ALMOND HALF-MOON COOKIES

**Ingredients:**
1 cup butter, room temperature
2/3 cup sugar
1 teaspoon vanilla extract
1 teaspoon almond extract
2 1/2 cups flour
1 cup almond flour
1/4 cup powdered sugar

**Directions:**
Preheat oven to at 350°F/176°C.

Cream the butter and sugar until light.

Mix in extracts.

Mix in flour and almond flour.

Take tablespoons of the dough, roll each tablespoon into a small ball, and shape into half-moons.

Put onto parchment paper.

Bake 15–20 minutes or until a light golden brown.

Dust with powdered sugar.

Annabel Bircher was frustrated. When she'd read about the Wall Street crash in 1929, she didn't think it would have any effect on her and the factory. How wrong she'd been. Tariffs had been put on almost everything. Her cheap Canadian wheat had become too expensive to buy.

Although she wouldn't have admitted it to anyone, what bothered her most was that Olaf Stevenson no longer had any excuse to cross the Atlantic to meet with his international customers, because he didn't have any.

Before the crash, she'd looked forward to his visits, which lasted far longer than needed. He had a face from which she couldn't pull her eyes away. His attraction was more than his looks. He made her laugh, something she did rarely when he wasn't in Einsiedeln. That feeling of gaiety when she was with Olaf was something she treasured.

At times she wondered if Dieter was unfaithful to her. He was away on party business more than he was home. They now had separate rooms, although maybe once a month there would be a knock on her door after she was in bed, and her husband would enter wearing a clean pair of pajamas. On those visits, he always cocked his head; that told her he didn't want to talk about politics or the company. She wondered if he knew he was being transparent, or if he thought she wanted him because she would answer the head cock with open arms.

For a man in his seventies he was still a sexual animal. Most of her friends with older husbands considered this part of their duties long past. They felt relief to be free of that chore.

It wasn't that Annabel was particularly interested in sex anymore, but it was part of her wifely duty. At fifty-three, and unlike most of her friends, she looked younger. She had maintained her slimness, the gray in her hair blended nicely with the blond, and her skin was unlined. It could be, she told anyone who asked, that working was what made the difference. Since none of her friends worked, the theory was unprovable because the sample was too small to be scientifically viable. Still, whenever Dieter was pumping away, she'd imagine it was Olaf.

Dieter was in France meeting with the fast-growing French socialist movement spurred by the unrest of the Depression.

Annabel was in her office going over the books with the accountant, one of her least enjoyable chores. Shortages, plus the fact that the country was no longer exporting watches, chocolate, and machinery in the same amount, meant that the Swiss people were spending less. Bread sales remained steady, but cookies and other pastries were an option that housewives struggling with the economics of a limited food budget could forgo.

Zurich hotels continued to buy her luxury cookies but not in the same quantities, as rich tourists had given way to bank clients, who were fewer in number.

Thus, their numbers were down overall.

Dieter had suggested reducing staff. He was such a good socialist until it came to his own pocketbook, a fact that Annabel did *not* point out to him. Annabel's preferred action was to meet with the union and, once they knew the situation, try to cut back hours rather than have a staff reduction.

She'd already cut back her own salary and was postponing the need for new equipment. This was not a decision she was happy about, although Herr Schmitz, her mechanic, could breathe new life into any piece of metal no matter how often it broke down.

There were times that Annabel wished that she'd had a regular education heavy on math, history, and economics. Although she tried to read up on all those subjects, she found it hard slogging.

Just as the accountant was explaining the cost of repairs for the roof of the building, Annabel translated his words into a very unladylike but unvoiced *Sheiß;* her secretary, Herr Bauer, interrupted them.

"I'm so sorry, but there's a visitor. He's not got an appointment." The man sniffed as if the visitor was in need of a bath.

"And who is it?"

"Herr Stevenson. He used to sell us wheat."

Annabel jumped up so fast she knocked over her chair. "We'll finish later," she told the accountant, using her hand to motion him out.

Olaf had light lines around his eyes that had not been there when she'd last seen him three years ago, although it seemed much, much longer. They exchanged the typical three-cheek kiss of friends rather than the handshake of business associates. Annabel would have preferred to hug him. It was one thing to think improper thoughts, another to act on them.

"What a surprise. What are you doing here?" She led him to the round table in one corner of her office. He sat without a formal invitation. "Coffee, please," she called to her secretary, whom she was sure was listening at the door. "He takes milk and one sugar."

"You remembered."

That she did remember shocked her. "What brings you here?"

"My grandfather died in Sweden. I needed to go to settle the family farm since his sons, my uncle and my father, are too old to travel."

Annabel knew that Olaf was her age. "And your wife?"

He frowned. "She died last year. Cancer."

"I'm so sorry." In their personal exchanges during his earlier visits, they had discussed their spouses, almost disloyally.

When Olaf said that his wife was an excellent mother, she

read into it that she thought her maternal duties were greater than her wifely ones, or at least that was what she half-hoped.

"By the time she died it was a blessing."

"But all that doesn't explain why you're here. Your wheat will be far too expensive with the tariffs."

They were interrupted by Herr Bauer, who put the coffee down. When Annabel told him to shut the door behind him, he sniffed. She thought Dieter insisted that they keep the man because he was about the only one she couldn't bend to her will. She also suspected he spied on her, for more than once when she left before him her papers had been rearranged ever so slightly the next morning. She'd begun memorizing where certain things were. Too often a pencil was not where she'd left it, or the papers which she'd arranged just so were no longer just so. Probably, she thought, he was reporting back to Dieter.

She and Stevenson talked about economics, how the wheat prices had fallen, but that at least it was a commodity that would always have some demand. She told him about some of the problems her company was having.

Annabel glanced out the window. When had it grown dark? Olaf had been there at least three hours. She went to the door to see that her secretary had departed. The sounds from the factory floor had ceased. Only one shift worked these days.

"May I buy you dinner?" Olaf asked, "I've kept you far too long."

Trying to stay calm, she said in what she hoped was a neutral tone, "Yes, thank you." As he helped her on with her coat she told herself that she was far too old to be having these feelings.

# CHAPTER 13

*Day 13, Saturday*

Brett Windsor's house was more like a small chalet, located on a street that ran parallel but about four blocks over to the one where the Young-Perrets were staying. Several cars were parked outside when Roger and Annie pulled up. Sophie had fallen asleep in her car seat and did not wake even when they secured her in the crib provided by the Windsors.

Although Roger had been less than enthusiastic about going, Annie persuaded him that it would be good for him to get out of the house and talk to someone other than a baby. All week she had worked hard to get the voluminous material under control. It was even harder with all the mutterings about Fritz whenever she walked through the company's corridors, but she refused to play the theory of what happened.

"Hanneli and Gisela used it when they were babies," Trudi Windsor said. "We'll set up our old baby monitor in case she wakes and is frightened being in a strange place."

Downstairs there were three other couples speaking a mixture of English and Swiss German. Annie tried to memorize the names lining them up with the faces.

Jason (American) and Marianne (Swiss) Costello. Alexander (Swiss) and Jennifer (American) Gerber. Kris (Swiss) and Heather (American) Herz.

Since they were all in their thirties and were dressed in jeans and sweaters, as were Brett and his wife, Annie knew because she met them all at the same time she would forever be confused on who was who.

Brett handed everyone a *Kir Royale* as an *Apertif.* They were seated on the three sofas that were placed around a full-wall, stone fireplace, which threw heat from a fire built with logs larger than most people's torsos. The conversation was mainly about their children, who seemed to go to the same schools and play together.

"I hope you're not too bored," the woman Annie hoped was the one named Jennifer said. "We're not used to having anyone new come into our little group."

"Not at all," Annie lied. She was almost afraid to look at Roger, who was both older and without any German. He reached for her hand, a signal that all was well.

"Let's stay in English for Roger," Marianne said, confirming Annie's long-held belief that women did more to make people feel comfortable than men did—not that men were mean, but that they just didn't think.

"I'd appreciate that," Roger said.

Trudi called everyone into the dining room. In the center of the table sat two *raclette* machines. One was the old-fashioned kind, H shaped, with the bottom bar of the H having a heating unit to melt the large semicircle of cheese to scrape over the boiled potatoes set in a nearby basket. The other's heating unit was below a small metal circle. Little metal dishes were covered with cheese and put on the heat until the cheese melted. Platters of dried meats, small pickles, and cocktail onions were placed so all could reach them without effort.

"We thought we'd do a traditional Swiss winter meal for Roger," Brett said.

"Thank you," Roger said as he glanced at Annie. She read it as he was telling her that even we French know about *raclette.*

When they were seated, Kris asked, "So what's the story on

your murdered boss, Brett?"

"I don't know any more than you do. The police are questioning all employees, but they haven't gotten around to me yet."

"I think it was the sister," Marianne said. "There was always bad blood between them."

"Marianne, Trudi, and Petra were all friends growing up," Brett said in Annie's direction. She wondered if that was the friend he had mentioned in the restaurant as the source of his information about the Bircher family.

"Petra doesn't seem the type to murder anyone," Jason said.

"How well do you know them?" Annie asked Marianne.

"Our family lived down the street from Petra's family. Our parents socialized a bit, but no one would call them friends. As kids Petra and I played together, but after we turned thirteen we developed different interests," Marianne said.

Since Annie was the newest to the group, she was given the first scraping of cheese and urged to eat without waiting for the others. She wanted to ask more about the Bircher family, but before she could, the conversation shifted.

"I've made my appointment," Jason said.

"When?" Jennifer asked.

"In two months, right before Christmas, in Bern."

"Jason and I are both renouncing our American nationality. That way we can keep our bank accounts."

Annie didn't need to ask why. Dual citizens were renouncing in record numbers because of the United States FATCA legislation. Banks, rather than go through the costly US-dictated procedures of reporting every financial move of American citizens living overseas, were simply refusing to do business with American expats. Longtime customers of most of the Swiss banks, and even those who had postal banking accounts, were told they were no longer welcome as clients. Americans' insurance policies, mortgages, and pension funds were all being cancelled.

Annie told them how her father, after years of doing business both private and professional, had been turned down for a car loan. "My mother's account had been closed."

The elder Youngs, Annie knew, hated the idea of renunciation but didn't like the other choices available to dual citizens like themselves. Her parents had told her that at almost every social gathering of Americans in Geneva where they lived, the question of renunciation had come up with "when" being more often used than "if." She hadn't expected it out here in the heart of Switzerland, where there were fewer Americans.

"What about you, Brett?"

"I'm not a dual. I've taken the route of putting everything in my wife's name: the house, all the bank accounts. If she didn't give me an ATM card I would be penniless or at least centimeless."

"Whew," Alexander said. "That means you have put a lot of trust in her."

"My only other choice would be to move our family back to the States, but Trudi has lived here all her life except when she was studying at BU, and she doesn't want to move."

"It's good in one way," Trudi said, as she made sure the semicircle of cheese was at a proper angle to melt. "I can guarantee he'll be awfully nice to me."

Brett reached over and patted his wife's hand, but he wasn't smiling.

# CHAPTER 14

*Day 14, Sunday*

Brett Windsor watched his wife Trudi unload the dishwasher from the party the night before. She held each champagne glass up to catch the light streaming through the kitchen window, checking for water spots, much like they do in television commercials. If nothing else Trudi lived up to the stereotype of the perfect Swiss housewife. "May I help with something?" he asked.

She lifted another glass. It must have passed muster because she put it in the box where she kept the good glasses between parties. "You don't put things away in their right place."

Brett swallowed to keep any nasty rejoinder from escaping his lips. If he were to save his marriage, he needed to play it cool, even if playing it cool had not been his method of operation for a couple of decades in anything. "I'm here if you think of something you want me to do."

He went to his desk and started going through the mail for the week, which he did every Sunday morning before he took the girls for a long walk. Sometimes Trudi joined them, but she often used the time to scrapbook without interruption. Scrapbooking had become her passion, making albums for friends from photos she'd taken. He wanted to point out to her that she could do the same thing online had she been willing.

This weekend both Hanneli and Gisela were at a sleepover, which had allowed him and Trudi to sleep in.

"What would you like for breakfast?" Trudi called from the kitchen.

"Do we have bacon and eggs?" He'd introduced her to an American breakfast and Sundays were usually bacon and eggs or waffles with real Vermont maple syrup.

"Yes."

He knew better than to offer to make them. He would never be able to leave the kitchen as neat as she demanded. That would lead her to slam anything slammable as she "cleaned up the mess," even if he could see no mess.

Sometimes he wondered what had happened to the carefree girl he'd met at Boston University in the April before she had returned to Switzerland in May. Letters had crisscrossed the Atlantic. The following year he had transferred to the University of Neuchâtel, partly because that was where she was studying. It all seemed like a lifetime ago.

His father and stepmother certainly didn't mind that his tuition went from several thousand dollars to almost nothing.

He'd hired Trudi to help with his French, or so he'd told her. Only after he confessed his other motive—getting her to be his girlfriend, did she agree to tutor him. He found her a harder taskmistress than anyone else would have been.

They'd spent the next summer trekking through Europe sharing a sleeping bag and laughter. Letters once again flew across the ocean when he found a job in Boston after graduation. Sometimes they even broke the bank with a long telephone call in those pre-email, pre-Skype days.

From the beginning of their relationship, Trudi said that she wouldn't live in the States and she insisted that he know at least two languages of her country if they were to be together.

The permit problem was a hassle. His father and stepmother had died in a car accident outside of Zurich during his last year at the university, severing his formal connection with the country. It also meant the end of his *Permis C* that allowed him all the rights of a Swiss citizen except voting. He'd been out of the country too long while he was studying to maintain it.

Marriage had been his option to be able to stay in the Alpine country and to be able to work. It was an option he would have selected even if working permits weren't involved.

He didn't know when their current problems had begun, but he was hoping they could still work through them. He loved her. Not the way he had in the beginning, but she wasn't like she'd been in the beginning. Maybe the woman he loved didn't exist anymore, but he had no intention of giving up on his marriage yet.

After his parents' divorce, he'd sworn he would never get divorced. He'd never do to his kids what they'd done to him and his brother—all those weekends shuttling from one house to another before his mother died.

Neither had the adjustment been easy to his new stepmother nor the move to Zurich. Although his stepmother had tried to be good to him and his brother, better than his own father, who was too busy to spend much time, it was easy to see that she preferred her own daughter to these two boisterous boys who came as part of the package.

Brett thumbed through the usual bills: the monthly health insurance, the car, the television subscription. Halfway through the pile he saw a letter from the bank that held their mortgage, now just in Trudi's name because of the pressure from the United States on Swiss banks. Her family had been doing business with the bank for probably over a hundred years, which let them shift from his and her names to just hers. He used the letter opener to slit the envelope.

"Shit! *Merde! Scheiß!*" They were asking for substantiation of Trudi's work, even though the manager there knew she still didn't have a job.

When they transferred the mortgage from the couple's name to hers, it was on condition she would find work, even though they knew that Brett's salary would be covering the payments. It was only the small town, long-term relationships that allowed this rule breach. Brett had been grateful that the manager had broken a rule or two to give them room to maneuver. The alternative would have been for the bank to demand immediate full payment on the mortgage, which they could not possibly pay and meant that the couple would lose the house.

Considering all the rules being broken by banks worldwide this was a tiny infraction, Brett knew, but the manager had taken a risk for them. Brett looked at the letter and realized that he had no choice but to push his wife to find work. The manager had made it clear that he would not require the normal salary level to justify the amount of the mortgage, but there had to be some piece of paper confirming that Trudi had income of her own.

The reality was that Trudi refused to work outside the home. He would never say she didn't work inside the home, which was spotless. Meals were on time and nourishing. She spent a great deal of time with the girls, but they were now both in school. Her excuse to not work was that the girls came home for lunch when she would give them a good hot meal, and his suggestion that they go to the canteen run by an American woman, who saw a great opportunity with the vacuum left by sending children home at noon, didn't sway his wife all that much.

"It gives us time to talk, communicate," she would say. He had to agree that time with the kids was important and that despite their Sunday forest walks as a family in spring, swimming in summer, mushroom gathering in autumn, and skiing or ice skating in winter, he didn't spend as much time with them as she did. And he didn't know how to play with them as she did.

His wife was truly a creative mother, unlike his own mother, who before her death was often too tired to do much with him other than to drive him to his Little League games, then go home and do whatever chore was the most pressing.

Had the mortgage remained in both their names, Trudi's working wouldn't be an issue. He liked their division of labor for the ease it gave their lives—or he had until now.

"It's your fault for being American," she'd said once.

"I can't renounce unless I have another nationality, and I can't get my Swiss nationality before the bank will call in the mortgage," he'd replied. The argument had accelerated until he'd said, "Tell you what, next time I'm born, I'll be born here." He'd slammed out the door.

He reread the letter and put it back in its envelope. He just didn't want to have a fight today. The weather was too beautiful and he was facing a horrendous week at work. What he wanted was a bit of calm.

"Breakfast is ready."

He went to the table, which had been set properly as it always was. The smell of bacon and coffee reminded him of before the girls were born, when Trudi would bring Sunday breakfast back to bed and they would make love.

How long had it been since they made love? Or even had sex?

Too long.

He sipped his fresh-squeezed orange juice.

As his wife reached for her napkin, he reached out and stroked her hand. "The kids won't be home until tonight. What would you think—"

"If you're thinking about sex, forget it."

"I was thinking more about making love."

"I'm using the time the girls are gone to clean their rooms."

# Chapter 15
# 1935

## Orange-Chocolate Cookies

**Ingredients:**
1 cup flour
3/4 cup unsweetened cocoa powder
1/2 teaspoon salt
2 tablespoons unsalted butter, room temperature
1/2 cup + 2 tablespoons granulated sugar
1 teaspoon pure vanilla extract
1 tablespoon orange zest

**Directions:**
Preheat oven to 325°F/162°C.

Line two baking sheets with parchment paper.

Sift dry ingredients together.

Cream butter and sugar until light and fluffy.

Add vanilla and orange zest.

Add flour gradually until well mixed.

Roll out dough between two parchment sheets.

Cut into desired shapes and put on baking sheet leaving about an inch between.

Bake 13–15 minutes.

★  ★  ★  ★  ★

The crisp, white linen duvet cover smelled of bleach. Outside the Zurich hotel room she could see the lake and snow-topped mountains. The sky was a brilliant blue. She stretched. At her age Annabel was amazed at the sexual pleasure she'd experienced the night before.

Sex was no longer sex. It was making love. It was becoming one with another person.

The sound of running water in the bathroom ceased and Olaf Stevenson walked out. A giant towel tied around his waist covered his legs. Even at fifty-five he was well muscled, which was emphasized by the lack of body hair.

He dropped his towel and crawled across the bed on all fours, growling, and making Annabel giggle.

"I love it when you giggle," he said. "It makes you seem like a young girl, a beautiful young girl."

Giggling had never been a part of Annabel's personality even during the period when she'd been trying to be a typical empty-headed wife, but Olaf made her laugh so much.

He pulled down the duvet and ran his forefinger over her stretch marks. Annabel still had a flat stomach. Her breasts, which had been almost nonexistent in her twenties and thirties, popped out during menopause and therefore had escaped the gravity that women who had had breasts from their teenage years suffered.

Olaf put his mouth over her left nipple.

"We should be going. Our first appointment is at ten and I'm hungry."

"I'm hungry for you."

"You always are."

"Okay, Chief." Olaf stood up and started to dress. "Let's run over our plans."

Aside from his being a wonderful lover, Annabel never regretted hiring him as a buyer for the business. Dieter had fought the idea because Olaf spoke none of the Swiss languages, but Annabel had hired a tutor, who for three solid months drilled him every day in Swiss German. Then another tutor appeared and spent three more months drilling him in French, so that now he was fluent in both.

"We're paying him to learn. What if he goes back to Canada?" Dieter had said.

"He won't."

"He's a salesman, not a buyer."

"Then he should know what tricks a salesman would pull."

Annabel had been correct. Not only had Olaf become fluent, which he said was easier because he already spoke English and Swedish so the third and fourth languages were simple, he had been good at building relationships with vendors. After the first year, he was the one who had suggested that he try sales, too, and despite the Depression he had opened five new accounts, although one had to be closed for lack of payment.

Dieter had admitted that Annabel had been right. She always credited her husband with the ability to admit where and when he was wrong, never saying "I told you so"—other than in her head, where she chanted to herself.

Now Annabel was grateful that Dieter was so preoccupied with his politics that not only did he ignore the business, he never realized when Olaf and Annabel became lovers.

Because of Olaf's position, it was natural that she would travel with him on some sales and buying expeditions, staying overnight in hotels, always booking two rooms on different floors, mussing the beds in the unused room in case any maid might later be called on to testify in a divorce hearing.

Annabel hated the extra expense, but prudence comes at a price she would say.

Annabel dressed and returned to her own room, making sure

the hallway was empty and taking the stairs. She took her nightgown from her purse and dropped it on the bed, then wet her toothbrush before picking up the phone to call Olaf, placing the call through the hotel operator.

"Ready for breakfast?"

"Of course, meet you in the lobby in five minutes."

Let the operator listen in. Annabel often thought it was guilt more than fear of detection that made her so cautious in creating the appearance of innocence.

Before leaving she glanced at herself in the mirror. The reflection was a very proper middle-aged woman. No one would guess that she'd been crazy with passion an hour before as well as the night before and the morning before and . . . God how she loved these business trips.

Olaf said she had a switch. One minute she'd be his lover and the next minute she'd be a business owner. As a business owner she needed to think about bringing Theo into the business now that he had finished at the London School of Economics.

He'd be coming home in another week with his English bride, the fair-skinned, blue-eyed Jemma. Had she thought it out, she might have suspected that he was of an age that he might fall in love.

She'd picked out a girl for her son, the Swiss daughter of the long-time mayor. The girl had had a crush on Theo before he'd left for London to study. They looked on track for an engagement.

Annabel felt sorry for the girl, but better that her son married for love, as she wished she'd done. The mayor had been huffy about the whole thing, but his daughter had been pursued by a local bank manager with good prospects for advancement, leaving everyone satisfied. Annabel could imagine in another decade someone might remember and say, "Theo might have married a local girl, but she was more interested in someone else."

Whatever they said didn't matter.

Her son was coming home. Maybe she would become a grandmother, although that made her sound older than she felt—much older.

# CHAPTER 16

*Day 15, Monday*

Annie was more than ready to go back to work in the office on Monday. Trying to organize what she'd done the previous week into some sort of story line so far, has left her little time with Sophie. What she had wasn't good, because of the baby's teething and general crankiness.

She felt guilty for not accomplishing more. She felt guilty that she hadn't made her daughter happier.

In one way she was glad that she could escape, which also made her feel guilty. Although the baby had been quiet and slept well during the party at the Windsors' on Saturday night, on Sunday morning Sophie was majorly out of sorts. As Roger had predicted, she had developed a diaper rash. He told Annie he was taking her out for a drive. Sophie was one of those babies who fell asleep almost before the car left the driveway, leaving Annie free to work from notes she'd brought home.

That she hadn't accomplished more was her own fault. She'd used some of the time to take a nap, a precious commodity these days. Even the dogs had curled up next to the bed as if glad for a moment of tranquility without a screaming baby.

After the door closed and she heard the engine start, she once again appreciated her situation. The same feeling existed Monday morning. She could diaper her daughter, dress and feed her, then put her coat on and disappear for the day, leaving

Roger to handle the rest of the household chores and the fussy baby.

Never, ever, would she have dared to tell him how happy she was that his heart attack made his early retirement a necessity, not that she was glad that he had a heart attack. When she had thought that he might die, she'd been terrified. Since it had taken her so long to commit to him, she was not ready to lose him. Her good feeling about him this Monday had nothing to do with his househusband efficiency. She just plain loved him for reasons that made no sense to her.

Because the weather was so clear, she decided to walk, which gave her time to switch from mother/wife mode to writer/ historian mode.

She was equally thankful that the house-sitting made this assignment even more profitable. Not only did they not have to pay for lodgings, her agent was giving them money for the duration because they were taking care of the dog, although Curie was no problem. She and Hannibal spent most of their time romping in the garden or sleeping by the fire.

She entered the factory and the receptionist handed her a note. It read, "Please see me as soon as you come in, Frau Ritzman."

"As soon as you come in" precluded going upstairs to take off her coat or getting a cup of tea.

Frau Ritzman's secretary's desk was empty, but Petra was visible through the open door of her office. She was dressed in black slacks and a black sweater again, but this time there was no scarf and no jewelry. She spied Annie and beckoned her in.

After the normal greetings, Annie said, "I'm sorry about your brother."

"Thank you. I'm sure you heard the rumors that we were at each other's throats almost all the time."

Annie was tempted to deny them, but she felt truthfulness

was called for: maybe she could be diplomatic. "Is there a company in the world that doesn't have a grapevine?"

"Probably not." Frau Ritzman looked beyond Annie. "Ah, you're back," she called to her secretary. "Can you bring a pot of tea, please?" And to Annie, "Tea is all right?"

Annie nodded. Frau Ritzman waved for her to sit down. The desk, which was elaborately carved with animals and trees, would have looked good in a formal study from the 1880s. The chairs were upholstered with a green and yellow chintz pattern that worked well with the soft green walls and dark green drapes. Annie knew from past experience they were comfortable. Petra wasn't the type of executive who tried to dominate by setting up an uncomfortable situation with those to whom she wanted to talk.

"The police aren't through questioning all the employees. Have they come to you yet?"

"They came to the house after they found the car. We're staying a few houses down from the lake where the car went into the water."

Frau Ritzman nodded. "I didn't realize that. They may want to come back to you."

"I can't be of much help, although I was with him shortly before the car went into the water, I think. He picked me up on my walk home."

"And you went to the *Gasthaus* for a drink."

Small town, Annie thought, remembering her first few years in New England, where her mother knew her grades before she brought the report card home. It was the same in Argelès-sur-mer. Roger's retirement was known before the paperwork had been submitted, although neither of them had said anything to anyone. The flow of information in any small village was probably as fast or faster than anything on the Internet.

"Let's say that he thought I might like to take sides, which considering this is a short-term assignment was more than optimistic."

"And if you had to take sides?"

This was one of those situations that Annie hated. She was being pushed to take a position in a situation in which she had no stake. Then again, what did it hurt to say what she thought? "In principle, Frau Ritzman, I support small companies over big multinationals. I like companies that care about their employees. I believe in co-ops even more. So the idea that this would be turned over to some firm without the history, and no interest at all in the community, would make me lean in your direction."

"Please call me Petra."

Annie nodded, but had no intention of switching from *sie* to *du*. Petra, she was sure, would still want some formal barrier.

"I certainly would be richer if I sold to a multinational."

"Is that your goal? Money?"

They were interrupted by Frau Küper with a tray bearing a tea set. She set it down and poured two cups, asking about cream, sugar, lemon. Both women wanted it black.

"Isn't that the Rosenthal Petite rose pattern, turn of the twentieth century?"

"I'm impressed," Petra said. "It has been handed down from my grandmother. Unfortunately, there are only a few pieces left from a complete service for twelve." She blew on her tea. "You know your antiques."

Annie didn't say that she only knew that because some had come up for sale when she was doing a project for a Geneva auction house.

Petra took out a green folder that was fastened with corner elastics. She opened it. There was about an inch of papers. Annie, who could read type upside down, noted that her name was printed in the upper right-hand corner. "My file?"

"You are astute, which your file says. Before we hired you, we did do an investigation."

Annie found that admission vaguely annoying, but if Petra were going to mention anything Annie hadn't told her that was in the file, what choice did the woman have? "Did you hire a private investigator?"

"With the Internet it isn't necessary. You've got a blog. You've published two books. There's social media where you're listed."

No secrecy, these days, Annie thought, but she'd known that every time she put something on the Net. However, she was very careful about what went up there. Even in her blog, when she wrote about family things, she paid close attention to what might cost her an assignment—or worse—embarrass her friends.

"Your husband was a policeman."

Annie nodded.

"He worked for 36 in Paris."

Annie nodded again. The 36 was one of the best detective forces in France. The name came from the number of the street where the headquarters stood overlooking the Seine, 36 Quai des Orfèvres. Had Roger's first wife not been killed by a man just out of prison, a man who had been put there by Roger, he would never have moved to the South of France. Argelès was a much better environment to raise his then pre-teenage daughter alone. She guessed that Petra knew all this.

"Would he come to work for me?"

"Doing what?"

"I've learned that I am under suspicion for Fritz's murder. I had the most to gain. As much as they can figure time of death, I have no alibi. My kids were at a sleepover and my husband was staying overnight in Zurich because he had both late and early morning meetings."

"You haven't been accused."

Petra shook her head. "They keep coming back with more

questions. They are worse than *Columbo,* only the detective in charge doesn't have an old raincoat or a cigar."

Annie smiled. In every country she had lived, the program had been dubbed into the local language.

"I want to be cooperative," said Petra, "but I need to protect myself."

"Have you hired a lawyer?"

"Yes," she sighed, "but that probably makes me look guilty . . . preparing for the reality of arrest and all that. I'd still like to see your husband conduct an investigation."

Annie had two thoughts: One, Roger would love it. Two, she'd lose her babysitting househusband.

"I'll ask him, but if he says yes, we'll need a babysitter and I don't know anyone around here."

"Your daughter would be welcome in our company *Kinderzimmer,* which is free to our employees."

When Annie hesitated, Petra suggested that she check it out.

The *Kinderzimmer* was in a building on the other side of the parking lot. Annie had heard about it, but she hadn't seen it except for watching employees dropping off their offsprings. The children didn't cling to their parents, but rushed in the door, which Annie took as a good sign of the way the *Kinderzimmer,* or *Krippe,* was managed.

Petra must have taken her silence for doubt. "Our staff is well trained. Or I can recommend a woman."

Maybe her mother would come from Geneva. But then again it might be good for Sophie to have more stimulation by having other children around. "I'll have to ask Roger about it—both if he wants the project and if he's okay about leaving Sophie with others. He's been saying how lucky we are that we don't have to."

However, she knew that Roger would love to be doing something professional again.

# CHAPTER 17

*Day 15, Monday*

After Annie left her office, Petra Ritzman sat for a long time at her desk and did nothing. Doing nothing was an abnormality. Her life was too full with the business, her three children, and yes, even her husband, to allow long contemplative moments or even short ones. She prided herself on being able to absorb information and make quick decisions and to have a majority of those decisions work out well.

She hoped Annie's husband would be able to do something to throw suspicion for Fritz's death onto someone else. The police had all but arrested her the other night. Walter had made a call to their attorney from his office while the police were questioning Petra in the living room. Like in all small towns, certain people have influence and influential people have pull. Her husband talked to the police and gave assurance that Petra wasn't about to run away.

However, Petra had overheard the police muttering that innocent people didn't need lawyers.

Run away? Good God, how stupid could the police be? She had a company to run, a company she had fought hard to lead. Although she hated to admit it, she spent more time thinking about the company than she did her children. It wasn't just a company, it was her family's heritage and she wasn't going to be the one to lose it.

"More tea?" her secretary asked.

Petra looked up, startled, and nodded. She helped the secretary put the tea things on the table.

She wished she could mourn Fritz, but she was glad he was dead, not that she would admit that to anyone. It was hard enough to admit it to herself. Nice people didn't wish relatives dead and Petra liked to think of herself as a nice person.

When she was little she had wanted a brother or sister. More than once, she was promised that one was on the way, but then her mother and father had said they changed their minds, it would be later. Only later did she realize that it was because of her mother's many miscarriages.

They hadn't told her Fritz was expected until they had placed the screaming bundle on a pillow on her lap and after making her promise to hold him tightly. They gave her the job of protecting him.

She wasn't jealous of the attention he had received from her mother, but she did resent how when her father came home, instead of sweeping her up in his arms as he had done before the birth, he went straight to the nursery to see "my son." Only afterward, would he come back downstairs and ask Petra about her day—unless he forgot or disappeared into his study to work. Before Fritz was born he would discuss many things with her, about her school work, her friends, a book she was reading, something that happened at the factory. After the birth he no longer did.

As her brother grew, her trips to the cookie factory were fewer and fewer. Fritz would be taken in her place. She would beg to go: Fritz would beg to stay. Neither of their tears made any difference to her father.

Her mother would try to comfort her, saying that she would grow up and have her own children and forget about the cookie factory.

It wasn't just the factory trips or her father's shifting of loyalties that made her dislike her brother—and God help her, even though he was dead, she had disliked her brother. He was the typical little brother, getting into her things, but unlike the brothers of her friends, Fritz had a destructive streak.

He'd taken a knife to her favorite doll, a rag doll the same size as a three-year-old and who wore Petra's clothes from when she was that age. The doll had blond yarn for hair, completely covering the flesh-colored scalp, and an embroidered face with a smile that implied that the doll had a secret. Her Aunt Mattie had made the doll for her. Although Petra had tried to fix it, the face was scarred and where the arms had been sewn back on the stitches were different.

Petra had played physical therapy with the doll. She'd asked a friend who had had PT for a broken arm how it was done.

If it had just been the doll, Petra might have forgiven and forgotten, or at least forgiven, but Fritz would also hit her when no one was looking. When she fought back, he would convince her parents that she had started it, leaving her angry that they believed him and not her.

Once he'd peed in her bed. Petra was accused of wetting her bed, and no matter how hard she tried no one would believe that it wasn't her pee.

When Fritz was eleven he was sent to L'Institut le Rosey, an exclusive school in the French part of Switzerland. "If he's going to run the factory, he needs the best business training," her father had said. "Le Rosey will prepare him for Cornell, and Cornell will prepare him for the Harvard Business School."

"But I want to run the factory," she'd said. Her father only laughed and reminded her that she was a girl. She could see no correlation between her gender and a lack of ability to do something. She'd even mastered peeing standing up to prove she was as good as her brother, although once she'd done it in front of her father, he told her never to do it again, so she'd returned to sitting. Sitting was more comfortable and she could read at the same time.

Fritz hadn't wanted to go away to school. Nor did he want to go to Cornell or Harvard Business School. Petra had tried to talk to Fritz's best friend and have him suggest to Fritz to flunk out, but the friend refused to do it.

Fritz, however, had a certain pride in being the best at what he did: football, grades, etcetera. Flunking out would have shown him not to be the best. Once he was the best, he stopped whatever it was. He'd proven what he wanted to prove. No more need to extend himself.

Petra did not resent him for being handsome, for both her mother and father had always told her how pretty she was. Being pretty plus her social standing would give her a good husband, the assigned family goal for her future, they kept saying. They were right. Walter was a successful investment banker.

Sometimes she thought Walter and Fritz were in collusion to make the sale of the company a reality, although she had no proof other than what she thought was her own paranoia. Too often when she entered a room when it was just the two of them, they stopped talking.

Her marriage was another thing she had to deal with. Maybe Annie's husband could also check to see if Walter's need to stay overnight in Zurich more and more frequently had little to do with late evening or early-early morning business meetings.

She wasn't sure how she would feel about a divorce. They didn't fight, and they did parent their children well. Their sex life was predictable but pleasant. They shared holidays—three weeks in the South of France in the summer and two weeks skiing in Austria during the winter school break. That amused her since skiing was within a half hour drive, but Walter liked being in the Austrian hotels and far away from his own work.

The children were of an age that she and Walter had been

talking about sending them to Le Rosey, where her husband had gone as well as her brother. Walter thought Einsiedeln a bit provincial and the contacts at Le Rosey would carry the children throughout their lives. Same old, same old: her father and her husband played the same mental CD over and over.

Petra could see the advantage. It would free her up for the business, although she would miss her *babies* dreadfully. She liked her kids—liked as well as loved. They made her laugh, were well behaved. The *Kindermädchen* took care of all the mundane parts of child rearing. Although the children were now a bit old for a *Kindermädchen*, Anita had come from the States when Petra's daughter was born, stayed with them, and married a local, who also lived in to maintain the house and garden. They were family, more family in terms of loving than the blood that she shared with Fritz.

Now Fritz was dead and she was glad she could continue with her plans to develop the company the way she wanted without his interference.

# Chapter 18
# October 1938

## Oatmeal Raisin Cookies

**Ingredients:**
3/4 cup softened butter
3/4 cup white flour
3/4 cup packed light brown sugar
2 eggs
1 teaspoon vanilla extract
1 1/4 cups regular flour
1 teaspoon baking soda
3/4 teaspoon ground cinnamon
2 3/4 cups rolled oats
1 cup raisins

**Directions:**
Preheat oven to 350°F/176°C.

Cream butter and sugars until smooth.

Beat in eggs and vanilla until fluffy.

Stir in dry ingredients except for oats.

Beat into butter bit by bit then add oats and raisins.

Drop by teaspoonfuls onto ungreased cookie sheets.

Bake 8–10 minutes.

"Do we have to listen to the news every morning?" Annabel set the white porcelain coffee pot down on the sideboard then picked up the cup she had just filled for Dieter and placed it in front of him. The question annoyed him.

They had let the maid go after the children had moved out, making do only with the cook and a cleaning woman who came in three times a week.

Her suggestion.

Dieter felt as long as things were done properly, it didn't matter all that much to him.

"But I like the news, and thank you for the coffee."

"Just once I'd like to eat in quiet. Maybe talk."

He felt tired and old, but then he was seventy-eight and still working for the Socialist Party in the same way as he had for half a century. Sometimes it seemed progress was metered out in single raindrops. Quitting was not an option. He knew if he had to retire he might as well crawl directly into his coffin.

Once for what? Oh yes, no radio at the table. Annabel did not ask a great deal. Like most of the couples he knew they had worked out their lives to accommodate each other as much as possible. He'd given in on her working long ago, although he remembered how much he had hated the idea, not just when it was introduced but for several years thereafter.

Her working made it look like he couldn't care for his family, but slowly he had come not just to accept it but see some advantages. In fact, the biggest advantage was that he didn't have to do much with the factory. What so impassioned both his father and his wife about the factory, he would never understand.

With each passing year, they had grown in friendship but not in understanding, which seemed contradictory, but in a strange way it made sense to him, without being able to explain it to anyone, including himself.

He still envied men with compliant wives who stayed home. Alice, his mistress, was content to stay in the flat he had rented for her in Bern and wait for him. They'd been together now for almost two decades. There were times that he wondered what would happen if Annabel found out, not that he was capable of anything sexual. He was sure the reality would be far more vicious than anything he could imagine.

At least Annabel no longer objected to his time away from the factory. In fact, she had seen the advantages of his putting some of his theories into operation behind his back.

One of those was putting George, the union leader, on the board. He could see what the management was trying to accomplish and the problems that they faced, and in turn he could communicate to the workers what was reasonable to expect. On the other hand, he was equally quick to see that his members received their share of the gains. A year-end bonus was given to everyone, varying depending on how well the factory did.

Annabel had fought him—tooth and nail, to use a cliché—against bringing George on board, but she admitted Dieter had been right. Give her credit, she would always admit when she'd been wrong.

It had crossed his mind that her fighting him was not sincere; if she disagreed it was to convince him to do the opposite of what she didn't want. There had been a period when he was younger that if she'd said, "I want red," he would reply, "I want blue," even if he wanted red: stupidities of youth.

On the other hand, Annabel's business sense had been a total surprise. When they were first married she'd seemed so irresponsible and, well, he wasn't sure how to phrase it, superficial? But she had been so much younger than he was. He hadn't been in love with her, but his parents put so much pressure on him to marry that he decided to give in. A young wife would be malleable, or so he thought. Had he been wrong! So wrong.

More and more he kept thinking about the past and more and more it was interfering with the present. Maybe that was what happened at his age.

He looked at his wife, who was holding her coffee cup in front of her face, taking in the smell. How shocked he'd been that when his father died, she'd insisted on going to work in the factory. He'd thought she'd make a complete mess of it. She'd done anything but. In for a penny, in for a pound, was her philosophy. Granted, she was better on the production side, adding that entire line of cookies and a cake here or there. She researched to find more efficient equipment that reduced their cost. They'd made a good team, although he felt he was the only one who believed that they were a team.

He sighed.

"Now you're sighing because you can't listen to your news." She waved her hand toward the radio.

He stood and walked over to the radio, dropping a kiss on the top of her head. She was still a good-looking woman. She hadn't thickened as many of his colleagues' wives had and her skin was only minimally lined around the eyes, mostly from smiling.

The announcer came on midsentence. "The German Wehrmacht has overtaken Prague, bringing it under German control . . ."

The couple listened, all movement forgotten.

"I knew it, I knew it, I knew it," Dieter said. The subject of Germany had been *verboten* in the home. Like many Swiss, Annabel thought Hitler was good for Germany, bringing order and helping the people out of the devastation and poverty brought on by the Great War. The socialists and the trade unions saw Hitler as a threat. "There's going to be a war, as bad if not

113

worse than the last one," Dieter said.

When the news stopped, Annabel buttered the toast that had grown cold. "I don't think so. What can it gain Hitler? Wars are expensive."

"Nothing good will come of this."

# CHAPTER 19

*Day 15, Monday*

Roger watched his wife hold Sophie on her lap as she spooned the baby's dinner, which had been processed down to pulp from their own regular meal, into her daughter's eager mouth.

His first wife and their French friends said the way to keep children from being finicky eaters was to feed them mushed-up table food as soon as they were on solids. Roger had said his daughter, Gaëlle, had been fed that way because it was easy and saved a fortune on baby food that contained who knew what. The truth about it preventing fussy eaters in the future would have to wait until Sophie became a toddler. At the moment, she ate whatever they put in her mouth.

"The *Krippe* at the factory looks great," Annie said. "I can pop in and see her during the day if I have a moment."

"Then you don't think I'm letting you down as babysitter, nanny, and governess?"

Sophie spit out the last mouthful she'd been given, hitting the towel that Annie had the foresight to put over her clothes. She tried once more with the same results. "Guess you're through, Pumpkin."

She washed off whatever needed to be washed off and put the baby on a blanket far enough from the fireplace that Sophie wouldn't hurt herself, but close enough to be warm. Several toys were on the blanket and Sophie held one and alternately looked at it and tasted it.

She and Roger then dished out their own dinners, a hot potato and leek soup and salad.

"You've missed working," Annie said.

"And Switzerland's flag is a white cross on a red background," Roger said. "I was too young to retire."

Annie resisted saying that after his heart attack he was no longer fit enough for police work. Mentally he was fine, but he had been warned against sudden bursts of exercise. Running after a criminal might qualify as a life-threatening activity. The decision was not his to take. The system decreed that he must retire when he couldn't get medically certified as fit for duty.

"Who do you think killed Bircher?" Roger carried the dishes to the dishwasher.

"Petra has the most to gain. Hiring you could be a ploy to look innocent."

Roger put the dishes in the dishwasher. "Or maybe she doesn't think much of the Swiss police."

Annie finished clearing the dishes on the countertop between the table and the dishwasher. Roger's stacking of a dishwasher was a work of art, while Annie's was haphazard at best. "Her brother didn't seem very likeable. Okay, he was surface charming. Very. And some people could have fallen for it. Easily."

"We both know the type. Tell me more about the company."

Annie did both, going into the history and the story of Petra's plans and Fritz's plans for the future of the company.

"No common ground."

"The day after tomorrow, I'll meet with Petra and see what I can do, if you arrange for the *Krippe.*"

They both glanced to where Sophie had been placed near the fire. Their daughter was sound asleep.

# CHAPTER 20

*Day 16, Tuesday*

The Abbey was filled for Fritz Bircher's funeral. Gold-leaf cherubs and designs covered the white walls and soaring ceiling. The closed casket was carried by eight employees of the company, whom Annie recognized by sight but not by name.

Roger had deliberately chosen a place to sit where he could observe all those attending the Mass. He had accepted the assignment from Petra.

Fritz's body had been discovered in a snow bank in a forest not too far off the road leading to Einsiedeln. A dog, out walking with his mistress, had dug through the snow.

Petra had said there was a parking place not far from the spot, where she used to go when she was taking her children to pick mushrooms. The police had released the body fairly quickly but had asked the family not to cremate it.

Any hopes of finding tire marks were vanquished by the snow, although the general attitude was that Fritz had been shot in his own car. Bullet holes (three) had been discovered in the upholstery. Roger had not been able to find out how many bullets were in Fritz's body.

The body had been transported to the spot by unknown means, maybe in Fritz's car, maybe in another vehicle. His car had been taken to the lake and pushed into the water. "The murderer probably didn't count on the lake being too shallow to cover the car." A small part of the roof had remained visible, he'd told Annie before the service.

His information came from Petra because the police had refused to talk with him.

"As for blood being in the car, I'm not sure it could be proved. The windows had been cracked just enough at the top to fill the car so that even Luminol might not be able to detect the blood."

The two places they had selected were toward the back of the Abbey where they could watch people file in. Annie knew if this were Roger's investigation, he would have someone photographing everyone who attended. The police might have been doing that, but if they were it was so subtle, no one could tell. She glanced around to see if she could spot any cameras, telephones, or tablets but didn't see any.

"I wish I were more familiar with who is who here," he whispered as Brett and Trudi entered. They were the only other two people he recognized until Marianne Costello from the *raclette* party the Saturday before walked by with two unfamiliar women.

Annie, on the other hand, recognized the workers from the plant. She guessed that the other people attending who did not work at the factory were locals who commuted into Zurich each day. How they knew the Birchers was unknown.

A television crew had been stationed outside, but they were kept at a distance by the private police that Petra had hired to protect the family. Annie guessed, by the notebooks and pens being used by a man and a woman, that a couple of reporters had slipped through.

Annie nudged Roger. "That's Christopher Auer, director general of ZPFI."

"Where you worked about three years ago?"

"The factory must represent a fairly large account for him to come to the funeral," Annie said. "Or maybe that's where Walter Ritzman works. I know it's a bank, but I don't know which one."

"If it's a bank it could be involved with the negotiations for the sale," Roger said. "Remind me to ask Petra, er Frau Ritzman."

Annie watched Brett and Trudi Windsor make their way to the front where the officers of LK had been instructed to sit. When he tried to take his wife's arm to direct her to a pew, she shrugged him off.

A chorus sang what Annie thought might be Bach's Mass in B Minor. Her tastes in music ran more along the pop, jazz, and gospel lines, although both her mother and father had insisted she at least be aware of the classics. For a second she imagined a gospel group singing "Cross the River Jordan" or "Amazing Grace," which would not only be out of place in the Abbey but totally out of character with the little she knew of Fritz.

Annie glanced at her watch. The funeral was scheduled for fourteen hundred hours. It was now fifteen minutes later, very un-Swiss. Everyone moved about in their seats. If it were a rock concert, people might have stamped their feet or made catcalls to get the show started.

The family entered. Petra walked down the aisle to the front row. She was wearing a black dress. A veil covered her face. A man, whom Annie guessed was probably Herr Ritzman, looked solemn as he held onto her arm. A teenage boy of maybe fourteen and a girl not quite in her teens followed. They too were dressed in black. Probably Petra thought her five-year-old daughter was too little to attend. The family made their way to the front row without looking at or greeting anyone.

The Mass was traditional. No one gave any eulogy. At the end of the service, the coffin was carried out by the same pallbearers, followed by the family. Then row by row, starting from the front, people shuffled out.

Annie noted that no one was snuffling into a handkerchief nor were they red-eyed. The closest feeling she could detect was solemnity, but that was normal for the occasion.

By the time she and Roger worked their way out of the Abbey, the hearse had already pulled away for the cemetery.

"What did you learn from that?" Annie asked.

"Nothing," Roger said.

# CHAPTER 21
# 1940

## PECAN-PUMPKIN SPICE COOKIES

**Ingredients:**
1 1/2 cups packed light brown sugar
1/2 cup butter or margarine, softened
2 eggs
1/2 cup cooked pumpkin
3 teaspoons vanilla
2 3/4 cups flour
2 teaspoons baking powder
1 teaspoon ground cinnamon
1/2 teaspoon salt
1/2 teaspoon ground ginger
1/4 teaspoon ground nutmeg
1/8 teaspoon ground allspice
1/8 teaspoon ground cloves
Pinch of ground cardamom
1 1/3 cups finely chopped pecans

**Directions:**
Preheat oven to 350°F/176°C.

Grease cookie sheet.

Beat brown sugar, butter, eggs, pumpkin, and vanilla together until fluffy.

Stir in dry ingredients.

Add pecans.

Drop tablespoonfuls of dough onto cookie sheet.

Bake 10–14 minutes or until edges are lightly browned.

The perfume of the lilacs outside the window of the dining room overrode the smell of bacon coming from the kitchen. Dieter sat opposite Annabel, with a newspaper separating them. She could read the headline: "Winston Churchill: *Neuen Britischen Premierminster.*"

He was home for three days before returning to Parliament, which was meeting to discuss the situation concerning the German successes in Norway at the expense of the Allies. Dieter talked constantly about the *Geistige Landesverteidigung,* the spiritual defense of the country that saw his beloved Socialist Party align with the entrepreneurs who had often different goals. Many who early on had been sympathetic to Hitler had changed their opinion and were more concerned that Hitler might consider Switzerland as his next target.

They were eating porridge sweetened with honey. Sugar was harder and harder to come by, although most of the beet crop in the country was being converted to sugar. Thank goodness for Olaf, who was still able to buy enough sugar for some of their pastries, although the kitchens were experimenting with recipes using the sweeteners that they could get with less effort.

Dieter had said many times that things would get worse, a lot worse before they got better—so repetitive that Annabel wanted to scream, but then again at least it was something to talk about. He no longer showed any interest at all in the factory. While this would have annoyed her before, it now gave her a freedom to solve problems using Olaf's wisdom, which was far more business-oriented than Dieter's would ever be.

Dieter reached around his paper to pick up his cup of hot chocolate, but left his bacon and porridge untouched. He was getting thinner and thinner and his complaints about stomachaches, which had gone on for years, were increasing.

"I do wish you'd make an appointment with the doctor," she said.

"I haven't time." The words came from behind the paper.

Annabel put down her napkin. "I need to get to work."

Annabel had been a familiar sight to the residents of Einsiedeln each morning since she began at the factory. She walked the ten minutes it took to get from the house to the office, or as she described it, "I stride. It's good exercise."

Usually, she was one of the first people in, but this morning, she was beaten by Theo. He now occupied his father's desk and had taken over most of his father's responsibilities; he was fast moving in on Annabel's, much faster than she was willing to concede.

Theo was doing well in his job despite his annoying habit of thrusting himself into some conversation where she felt he would have been better saying nothing and listening more. "Aren't there things you want to do other than work, *Mutti*?" he would ask weekly.

Annabel, who had no intention of retiring and turning the company over to him just yet, would say, "I love to work, so it isn't work." Sometimes she thought that Theo might not be as bright as she thought, since he hadn't really varied the conversation all that much. She'd debated writing out the conversation word for word, since they had it so often, and simply handing the paper to him the next time he brought up the subject of her retirement. "Read this. It will save us both going over the same old sentences," she would say. So far she'd resisted, but she had picked up a pen and paper a few times and wrote out at least the two first sentences before changing her mind.

Sixty was not that old. Many people in Einsiedeln reached their nineties and a few even were walking around in their hundreds, albeit with canes. Even her husband wasn't old in his head, although physically he seemed to be shrinking.

Besides, there were things she still wanted to do with the company once this damned war was over.

"Good morning, Theo," she said as she passed his office.

"Good morning, *Mutti.*" He closed the ledger he'd been reviewing and followed Annabel into her office. "You're later than usual. Is everything all right?"

Despite his desire to take over the company from a parent who didn't want to let go, Annabel adored Theo. He'd been an active little boy, good at sports, good with his studies. He'd done well at university but on vacations he'd always come to the plant. He had learned every piece of machinery, knew every worker's name.

When she was ready to let go, he'd be ready. He was ready now. She wasn't. Her son would just have to accept that.

His attentiveness as a son was equally commendable. Some of her friends complained that once their sons married they barely saw them. Theo and Jemma, who lived three doors away, were regular visitors, always calling beforehand to check if it were convenient.

Annabel had liked Jemma from the first time she'd met her. She came from London and she and Theo had met when he was at the London School of Economics. Jemma's brother had been Theo's classmate.

Her son's one vice was a quick temper. Jemma knew how to subvert it with a word or a touch.

Annabel felt that Jemma was frustrated as a wife. She wanted to be more active in the company, but Theo had said one woman running the family business was enough. Had Jemma not had miscarriages, but had had babies, she might have been more content. Annabel understood the desire to be more than just a wife. More than once, Annabel had seen business law books open and she knew that Theo was not the one reading them.

Maybe that would keep Jemma interested, although married women attending university were not totally unknown.

Even if women doing unheard-of things appealed to Annabel, her son and daughter-in-law would have to work through their own issues. She refused to interfere, although Lord knows she wanted to offer her "better" ideas.

Her husband would say their children had to lead their own lives. She had never complained to Dieter, because he wasn't aware of any of the undercurrents that went on in the family. Amazing that a man with such political acumen would miss the subtleties around him, but he did. Thus Annabel relied more and more on Olaf not just for business talk but family talk.

"I'm worried," Annabel said to Theo.

He moved his head in a motion that said, "I'm listening."

"Your father isn't well, but he refuses to take time to do anything about it."

"Getting either you or Father to do anything you don't want to is harder than moving the Rock of Gibraltar to South America."

Annabel smiled at that. Her son was always great at analogy. It worked well when he was discussing ideas with the staff. "I don't suppose you would be willing to talk to him?"

"I'll try when he gets back."

They were interrupted by the rest of the office staff arriving almost as a group: footsteps, doors opening and shutting, desk drawers being unlocked, papers rustling. The weather was so warm that coats were no longer needed. People settled directly after exchanging the ritual handshakes required at the beginning and ending of each day.

The next sounds were typewriters, the noise clattering through the open doors of the various offices. Short bursts of conversations were overheard as one staff member would request this or that document or bit of information from a coworker.

Theo returned to his office.

Annabel picked up the inventory list to decide on their manufacturing capabilities. She was looking forward to having lunch with Olaf, back from a combination buying-selling trip. Dieter had finally agreed that the Canadian had more than justified his salary, saying he held two posts in one and freed Dieter from many of the chores he so hated.

Annabel wanted to reach out and take Olaf's hand, but wouldn't. They'd managed not to arouse suspicions. He was never in her office with the door closed. They nodded when they met in the hall. Although they would sometimes eat lunch together, more often it was in the cafeteria with other staff. Annabel made sure that she went out to lunch with other senior staff with the same frequency she did with Olaf.

Only when they could arrange to be out on business at the same time did they allow themselves to act like lovers. When Theo talked about her retirement, the only thing she would have wanted was to spend the time with Olaf, which was not something she would ever say to her son. She did enjoy imagining his shock if he discovered her affair, but that was where the event would stay—in her imagination.

# CHAPTER 22

*Day 17, Wednesday*

"I honestly don't know how much I can help you." As he sat across from Petra in her office, Roger thought how efficiently she used the desk as a barrier. It was almost large enough to turn into a bed, albeit a hard one. This was their third meeting in as many days.

Petra held a capped fountain pen in both hands as she listened to Roger. The grandfather clock in the corner of the room tick, tick, ticked. Finally she spoke. "There were times, many, many times, I said I'd like to kill my brother, but I never meant it literally." She spoke in English although she'd offered to speak in French. He quickly realized that her English was stronger than her French and there was something about both of them being in a second language that was a great leveler.

"We all say that at some time about someone. I've done it myself." Roger had even said that about Annie from time to time, but he would never do anything to hurt her, even when she drove him crazy with her insistence on her independence.

"But I do have a motive."

"You wouldn't have to share the business."

Petra nodded. "Or sell it."

"That seems to be the prevailing view—that you would do almost anything to stop the sale."

"What is disturbing is that I can't prove where I was when he was murdered, because they can't determine the time of death exactly. The last time he was seen was with your wife in the *Gasthaus*. When he was found his body was frozen. Solid." When Roger frowned, she said, "He was found in a snowbank. The temperature . . ."

"Was well below zero." Roger made a mental note to stop finishing her sentences. He knew the temperature, because proving time of death of frozen tissues was next to impossible.

"They do have an idea of when his car went into the lake but that doesn't prove he was dead at the time. He could have pushed the car himself. Why he would want to do that doesn't seem reasonable no matter how you try to explain it."

"But that wouldn't explain the bullets in the upholstery."

"True." Petra nodded.

"However, that means you can't establish an alibi at all unless there's someone who can testify where you were every second between the time he left the *Gasthaus* and when the body was found, including allowing time for it to freeze. Or rather when the car was found, which shortens the time period considerably."

"Impossible. I was alone at home in the evening. The children were there, but in bed, and the *Kindermädchen* was out with friends."

"Your husband?"

"Walter was staying in Zurich." When Roger frowned, she added, "My husband."

Roger wasn't sure how he could proceed. This wasn't his territory. "Frau Ritzman, I don't speak German. The local police certainly have already made it clear to me when I went to the station that they won't appreciate a retired French detective poking around in their investigation. I'm not sure how I can question any suspects if they speak neither French nor English."

Petra said, "You could start with my brother's girlfriends. He had two: both speak at least four languages. Fritz didn't like

128

stupid women, but he also wanted them compliant."

Roger sat up in his chair. "Did they know about each other?"

Petra shrugged. "It's a small town. I've had both at the house for dinner at different times. Charlotte Bachmeier was the one I preferred, but I never let on. Fritz would have dumped her immediately so I acted rather distant with her. Whenever he said he was bringing her as his dinner partner, I'd roll my eyes and sigh."

She's clever, Roger thought. As he glanced out the window he could see that it had begun to snow. He wondered how Sophie was making out in the *Krippe*. They had not left her often and when they did it would be either with Gaëlle or with Annie's parents. She was a baby who would go to anyone, and she'd seemed so interested in the other children who were there that she didn't even notice when he left.

"Christianne Adler, I didn't like. I think she was hoping to marry Fritz's money. I pretended I preferred her."

Sibling rivalry with a little psychology thrown in, Roger thought. "Do you think they would talk to me?"

"I can ask them." She picked up the phone. During each call he guessed that she asked how they were doing and they must have asked the same because the reply seemed to be, "As well as can be expected. The shock will take a long time to subside." At least that was what he guessed by Petra's tone.

She confirmed how the conversation went after she hung up.

Roger noticed she didn't use the word "grief." Still, he wondered how this small but compact woman would have the strength to drag her brother's body from his car and then push his car into the lake. He had to have outweighed her by at least thirty kilos. Roger didn't rule out the possibility that she might have had an accomplice. His instinct told him that if she had killed her brother, she would have acted alone.

When Petra had finished talking to the women, she wrote

down two addresses and times. "They'll see you. Do you have GPS or should I give you directions?"

"I've a GPS," he said.

# CHAPTER 23

*Day 17, Wednesday*

Roger Perret pulled up in front of Charlotte Bachmeier's four-unit apartment building. He assumed that under the snow on the ground the place was well-landscaped, based on the way small pines flanked the flagstone tile walkway that didn't have a snowflake remaining. The concierge must stand by with a shovel and broom waiting for a flake to descend.

The woman would be home during the day for it was a school holiday week. Petra had said Charlotte was a teacher.

He didn't have to ring. Because a person was leaving, he was able to step through the security door. The mailboxes to the left told him that he wanted the apartment on the left, one flight up.

"Charlotte Bachmeier?" Roger asked as a natural blond, slightly shorter than the average Swiss woman, opened the door that bore her name on the plate over the hall light switch.

"Yes."

"I'm Roger Perret. Frau Ritzman . . ."

"Petra phoned to say you'd be stopping by." She stepped back, letting him into her neat but small apartment.

There was a matching gray sofa and chair, a medium-size plasma TV screen. The drapes were a gray and red geometric print, and red print cushions were scattered around the room. They were big enough to sit on if one didn't want to sit on the couch or on what he guessed was a real oriental red rug. If it were real, it would be worth more than all the other furniture together.

Three bookcases were chock-a-block with books, most in German, some in English, some in French. One large modern painting adorned each of three walls. The fourth wall had sliding doors leading to a balcony that overlooked a walled-in garden with a bare tree in the center and a waterless fountain.

Four doors probably led to the kitchen, bedroom, toilet, and bathroom, or so Roger guessed.

Petra had said Charlotte taught the sixth year of primary school. In one corner was a modern-designed desk with paper in neat piles and a laptop. A paper tablet was on the glass coffee table in front of the couch.

"We can speak in French or English, whichever you prefer," Charlotte said.

"Your choice."

"English. I listen more to the BBC than the French channels. They have wonderful mystery series. I love mysteries . . . books and dramas . . . not real ones . . . coffee?"

"Please."

Charlotte opened a door and left it open. Roger watched as she made coffee in a kitchen that was as pristine as the rest of the flat.

Once seated, he started to explain why he was there.

"I know. I have talked to the police. I can imagine that Petra is not satisfied with the progress. She needs control."

"You don't like her?"

Charlotte sat back on the couch, tucking her feet under her. "I admire her more than like her. She's accomplished a lot. Those who work for her really like the way the company runs, especially in today's world."

"I asked about how you felt about her."

"She was nicer to me when Fritz wasn't around. I ran into

her once in the Migros and she suggested we have a cup of coffee. We talked about the kids I was teaching, her kids, just like friends. But when Fritz and I were at her house for dinner she was really cool to me."

"You must feel terribly about Fritz's murder."

She sighed. "I never knew anyone who was murdered. I try to imagine what it must have been like for the woman who found the body."

Roger observed that Charlotte spoke almost as if she were talking about one of those mystery programs she saw on television. He waited for her to continue. When she said nothing, he asked, "Were you in love with Fritz Bircher?"

He didn't expect her to laugh, but she did.

"Do I take that as a no?"

"Definitely. I'm a schoolteacher. Most of my days are spent with eleven- and twelve-year-olds. And I like my work. Most of my friends have already married, and I don't get a chance to date that much. Fritz was fun, he had a great car, but . . ."

"But?"

"He wasn't husband material. In fact he wasn't even boyfriend material. I know he was seeing Christianne Adler and at least one other woman whom I don't know." She got up and took the coffee cups into the kitchen and brought them back refilled without asking him.

"Fritz was a spoiled brat masquerading as an adult. He was also a great dancer. I like dancing, going to films, and it is fun to go with someone."

When she sat down, she smiled but it wasn't a merry smile. "My friends thought my seeing him made me a little glamorous. Teaching is anything but glamorous." She picked up her cup and held it near her lips without drinking any of the liquid. "He brought a little fun into my life."

"Do you have an idea who might want him dead?"

"I would have to say Petra, except I can't imagine her killing anything. I heard a story about how she bawled her eyes out when they had to put down the family cat, but that could be rumor. You know how it is with prominent people. All kinds of stories get told and retold and with each retelling more details are added."

Roger did know.

Roger's next stop was Christianne Adler's apartment—or rather, the room that Petra Ritzman said she rented. It was on the top floor of an old home. An elderly woman answered the door. When he asked for Fraulein Adler, he thought she said something like, *"Sie ist nicht hier,"* but he couldn't be sure.

Then a dark-haired woman pounded down the stairs. Roger had no idea what she said to the elderly woman, who sniffed. The two spoke and although he understood nothing, he could smell the rancor. The old woman stomped down the corridor and slammed a door behind her.

"Are you Roger Perret?"

"Did Petra Ritzman tell you about me?" He wondered if Petra had made a second call to the women after he'd left her office.

"She said you'd be by. My landlady doesn't allow me to have male company upstairs, but we can talk in here." She led him into a room that could have been from the 1930s or 1940s. Everything was dark, including the lamp that had a dark blue shade with a fringe hanging down: a dusty fringe, he could see in the limited light.

"Gloomy isn't it?" She plunked herself down on the sofa and pointed to a chair. "I suppose you want to ask me about Fritz."

She did not invite him to take his down jacket off. The room had a floor-to-ceiling gray-tile, ceramic stove with a woodpile next to it. He could see a fire burning through the grill. He guessed that the temperature in the room was at least eighty degrees. He unzipped his jacket.

She began to cry, dabbing at her dry eyes with a shredded tissue. "Poor Fritz. We were talking about getting married."

"Really?" He wanted to ask about the other women, but thought it better to wait. "How long had you been dating?"

"About a year. I work in a boutique here in the village. He came in to buy something for his then girlfriend and ended up with me as his new girlfriend. I didn't see him as much as I would like, because he was always so busy with work. But once the sale of the company went through we were talking of going to live in Saint Thomas or maybe Florida . . . someplace warm with palm trees. Have you ever been there?"

Roger shook his head.

"He took me to Florida and Saint Thomas on holiday last November. We looked at houses to buy. Fritz said after the sale we'd have enough that we would never have to work again as long as we lived."

"Did he get so far as to buy you a diamond?"

"Every time we were ready to go shopping, his bitchy sister came up with some meeting that he just *had* to attend."

Roger knew that jumping to conclusions was not a good thing, but he suspected that Christianne was being strung along.

"If you can't have men here, where did you and Fritz . . ."

"I'd stay overnight at his place." She blew her nose, a dainty little blow.

"Did you know he was seeing other women?"

She jumped up. "That's a lie. He only loved me, he told me. People love to spread false rumors, especially if they're jealous."

"Who was jealous?"

"His sister. She pretended to like me, but I saw through her."

"But why would she be jealous?"

"Because Fritz loved me. She was stuck with that boring old banking husband of hers."

Roger decided to keep changing the subject. "What do you know about their disagreement on the business?"

"Not much. I just know they were going to sell it."

"Why do you think he wasn't seeing other women?"

"Because he said so. Now please go. This is much too painful."

Roger stood up and left.

# CHAPTER 24
# 1940

## DECORATED SHAPED SUGAR COOKIES

**Ingredients:**
1/3 cup butter
1/3 cup shortening
3/4 cup granulated sugar
1 teaspoon baking powder
1/8 teaspoon salt
1 large egg
1 teaspoon vanilla extract
2 cups flour

**Directions:**
Preheat oven to 375°F/190°C.

Cream butter, sugar, and shortening until light and fluffy.

Combine baking powder and salt until well mixed.

Add egg and vanilla.

Add flour.

Divide dough in half.

Chill for 2 hours.

Roll out dough to a thickness of 1/8 inch.

Use cookie cutters to make desired shapes.

Bake 7–8 minutes, until edges are firm and bottoms are lightly browned.

Frost or use colored sugar to decorate.

The air was crisp although it was only the first week in September. A few trees had turned yellow and it was possible for Annabel to kick the leaves that had tumbled to the ground in the wind, just as she had when she was a little girl. She inhaled that special smell that leaves have when they first fall to the ground. This was the time of year when the sky was a blue so dark that it looked as if layers of color had been painted over each other until the color became opaque.

Annabel had always thought of the autumn as the start of the new year, not January first. It was when school had started, first for herself, then her children, and now her grandchildren were toddling off on their first academic adventures, although kindergarten was hardly academic.

Everything seemed so peaceful. But the conversation at the breakfast table was talk of bombings in London, Belgium, and Berlin. Each national side scored a bit, but for what? It was all destruction in her book.

Dieter, who still was complaining about his stomachaches, was furious that the Jews in Germany had been ordered to wear yellow armbands. She found it amusing that her husband, who would never consider asking a Jew to their dinner table, was so incensed. "But, if they can do it to them then they can do it to any group. Sometime, someone may want to persecute everyone named Dieter or those who like chocolate cookies," he said. Annabel's favorite cookie forever had been dark chocolate ones.

Her reply had been her usual, "Yes, dear," as she drank the last of her tea and gathered her papers to leave. She looked forward to the walk—it was her thinking time—a transition from home and work.

She passed her next-door neighbor, who was heading away from the center of town pushing her infant daughter in a straw pram that had to be at least one hundred years old. "Let's enjoy the fresh air before winter sets in," the neighbor said.

Annabel agreed. Her mind had shifted toward work and away from her husband's political opinions or the weather. Maybe it was the right time to turn some more of the responsibilities over to Theo. He was proving to be a good manager. He had enough of his father's socialist leanings to get the maximum out of the employees. If only the flow of supplies was better.

But she worried: besides not having the excuse to spend time with Olaf, once she was retired how would she occupy her time? What would a day be like without dealing with hundreds of little work-related details?

Although she had never liked awkward situations, her relationship with Olaf was one. She loved him, plain and simple. That she would do nothing about it was just as plain and simple. If she broke her marriage vows emotionally and physically, it didn't mean she would ever leave Dieter.

It was neither of their faults that instead of growing together, they had grown apart. Granted, they were still considerate of each other. They were always polite. Their conversations about politics on his side, work and the family on hers, were more about keeping the other updated on things that they might need to know rather than any real sharing of spirit.

At social events, each backed the other up like a well-choreographed dance.

On one level, Annabel felt that in comparison to some other marriages, hers could be a lot worse. Maybe, even if she and Olaf were married, they would also grow apart, especially if he were working and she was waiting at home for him each day.

Waiting at home . . . what a horrible, horrible thought.

What if she cut down to half days for a month as a trial? But what if she couldn't stand it? How discouraging would it be for Theo if she wanted to go back to full time?

The closer she got to the factory the more people, who were also going to work, greeted her. It wasn't as if Theo wouldn't do a good job. His strategic thinking was not as strong as hers, but his ability to absorb numbers and their significance exceeded hers. In working his way up the proverbial ladder, he'd won the respect of all the employees.

He would never be simply a figurehead like his father. It wasn't that the staff disrespected Dieter, they just knew he was there only because his name was Bircher and that his heart was in Bern, not in Einsiedeln. Theo's head was entirely in the factory . . . almost too much, she thought.

Annabel made it a point to greet every group of workers as she walked through the plant. Because of the difficulty in getting supplies thanks to the bloody war, there were fewer employees. She hadn't fired anyone, but when someone retired, she didn't replace them. Profit margins were down, but were still enough on the plus side.

Annabel's day passed like all her days. She would look up after what felt like a few minutes and it would be lunchtime. After lunchtime the afternoon would disappear and the evening began without her finishing what she'd wanted to accomplish.

Tonight there would be no rush to get home. Dieter was going to spend the next few days in Bern. He had asked her to join him for a dinner on Saturday night, and she'd agreed, although listening to politicians pontificate was not something to which she ever would look forward. She did it because it was on her list of wifely duties to perform.

At home, she wanted only a light dinner: a slice of toast and maybe some tea and some of the first apples and grapes of the season. At least local produce was still readily available.

Before eating, she drew a bath, appreciating that they had installed a powerful hot water heater, a real luxury. It needed enough water pressure to trigger the pilot, necessitating the tap be fully open. This time she let the tub fill almost to the top.

Her body was not bad for a woman of her age: a few faded stretch marks ran from her belly button, a bit of cellulite on her thighs, but she wasn't overweight. Olaf had told her she looked damned good. "Damned" was his word. Despite "acting like a man on the job," as Dieter said, she had always tried to remain ladylike in her speech.

Dieter never said anything about her looks. They had not had sex for years. Was it a question of him not being able to? Some of her friends were thrilled when their husbands couldn't perform that way anymore, relieving them of the chore.

Dieter could have a mistress. In one way she hoped he had. Not that it made her any less guilty for her adultery but it would make them even.

A hot water bath was a miracle in her mind, draining any tiredness from her. She shut her eyes and let her mind drift, imagining a walk in the mountains when violets were covering the hillside.

A knock at the door brought her back to reality.

"There's a man at the door for you," Maria, the maid, said through the wood. They had gone back to having a maid, partially because Maria's husband had been killed. He had gone to Spain to fight in the Spanish Civil War then to France to fight the Germans. "He was meant to be a soldier," Maria had told her. "Unfortunately, he was born in a country that doesn't go to war."

Annabel knew she couldn't give a job to every woman who needed to raise her family on her own, but she did the best she could. The hours at the factory would not have worked for Maria, whose eldest son had something strange wrong with him. Annabel allowed Maria to bring her son with her to work. She kept the child away from the main part of the household, something that would have been impossible at the factory.

Annabel scrambled from her bath. "Tell him I'll be down in a few minutes." She had planned to get into her flannel nightgown and crawl into bed with a novel. Flannel was as much a sign of fall as chestnuts being sold on the street corner, or the sound of gunfire in the mountains signaling the hunt was in full swing. Instead she slipped back into the clothes she'd been wearing all day.

The man was no one she knew. Although she wasn't good at guessing ages, she put him in his mid- to late thirties based on the smoothness of his skin. He wore a suit and held his hat in his hand.

"I'm Yves Longchamp. I'm in the Parliament with your husband."

Did Dieter send him as a guest, she wondered? The man looked distinctly uncomfortable.

"I've bad news. I was chosen because I had to come to Zurich and they thought it would be better not to tell you over the phone."

Annabel had no idea who "they" were. Before she could ask, Longchamp turned bright red.

"Your husband was crossing the street across from the Parliament. He was hit by a taxi and was killed instantly."

# CHAPTER 25

*Day 17, Wednesday*

Roger and Annie settled on the sofa in front of the fire. She had poured two glasses of red wine and had three kinds of cheeses cut up and arranged on a platter.

They had changed into pajamas. The fire in the fireplace threw a soft light that was supplemented by candles placed strategically around the room. The two German shepherds were curled up in the dog beds, although they were not in their own but each other's.

Annie felt cozy more than romantic . . . cozy and curious about what Roger had accomplished with Petra and with Fritz's two girlfriends. When they'd first arrived home, their efforts were focused on getting Sophie to bed. Neither felt like a meal, both having had large lunches.

Annie brought the two glasses of a pinot noir and a small round light-wood box.

"What's that?"

"You'll love it. *Vacherin Mont d'or.* I'll be back with the bread. Pour a tiny bit of wine on top of the cheese."

As the couple ate their cheese and bread and sipped their wine, Nina Simone sang, "I Put a Spell on You" in the background. They both yawned.

"So what did you find out today?" Annie asked.

"Instinct tells me that Charlotte didn't kill Fritz because she didn't care enough and Christianne didn't because she saw him as a meal ticket. She blew up at me when I suggested she might not be the only woman in his life."

"Not the smarter of the two?"

"Definitely not. What do . . . ?" Before Roger could finish his question, the doorbell rang.

The two humans and two dogs jumped up. The dogs barked until Annie said, "Shush," but they walked on each side of her as Annie opened the door before there could be a second ring and possible disturbance of the baby.

A man dressed in a suit and overcoat flashed a police badge, which offered information including the name Fritz Nagel and his title, *Feldweibel*—which meant he was the lead investigator, if Annie remembered correctly—and his photo. "May I in-come?" he asked in heavily accented English.

Hannibal let out a low growl.

"Good boy, go lie down," Roger said. The dog looked at him and obeyed. Curie followed.

Annie stepped aside and pointed to the living room. "May I take your coat? It is quite warm in comparison to outside."

He shook his head, but unbuttoned his coat and sat in a chair that was kitty-corner to the couch. "I see you are ready for the bed already." He looked at his watch.

"It was a wearing day," Annie said. She thought about speaking in German to him, but decided not to. His syntax made her wonder how good his English was and she thought she'd keep the advantage. "How may I help you?"

"I know who you are . . . who the two of you are."

"There's no reason to keep it a secret," Roger said.

"What I want to know is why you are in the murder case interfering?"

Annie glanced at Roger and decided to let him answer.

"I was hired to investigate."

"Do you have a license?"

"No, and maybe 'hired' is a bad word. I'm doing it as a favor."

"And how do you think you know more than the police know?" Feldweibel Nagel's tone was moderate throughout the conversation. He spoke slowly, and Annie wondered if that were a tactic or if he were struggling for the words.

"I used to head a murder division in Paris, and I've been a police chief for many years in a small French village."

Annie would have thought that the *Feldweibel* would have already known, since he'd said he knew who they were. Maybe he knew who, but not what.

"Which one?" When Roger told him, Feldweibel Nagel said, "I have several summers there spent. Camping."

Annie wanted to ask him if he had two bicycles on the back of a caravan, which seemed almost obligatory on every German or Swiss-German caravan on every campground in their village. She resisted.

Feldweibel Nagel stood. "I won't up-keep you any longer. As a former policeman you know why we don't appreciate you meddling in a going-on investigation."

Roger stood as well. He was a good five inches taller than the Swiss-German policeman. "I do understand, but perhaps we could work together."

"We here in Schwyz are quite able our own work to do."

The dogs, seeing people moving, stood. Annie noticed that the policeman had done nothing to engage them.

"I'm sure you are. It's just that I know you only have one murder or two a year at most and those are usually family violence."

"True."

"When I was in Paris we handled over twelve hundred a year."

Annie could see by the frown on Feldweibel Nagel's face that this was the wrong tack.

"Are you saying we are incompetent here?"

"Not at all, but an extra pair of eyes never hurts."

"I will about it think."

Annie knew that he would think about it for a nanosecond and reject the idea.

"Until I decide, please let us to our work without any . . . any . . ."

"I will not step on your toes," Roger said.

When Nagel looked like he didn't understand, Annie translated the phrase as "I will do as I please but stay out of your way," only she put it a bit more diplomatically, saying, "I'm helping a friend, but will be careful not to hamper the police."

Feldweibel Nagel buttoned his coat and went to the door. "I wish you a *Guten Nacht.*"

Annie locked the door behind him.

After they had settled on the couch, Roger laid his head in Annie's lap. "That was interesting."

"What's your next step?"

"I'll talk to Petra in the morning and see if she wants me to continue. I also need more information about her brother from her."

Annie scraped some of the cheese off the round, put it on a piece of the bread, and popped it into Roger's mouth.

"As crazy as this sounds," he said, "I'm beginning to understand why you enjoyed going away on assignment so much. This is great cheese."

# Chapter 26

*Day 18, Thursday*

Annie stared at Annabel Bircher's personal journal, which she'd discovered behind other books on a top shelf. When she'd begun working with Annabel's leather notebooks, they had been full of information: dates, amounts of money spent, dinners attended . . . but nothing personal such as discussions with her children and her husband. Annie settled back in the chair with a cup of tea on the table to her left.

Today's research would be even more interesting than before. She'd already developed a liking for this woman, although she feared some of the new material in the journal would necessitate a rewrite or at least additions to what she'd already done.

A separate set of journals involved only information about factory problems, their solutions, conversations with employees, and financial issues but without the meticulous detail that an accountant would have. Annabel was not a numbers person and her frustration with the accountant came through.

Over the years, Annabel had become more aware of cost-benefit analysis, although it wasn't the term she used. She probably didn't even know the phrase. Perhaps it hadn't existed in her time. Annie decided the phrase's development was not so important that she should devote additional time to researching it.

Her insistence on quality may have built the reputation of the company in the region, but it also lowered profit margins. Annie applauded her stance, but she'd dealt with enough numbers people to understand the conflicts. How she would deal with this attitude of the woman who had been a major contributor to the creation of Leckere Keks in this current writing assignment left her uncertain.

She'd been scanning the personal journal, much of which was useless except for the mention that Annabel's daughter married and had a child.

On page 102, for Annabel numbered her diary's pages, the words became incomprehensible. The language was one she'd never read—for a second she wondered if it could be a Slavic tongue, although none of the letters used by those languages were in the journal.

She went to a translation page on the web and typed the words into it, trying to identify them as Polish, Czech, Serbo-Croatian, Turkish, or Hungarian, then requested a translation into Swiss German.

Nothing.

She tried for the translation into Latvian.

Nothing.

"Am I interrupting?" Brett Windsor stood in the doorway. "I haven't run into you for the last couple of days and wanted to see how you were progressing."

"Up until ten minutes ago, perfectly. Look at this."

Brett took the journal. "Looks like a code."

"Why would a woman in her fifties suddenly write in code after keeping a diary from her childhood without one?"

Brett held up his hands. "You're asking me, an American male, to explain the thought process of a Swiss woman from a different century?"

"Good point. Is there anything else I can do for you?"

"Just wanted to know if you wanted to have lunch with me. I've an appointment at the bank, and I want to fortify myself with a good meal beforehand."

When he'd left after Annie agreed to meet him later, she picked up the diary again. The strange wording was not on every entry. Normal events were interspersed.

For years Annie had loved doing cryptoquotes, puzzles that involved a simple letter exchange. She knew things like *RS RJ* would probably be *IT IS* and *UVFU* would be *THAT.* Her parents gave her a book of the puzzles each Christmas, but she also did them online and only in English. She played other word games in French.

She typed Annabel's entry into her laptop and thought about the structure of Swiss German. Okay, those words with capitals were nouns. Three-letter words might be *der, die, das,* but they could also be the verb *ist.*

What about moving one letter down in the alphabet?

She looked at the code *HBG VDBRR DR HRS E?KRB ?ADQ HBG KHDAD HGM.*

She tried *JCH* . . . Okay, that wasn't a word. What about one letter before, *Ich* . . . *voilà,* she had it. The first sentence read, *"Ich weiß, es ist falsch, aber ich liebe ihn."*

Annabel had a lover. She loved him even if she knew she was wrong. And even if Annie hadn't broken the code, the fact that Annabel had used a code to describe her affair showed she'd needed to keep it a secret.

What the hell would Petra think of that? And surely she wouldn't want that in a book destined to be a marketing tool. For her own curiosity, Annie decided to devote an hour to the translation, then tell Petra.

# CHAPTER 27
## 1942

---

## CHOCOLATE MERINGUE COOKIES

**Ingredients:**
2 large egg whites, room temperature
1/3 cup granulated sugar
1 teaspoon vanilla extract
Pieces of semisweet chocolate, about 4 ounces, melted and
    cooled
1/2 cup finely chopped pecans
1/4 teaspoon salt

**Directions:**
Preheat oven to 325°/162°C.

Beat egg whites until foamy; beat in the salt. Slowly add sugar
and beat until stiff peaks form.

Add vanilla and cooled melted chocolate. Add nuts. Drop by
spoonfuls on a greased baking sheet.

Bake for about 9–10 minutes.

Makes about 2 dozen cookies.

Theo typed out yet another letter to the Swiss government in
Bern, not wanting his secretary to see what he'd written. She
had already left for home, her newly issued ration cards in her
purse ready to hit the shops before everyone else cleaned them

out of scarce supplies.

He wanted more flour. Before the war, the company had bought their flour from Canada and from Eastern Europe, but the war had dried up all those channels. Granted, Germany was still a major Swiss trading party, but battlefields disrupted cultivation. War is hell even if his country were only suffering indirectly, Theo thought as he banged away on the typewriter.

Unlike many men, he was an excellent typist. His mother had insisted that he learn typing along with every other skill in the factory. He had resisted, sulked, but that was water under the bridge. In retrospect, his mother had been right on the money on that one. More than once, knowing every splinter in the factory had helped in making the better choice when faced with a dilemma.

This time his knowledge wouldn't help without the basic materials needed. Production was suffering under rationing.

One solution of Theo's ideas was to ration what his clients could buy, which although explainable, meant lengthy negotiations as clients would cite how long they'd been loyal customers—so couldn't the quantity be upped a bit? He supposed that other companies were having the same problems, so changing vendors wasn't a possible solution for his clients. What Theo feared was that if he didn't handle the clients well enough, after the war was over they would look elsewhere.

Where once the factory had produced cookies primarily, it had now gone back to its original bread line as the main product, with cookies becoming secondary. Cookies required sugar. Cane sugar was almost impossible to come by and when he did locate a supply, it cost an arm and a leg . . . two arms and two legs. Beet sugar was being used as a substitute, but even that was in limited supply.

Honey worked as a sweetener, but there weren't enough bees in Switzerland to meet his needs.

Honey and beet sugar wouldn't be mentioned in the letter that he planned to file in his safe along with other copies of sent letters. When it came to availability of wheat, it didn't matter that agriculture had increased by at least half with almost every arable area under production for vegetables, cows, sheep, and goats. Or that was what the Swiss public radio station claimed. Their reports seemed to resemble the BBC, which were totally different from the propagandized German stations. Or maybe it was the BBC that was propagandized? Or both?

As for chocolate? Impossible.

His mother, who was still far more active in the company than one might expect at her age, had been good in developing recipes around whatever products were available. Mostly she worked from home these days.

He had discouraged her appearance at the factory. It was as if he were tilting at windmills and never coming a step nearer his goal of a more efficient factory when she was around.

Sometimes his head went in circles trying to balance numbers, unions, production, sales, and supplies. At the moment it was slowing down his thoughts. Tearing the paper from the typewriter, he started a new one.

Olaf Stevenson, he knew, would find whatever he could and get it at the best price he could. Still they'd be paying a pretty penny. He'd always liked that English phrase that Olaf had taught him. He'd seen a Canadian penny: it wasn't all that pretty.

With his father dead, he had to accept Olaf's place in their lives, although it had been hard at first. Jemma had encouraged him to ignore how soon after his father died that his mother replaced him with the big Canadian.

That was the word he had used to her—replaced. She was furious and had thrown him out of the house. It had been at a dinner three months after the car crash. An autopsy had shown

152

his father wouldn't have lived long with the stomach cancer that was probably responsible for his weight loss and paleness.

He had never understood his parents, and he wondered if one day his twins would say the same about him and Jemma, except he and Jemma were a team working for the same goals, only in different ways. His parents each had goals but they were so different. His mother was factory, factory, factory and his father was socialists, socialists, socialists.

His father's socialist politics made it harder for Theo each day at work. The unions were pushing for better working conditions despite the war. That had all started after his mother stepped back from the day-to-day operations.

How wrong he'd been to think that his job would be easier once she was out of the way. He no longer had arguments with her about costs, but where the work force had been docile, now the union had become a nightmare.

Every day their leader was in his office with a new demand.

Theo looked at the blank page. This wasn't going to work. He'd have to think about what he wanted to say tonight after the twins were tucked in bed. He stood up.

Walking through the hall, he noticed a window that someone had forgotten to close. Since they were on the second floor, he wasn't worried about anyone breaking in, but if they had one of those violent thunderstorms rain could soak the wooden floorboards. At the end of the hall was a long pole with a hook that people used to open and close the windows.

Before the war, a second shift would have been operating at this time in the evening, running until eleven at night. It is what it is, he sighed.

On this July evening, and one of the very few where he felt he could undo his tie and roll up his sleeves while out on the street, rather than remain properly clothed—reflecting his status—he noticed that families were out walking. Little boys were on bikes, and little girls pushed their baby-doll carriages. As he passed the park, a father was encouraging his son to climb the ladder to the top of the slide and the little boy was frightened. Theo didn't proceed until the little boy arrived victorious at the bottom of the slide and was hugged by his father.

Everything seemed so normal. It was hard to believe that the rest of Europe was in the middle of a major war, one that looked as if it were in no way ready to abate. The morning paper had carried the news that the Dutch government had gone into exile and that the Americans had bombed the continent. At least Switzerland was staying out of it—so far.

Outside of the war and how it affected the business, Theo had never been interested in politics. If he were to analyze why, he probably would blame politics for keeping his father away. Theo could count the times his father had been at one of his school or sporting events never mind his birthdays, as they say, on one hand and have fingers left over.

Already he knew he wouldn't be an absentee father. No matter how much work he had, he would be home to give the twins their bath, even if it meant going back to the office afterward. Tonight was the exception, the first since January.

He rounded the corner and could see his house, where his parents had lived and his grandparents before them and where he now lived with his family. The hydrangeas were in full bloom, bigger and brighter than he remembered in past years. The same with the geraniums which bloomed from window boxes. The whole world was coming apart and someone had forgotten to tell the flowers.

He could hear the sound of cow bells carried on a light wind from the nearby field. At least the acquisition of milk and eggs was never a problem. He had fought his mother tooth and nail when he wanted to buy a small farm to produce their own milk and eggs. She'd given in, and it had surprised him when she told him how right he had been.

His mother had moved into an apartment just away from the center of the village with Olaf. She'd turned the house over to him and Jemma. He'd expected she would die in the house. That she was anxious to be free of it had shocked him.

"Too much to take care of it." She'd put her arm into the crook of Olaf's arm. "I'll take Marie with me; we can use a cleaning lady. You can keep the rest of the staff."

The staff at that point was a part-time gardener and a cook. They hired a new woman to come in to clean twice a week and when the twins were born, they hired a nursemaid.

Jemma had wanted to take care of the babies herself, but the birth had been difficult and it had taken her several months to regain her strength. By then she saw the advantage of sleeping through the night and having the freedom to lunch with her friends without worrying about the children. Still they were hands-on parents and the nursemaid often complained that she didn't have enough to do.

Theo would have liked to lower her salary but Jemma wouldn't hear of it. What was it about women and money? They never thought of economy even in wartime.

As he turned the corner to the house he saw his mother walking up the street.

"My darling son," she said, kissing him three times, alternating cheeks. "I just left your lovely wife. She invited us for dinner on Sunday."

Theo wondered why Jemma had done that. Annabel would want to talk about the union and try to convince him to cave in. Give an inch and they'll take a mile, he thought.

"I'll see you then," he said with an enthusiasm that bordered on a lie.

# Chapter 28

*Day 19, Friday*

Brett Windsor kissed his daughters good-bye at the school entrance and watched them disappear into the building, their book bags bouncing behind them. God, how he loved them. Before he had kids, he never believed when parents said that once you had kids you were never free again, not that he wanted to be free. He just wanted to maintain the life he was living, and he couldn't do that if he were divorced.

His reasons weren't altogether selfish. If he were forced to leave the country because of lack of banking ability he could go back to the United States and search for a good job. It wouldn't be easy. He was a member of a couple of professional organizations, but he'd never made contact with any of the other members. Contacts help in job searches.

His contacts were limited because he hadn't spent much time in the States since he was a teenager, with the exception of university. In that sense, his life sounded a bit like what Annie had shared with him about hers. They were both third-culture kids.

He could try social networks, such as LinkedIn or some of the other professional boards. The thing of it was, he didn't want to go back. He wanted the life he had here, with a job he liked, his kids and his wife, whom he thought he could win back if he tried hard enough.

He wished he had applied for his Swiss nationality earlier,

but somehow he had wanted to be only American. It had given him a sense of independence. Now he thought he had been stupid to wait, but who would have thought that being American abroad would have become such a handicap? Even if he had filed papers the day the bank first called him, getting his nationality could take up to three years. He would never have been able to get Swiss nationality and renounce his American citizenship before the bank called the mortgage and demanded full payment.

He ran his fingers through his hair. As he sat in his car, he stared at the empty schoolyard. A man came over to the car and tapped on the driver's window. "What are you—oh, I didn't recognize you, Herr Windsor. Can't be too careful. Pedophiles and all that."

Windsor recognized the man as the custodian. His daughters played with the custodian's girl, although Trudi wasn't happy about it. She preferred the girls' friends be of "our class," while admitting the little girl was a lovely and well-behaved child.

"I'm glad you watch carefully. I need to get to work. I was just sitting here planning my first meeting."

The custodian nodded and patted the hood of the car as Brett backed up.

He had given up the hope that the renunciation of his American nationality wouldn't be necessary. He didn't want to never be able to live in the United States again. Brett hated having his choices cut off.

He put the car in gear and turned left to go the plant. Damn it. He'd left the latest issue of *The Economist* on the nightstand. It contained some predictions that Petra should see. Although she read English easily, she preferred to receive summaries of English press that might affect the Swiss economy and Brett had taken on the chore. It provided just another service to keep his boss happy—job security and all that.

He pulled into a driveway and headed back to the house. When he entered by the kitchen door, all the lights were off, and the dishes were still in the sink. Trudi hadn't said anything about going out. Her car was still in the driveway, but it wasn't impossible that she might have popped in to the neighbor's for a coffee and complaints about husbands.

He went upstairs without taking off his coat and only shoving his gloves in his pocket. When he opened their bedroom door his wife was under the covers sobbing. She jumped.

"Bastard, you nearly gave me a heart attack."

"Not on purpose. I came for . . ." He went to the nightstand and picked up the magazine. "I forgot it." Stupid thing to say: it was obvious. He sat on the side of the bed. "What's the matter?"

"Nothing."

"So part of your routine when everyone is gone is to make the beds, start lunch for the girls, and cry in bed?" He reached for a tissue in the box on her nightstand. She took it and blew her nose. He'd always marveled at how delicately she did it, so delicately he wondered if the action had any efficacy at all.

He reached for his phone and called the office. "I'll be a little late getting in," he told his secretary. "If Petra needs me, she can ring me on my cell." He tried to pull his wife into his arms, but she stiffened at his attempt to comfort her. "Talk to me."

"I'm miserable."

He could see that, but he stayed silent.

"I don't . . . I don't . . ." Although he thought he guessed what was wrong, he knew he couldn't do anything about it. All he could do is try to be the husband she wanted.

Trudi stood up. "I'm being silly." She started to make the bed, forcing him to stand.

He debated his next statement. It had to be said, so why not get it over with? If she had been in a good mood, it would put her in a bad one. Why waste a bad mood?

"Silly or not, you need to call the bank to arrange a start date." He had felt so lucky when the bank manager had offered Trudi a post to solve the employment issue with the mortgage. A community where generation after generation stayed, people knew each other and helped each other out. It was something that had no price. Even with Trudi working, her salary would not be considered large enough, but the manager had said that this limb was better than the previous limb he had climbed out on for them.

"I don't want to work. The girls need me at home."

"No, they don't." Oh God! They could almost record this conversation and replay it instead of going to the work of repeating it again and again.

Trudi glared at him.

"We can arrange for someone to be here when they get home from school, if that's your concern. Or we can send them to someone's house. Besides, if I come home early, the girls are usually in their rooms or at a friend's house."

"They like my lunches." She plumped the pillows.

"We've gone over that alternative." He watched her fold the two duvets in half. Their large bed had two half mattresses and they each had their own duvet. His wife made sure that neither had a wrinkle and were positioned identically under the pillows, which were also wrinkle-free. "Trudi?"

"What?" she asked in the voice he'd come to think of as her snapping-turtle tone.

"The girls need a stable home. They need two parents under one roof."

"Don't tell me again how much your parents' divorce hurt you." She picked up the bath towel he'd left on the chair and headed for their bathroom.

"Trudi!"

"I'll call the bank. I'm doing it not for you, but for the girls. So they can stay in this house."

When he arrived at the front door, he took out his gloves. His car keys fell on the floor. He turned to see his wife standing at the top of the stairs.

"It won't be as bad as you think. Nice people work at the branch. The girls will adjust."

She didn't say anything.

He opened the door.

"And for the girls' sake, we need to try to get along better."

The cold he felt was not just from outside.

# CHAPTER 29

*Day 19, Friday*

Annie lay on her stomach on a blanket in front of the fireplace. She was wearing sweats with "Université de Genève" written over the chest and down one leg. Sophie was also on her stomach and they were face-to-face as Annie handed her daughter toys to taste.

Outside a few snowflakes drifted down halfheartedly, but the sky was so overcast that the lake was invisible.

The landline rang and Roger's steps could be heard upstairs going to answer it, but Annie couldn't make out the conversation. A few minutes later he thumped down the stairs. "That was Petra. She wants me to follow her husband into Zurich. He's leaving their home in an about an hour. I may be gone overnight."

"There goes our family Saturday," Annie said, only half minding. There was justice in this, considering all the times she had blown off their time together for her own work. She stood up and got his coat and scarf from the pegs by the entryway. "Stay warm."

After he left, she realized that she was almost never alone with their daughter. When she wasn't working, they shared Sophie's demands. When she was, Roger did most of the work, while they both provided the necessary cuddles.

Sophie rolled over on her back, entranced with a soft beige stuffed lamb.

Annie went to the kitchen to make herself a cup of tea, which she put on the end table. Picking up her laptop she settled on the couch, ready to write. However, whenever Sophie gurgled, Annie found her attention switching from work to child. She loved looking at the baby. As her red hair was growing it looked as if it might be as curly as her mother's. Sophie's eyes would definitely stay blue. Had they been going to change, they would have done so by now.

This certainly was a strange assignment. If it had been the first family firm she'd worked for, she would have been shocked how relationships could play as big a part as the bottom line. Murder, however, was not a part of most family businesses.

Annie liked Petra, liked her principles where she considered her employees part of her success, not a handicap requiring her to give up part of her wealth. She hadn't liked Fritz in the brief time she'd known him, not just for his beliefs but his manner. That he was dead did not make her any fonder of him.

Sophie had fallen asleep. Annie covered her with a blanket, although the heat from the fireplace left the room cozy. She wondered if Roger would have thought the baby warm enough without the blanket. If Sophie were too warm, surely she would kick off the cover.

Back on the sofa she found the words racing from her brain to the screen. Good. The faster she finished, the faster they could go home. She'd written no more than five hundred words when she thought she heard a car pull into the driveway and a car door slam.

It was Roger.

She put her finger to her lips and pointed to the sleeping baby.

Roger hung up his coat and sat down next to Annie as she mouthed, "What are you doing home so fast?"

"When I pulled up by Petra's house to wait for her husband to leave, I saw the police take her out in handcuffs."

# CHAPTER 30

*Day 23, Tuesday*

On the Tuesday after Petra Ritzman's arrest, Annie was preparing to walk to work. As she tugged on her boots she couldn't help wondering what would happen that day. One of the owners was dead, the other had been arrested and was in jail.

She wondered if she still had a job, but she'd go in to work anyway and continue as if everything were normal.

The factory worked well with small groups each operating independently yet as a team. A strange arrangement that she had not seen before, but it seemed to work as far as she could tell.

"Have you seen my keys?"

Roger was planning on staying home with Sophie. With Petra arrested, he did not know if he should continue the surveillance of her husband, but he was not about to rack up charges without authorization.

"She also wanted you to prove her innocence," Annie reminded him as she searched for her keys, an activity that they both claimed would qualify for Olympic Games status.

"The police don't want me meddling." He checked the dish by the door. "No keys."

"She probably needs someone to meddle on her behalf." Annie started digging through her purse, producing a wallet, tissues, a pacifier, several pens, a small notebook, safety pins, and a bottle of aspirin but no keys.

"I haven't a clue as to what to look for. Had Petra not been put in jail, she might have been able to help or at least give me some direction." He kissed Annie on the forehead and tightened the scarf around her neck. "She seemed much more interested in having me follow her husband around than work on the murder, which in itself makes me think she is innocent."

Annie knew her husband's instincts in crime solving were usually right on. He was also good at finding keys—he put his hand into her coat pocket and gave them to her.

As soon as Annie entered the factory, she felt a strange buzz. Her first stop was the cafeteria to pick up a cup of tea before going to the top floor to research more records. Not only were people buying their first coffees and teas, but the cafeteria had been rearranged theater style.

When Brett Windsor tapped her on the shoulder, she jumped. A bit of the tea slopped over the edge of the Styrofoam cup. The liquid was hot enough to be uncomfortable, but not hot enough to burn her. He apologized.

"Not a problem. What's going on?"

"The attorney for the company is going to talk to us about work." He took her by the elbow of the arm that didn't hold the tea and ushered her to a seat at the end of a row. "The board that was behind the sale is insisting."

She was sure nothing that would happen would affect her directly or even indirectly, unless she wasn't paid for her work. Anyway she wasn't worried. Her agent handled those issues, but she guessed if she wasn't working and they had to stay because Sharon was still on holiday, Roger would mumble about the cold.

However, for the people settling into their seats, this was their livelihood. Some had worked for LK for their complete working lives. They knew nothing else.

"It's going to be interesting because of how Petra set up the company before Fritz came on board, something he hated."

"How?"

"Stock."

Annie tilted her head, waiting for more information.

"She and Fritz each held twenty-four percent of the shares. The lawyer has three percent, so things wouldn't end up in a tie. In a way it backfired on her because the attorney was more on Fritz's side than Petra's."

"And the rest of the stock?"

"Divided among all the employees. That gave the family veto power if the attorney voted with them, but it also gave the employees an interest beyond their paychecks. Way, way beyond."

Annie found the setup interesting. Roger would want to know this. She wasn't sure if the system increased or decreased Petra's motive.

Brett crushed his empty coffee cup in his hands. A few drops spilled on the floor. "Profits are split with the same percentages as the shares. So too are the bonuses, although bonuses for special things like the invention of a new process that saves money can result in a bonus that all the employees vote on."

"So how do the employees feel about selling to a larger company?"

"I never heard anyone say they were for it. No one! Not one! The company promised a large payout, but it was a one-time thing. Most of the employees realized that the payout wouldn't be enough to live on for the rest of their lives and other jobs in the area aren't as good as the ones here."

The seats were filling up with men and women carrying coffee cups.

In front of the rows of chairs was a table. At 9:32 a man in a dark blue business suit, light blue shirt, and blue-patterned tie walked through the door and over to the table. Annie guessed he was probably in his late fifties, although guessing ages was never her strongest skill. He put his briefcase on the table then sat down and began fiddling with the contents, pulling out some papers, then putting some of them back.

When everyone was seated he stood and spoke in a deep voice.

"As you probably know, the codirector Petra Bircher Ritzman has been arrested for the murder of her brother, codirector Fritz Bircher. She is currently in jail and will be arraigned later today as far as we know."

The murmur told Annie that most of the people had heard this, but the confirmation brought it into reality.

The lawyer cleared his voice. "One of her great concerns is that nothing affects the running of the company. In her absence, we need to appoint a manager. I have a talented young man in my office."

For the first time Annie noticed a new face seated at the right end of the first row. The man was also dressed in a suit and tie. He might have been in his mid-thirties. "I'm Tobias Grunner," he said when he stood.

Annie noticed that he had sheets of paper in his hand. He walked to the edge of each row and counted off the correct number and gave them to the first person to pass down the row.

Annie wondered why he didn't use a PowerPoint presentation.

"This is my CV. As you can see, I have a business degree from the London School of Economics. My specialty has been taking troubled companies out of trouble."

"This company isn't troubled," someone behind her murmured.

"Petra will be fine," another voice whispered.

The word "arrogant" flashed through Annie's mind. Her instincts on people were usually right; but she was off just often enough that she didn't rely on them totally.

A man, wearing the type of lab coat indicating he was

involved in the mixing or cooking of product, raised his hand. "Does Frau Ritzman know about this meeting?"

"We'll be talking with her later before the arraignment," the lawyer said.

Brett leaned over and whispered into Annie's ear. "I'd heard that Petra was going to fire this lawyer because he was on Fritz's side about selling out to York and James Capital."

So that was the company that had been pursuing them. Annie had done a project once for their European headquarters. If she remembered correctly, they had a reputation for buying a small company, making all sorts of promises, then stripping it of assets. Or was it that they increased profit margins by firing people and discontinuing pensions? Or both?

She thought that they owned many different types of manufacturers from food products to electronics. She needed to check them out on the Internet.

A woman stood up. A net covered her gray hair and she too wore a white lab coat. "What experience do you have running a baking company?"

Tobias Grunner gave a smile, or maybe a smirk. "I love good bread and pastries," he said.

"That wasn't what I asked." The woman's response brought mutters of approval from the employees.

"I've run several companies that make a variety of products or offer a variety of services."

"But not a baking company."

Annie admired the woman's persistence.

The lawyer interrupted. "If you look at Herr Grunner's CV you will see he is vastly qualified. He turned around . . ." He droned on about this and that company where the bottom line had been increased.

Annie whispered to Brett, "Ask him what happened to Gregor Lines."

Brett did.

"The company was not viable. It was sold off to the benefit of the shareholders," Herr Grunner said.

"What happened to the employees?" another worker asked.

The two men looked confused. "What do you mean?"

"What I said. What happened to the employees after the company was sold?"

"They were able to collect unemployment until they found new jobs," the lawyer said.

"How many found new jobs?"

"I have no idea. Now if we could look . . . "

"Ask him about Jenner Electronics," Annie said to Brett. She'd worked at Jenner at the time York and James Capital was stripping it.

Brett did.

Before Grunner could answer, a man Annie thought was named Daniel stood up. "How many companies that York and James Capital bought are still in business today?"

The lawyer stood up, putting his hands on the table and leaning much like a gorilla. "This isn't about the possible sale of this company. This is about who will oversee the day-to-day running right here, right now."

This time a woman stood up. She was overweight, something fairly unusual on the staff. Maybe, Annie thought, being around so many cookies stopped people from desiring sweets, just like working at an ice-cream store one summer when she was young had made her lose interest in ice cream for a couple of years. "We run mostly on our own. We don't need an outsider." This was from one of the youngest-looking employees.

"*Ja, ja, ja, ja*" and more "*ja jas*" were heard throughout the group.

"A company can't run on its own. Herr Grunner will be a good chief," the lawyer said.

This is getting interesting, Annie thought. The workers were calm, but there was a determination that could only come from people who had some control of their professional destiny as a matter of course.

This time a man in his fifties stood up. He was dressed in a forest green uniform with the company name embroidered on his shirt pocket. A heavy jacket of the same color and the company name embroidered in the same place hung over the back of his chair.

Annie guessed he was doing deliveries, although she knew that was another one of the jobs that rotated on the theory that by meeting the customers it gave an employee another understanding of why and how the product's quality should be only the best.

"I think you will find"—the delivery man spoke clearly in the local dialect—"that in this room there's forty-nine percent of the votes for the company and there's enough people according to the bylaws to make a quorum. Herr Bircher's will has not been settled so his votes are not available and I doubt if Frau Ritzman can vote from jail. I'm not sure she'd approve of this plan. I suspect"—he paused and looked around the room—"that any one of us can take over as leader until Frau Ritzman is ready to take up the reins again."

"Impossible." The lawyer's face had assumed a scowl, deepening the lines over his nose.

"Not impossible at all. We've voted on other things. We'd have voted on the takeover as well."

"Fritz was pushing to get the employees to vote his way and was frustrated it wasn't working," Brett whispered, but the woman next to them heard and nodded.

"Do the math," she said. "Frau Ritzman and the employees would have outvoted Herr Bircher."

"She's right," Brett said.

"Herr Bircher was making us all kind of offers so he could get the fifty-one percent he needed. All of it was hush-hush." She pursed her lips and said, "Herr Bircher was not too bright if he thought he could divide and conquer. Some of us are third- and fourth-generation employees."

"We're family," the man next to the woman whispered.

"Can we have quiet in the back of the room, please." The lawyer looked at where Annie, Brett, and the man were talking.

Brett stood up. "How many of you are against Herr Grunner, no matter how competent, running the company until Frau Ritzman is back in charge?"

Annie noticed that his voice had a certain resonance when he spoke to a group that it didn't have when it was a one-on-one conversation.

Every hand went up.

"We do need a coordinator, however. Do I have any nominations?" Brett asked.

"This is impossible," the lawyer said. He banged his hand against the table as if it were a gavel. Annie suspected that it must have hurt by the look on his face, but she suspected willpower kept him from rubbing it.

"No, it's not," Brett said. "I'm sure Frau Ritzman, when she is free, will back us up. Now who has a nomination?"

Three names came up, including Brett's.

"I insist Grunner's name be included. And mine," the lawyer said.

"No problem," Brett said. "We'll do it by paper ballot, so we have a written record."

Notepaper and pencils were found behind the cash register and distributed.

The vote was taken.

Brett insisted that the head of the union and the lawyer count the votes in front of everyone. When the lawyer protested, the employees started hollering at the lawyer until he acquiesced.

While the votes were counted, the room was deadly still. Every employee was staring at the table at the front.

The attorney had no votes. Grunner received only one vote. Brett had the remaining votes.

"Thank you both for coming," Brett said to the lawyer and Grunner. "If you tell me what time Petra will be arraigned, I want to be there and get a chance to talk to her. If she doesn't approve of what we just did and she wants Herr Grunner we will let you know, but we need to hear it from her, not *you.*"

The lawyer and Grunner pushed their papers into their briefcases, slammed the cases shut, and stomped out of the room.

"Everyone better get to work," Brett said. The scraping of chairs and the shuffle of feet quickly disappeared as the room emptied.

Annie sat there. She felt she'd just seen a casebook study of something, but she wasn't sure of what.

Brett came over to her. "What do you think?"

"Wow."

# CHAPTER 31
## 1965

---

### RAISIN BUTTERSCOTCH COOKIES

**Ingredients:**
1 cup softened butter
3/4 cup brown sugar
1/4 cup sugar
2 eggs
3 cups instant oats
1 1/2 cups flour
1 package instant butterscotch pudding mix
1 teaspoon baking soda
1 cup raisins

**Directions:**
Preheat oven to 375°/190°C.

Cream butter and sugars together before adding eggs.

Slowly mix in dry ingredients.

Add raisins.

Drop by spoonfuls onto an ungreased baking sheet and bake for 9–11 minutes.

Thomas Bircher tossed his backpack into the trunk of Jacqueline Fuller's Spitfire. The top was down. He wanted to jump into the car without opening the door, the way he'd seen heroes in the movies do, but he knew he'd probably end up kicking Jacqueline ("never call me Jackie") in the face.

"We're lucky, it's Indian summer and we've a three-day weekend. What more could we want?" Jacqueline said as she pulled out of the parking lot in front of the triple decker in Roxbury Crossing, where Thomas rented an apartment. What a relief to *not* be living in a dorm after his years at Phillips Andover and Harvard. It would be an even greater relief if he were not at the B-school. Sometimes he wondered if he would ever be free of ivy-covered, brick-building academia.

All he wanted at this point was to go back home—home to Switzerland. He had prayed he would not be admitted to any of the business schools he'd applied to, but Wharton, the London School of Economics, and Harvard had all accepted him.

His choice, which once would have been London, was Harvard because of Jacqueline, whom he'd started to date in their junior year. Let his father think that he'd acquiesced to the elder Bircher's wisdom.

Jacqueline was now working at H. J. Jameson, an educational publisher located on the Boston Common side of Beacon Hill. She had moved back with her family on the ritzy side of Beacon Hill after her graduation.

Thomas found her intriguing and not just because she packed so much energy into her five-foot, ninety-pound body. Nor was it her dark pixie-cut hair that never seemed to fall out of place, even after they'd been making love for what seemed like hours.

Although her physical attractions could cause an erection just thinking about them, it was everything else about her.

Her family, like his, was tradition steeped. Like many other families, they claimed Mayflower ancestry, although in their case, it was true. The family had been part of Boston society for as long as there had been Boston society.

Jacqueline more or less ignored this part of her inheritance, but she'd given in to being a debutante at least as far as the presentation at the Boston Cotillion. She and Thomas had almost broken up over the event, because he was not allowed to go. Her family was not overly impressed with her dating a foreigner, even one who appeared to be from a wealthy industrial family.

Mr. Fuller had asked, if she must date a Swiss, why couldn't it at least be a banker like himself? As for her mother, the welcome when he went to their house for meals always made Thomas want to put on an extra layer of clothing. How Jacqueline could be warm, funny, and irreverent coming from that environment he would never understand.

None of this bothered him as they headed to the family cottage in Maine for the Columbus Day weekend. He tried not to think about the work—another case study that he didn't give a damn about, except for the grade he would earn. It would have to wait.

All he needed to do was pass, because he never again had to worry about being accepted at another university. When someone had told him the joke—"What do you call the person who graduates with the lowest grade from Harvard Medical? Doctor!"—he'd decided he didn't care where he rated on the list of graduates. All he wanted to do was finish and get his father off his back, where he'd been riding for years, forcing him to come to America to study first at Phillips then at Harvard, and now at the B-school.

It was hard to tell which year he hated most. Phillips had provided a first-rate education, but he had been shackled with his twin sister, who rebelled by barely passing and sleeping with his friends. Only when he reported Mattie's slutty behavior to his father was he free of *that* responsibility. Still his father blamed him, saying it was a miracle that Thomas wasn't about to be an uncle.

Mattie had said it was impossible thanks to the pill. Well that had been six years ago. Mattie had shaken off the family yoke and moved to Paris, where she was living some disgusting bohemian life, according to his father. Thomas never heard from her.

His father had been silent lately, other than urging him to learn everything he could before coming back to Switzerland and the company. Any thoughts about his father being on his back because they'd be working together, he shoved out of his mind.

So what if when he and Jacqueline came back on Monday night, he would be up all night doing his part of the case study that his team was working on?

So what if he let down his teammates on the project? Only he wouldn't let them down, because he would have all the facts and figures already gathered in that all-nighter Monday.

Thomas put his hand over Jacqueline's, which rested on the gearshift. The trees along Route 93 had donned their brightest red and yellow dresses. Leaf-peeping was the excuse for the trip, but the couple's real goal was to make love as much as they could in her parents' cabin without fear of interruption.

That the two slept together was ignored by Jacqueline's parents, although she often did not come home at night. As long as they knew in advance, they didn't comment, although Jacqueline revealed her wish that sometime her mother's lips would grow so tight her mouth might have disappeared forever.

They stopped for lobster at a shack as soon as they crossed the Portsmouth Bridge into Maine. Jacqueline had bounced from the car and almost run into the restaurant with its weathered wood siding decorated with netting and lobster traps. Six wooden tables with matching benches filled the small building. Outside the window, the gray Atlantic was visible.

A man came out to greet her. He was probably in his fifties

based on his white hair, but maybe younger because his skin was unlined, unlike many of the locals who'd spent too much time at sea. He wiped his hands on his white apron then hugged the young woman, showing her more affection than Thomas had ever seen her father demonstrate.

"Jacqueline, what a surprise."

She introduced Thomas to Fred, the owner of the shack.

"She's been eating lobster here since she was a baby. I never saw such a young child put away lobster like she could," Fred said.

"Still can," she said.

Thomas, for all his time in New England, had never eaten lobster. He felt a bit silly with the plastic bib with the bright red lobster on it. Rather than ask her how to eat it, he watched as she broke off the small legs and sucked on them. Then she went to work on the claws using what he thought of as pinchers to break the shell.

He swirled his recovered meat in the melted butter just as she did. It was good, but he was nowhere near as orgasmic about it as she seemed to be. He hoped when he got her into bed, she would respond as well to him as she did to the meal.


The Fuller cabin was nothing like Thomas expected. The Beacon Street house was filled with antiques, artwork, and sculptures. The cabin was just that—a cabin. The outside was made of logs and Thomas could almost picture a covered wagon parked under the pine trees that surrounded the building, except he knew that covered wagons belonged to the western part of American history, not New England's.

"We should put the top of the car up in case of rain," Thomas said, but she had bounded ahead and either didn't hear or ignored him.

"Don't the trees smell wonderful?" Jacqueline fumbled with

the key until Thomas took it from her. The lock was sticky but he managed to jiggle it open.

As they stepped in, he saw a basic kitchen with a dividing bar and two stools on one side, light pine cabinets, stove, refrigerator, and a window looking out to the lake on the other. Thomas went to hug Jacqueline, but she had already gone to switch on the fuse box and close the refrigerator door.

"We'll need a fire tonight."

She was right. The inside of the cabin was shiver-producing. In the fading afternoon light the air outside was only slightly warmer.

As Thomas unloaded the groceries they had brought, Jacqueline built a fire and made up the double bed in the master bedroom, although there was almost no floor space left with the bed, two small night stands, and a dresser. One had to walk sideways between the bottom of the bed and the dresser.

"The good news," Jacqueline said, "is that my parents have an electric blanket, dual controlled even."

This is the woman I want to marry, spend the rest of my life with, thought Thomas. He pictured them walking hand-in-hand to pick up fresh baked *brotchen* on a Sunday morning. He thought of her greeting him at the door when he came home from the factory at night, and their children, a boy who would follow in the family business and a girl whom he would dote on because she so resembled her mother. Flights of fantasy were not Thomas's style, but Jacqueline's exuberance triggered something in him that he could not describe, nor did he want to.

He helped her make up the bed and as soon as they finished they switched on the controls, undressed, and did what they'd been waiting to do.

# CHAPTER 32

*Day 23, Tuesday*

"Petra would have loved that," Annie said to Brett after the employees had gone back to their jobs.

The smell of the early batches of baking cookies drifted into the cafeteria. The meeting had begun right before the first batch of the day's product had been oven-bound. In the time Annie had been working there, the smell had gone from tantalizing to something she almost forgot about. It was like when she visited her grandparents who lived in a pine grove. At the beginning of the visit the smell of pine was everywhere, but within a couple of weeks she no longer noticed it.

"She would indeed. I doubt if the sale will go through now but the running of this place will be difficult without Fritz or Petra. Sadly, I really only know marketing, so I'm not sure I'll do an adequate job."

"The employees had to have confidence in you, especially since you're an outsider." Neither of them needed to comment on the Swiss attitude toward non-Swiss in some of the smaller towns in the German section. It was less so in the French cantons, but it still existed. Only in the international cities of Geneva, Basel, or Zurich were foreigners readily accepted, although once they proved themselves to be integrated it seemed their origins were forgotten in the villages as well. "So what's your next step?"

"I need to call Petra's husband. He can see her in jail. I can't.

Although with any luck she'll be released on bail by tonight or at least tomorrow."

Annie stood and headed to the elevator to go back to what she'd begun to think of as the penthouse. Here it was another week, just starting out.

"Wait."

She turned.

"Will you go with me to talk to Walter Ritzman?" he asked.

Annie wasn't sure why, but she agreed.

Walter Ritzman was a good-looking man and his body movements made Annie think that he knew he was attractive. She could imagine him and Petra side-by-side for some glossy magazine spread dedicated to the successful business couple.

He had returned from Zurich early last evening for his wife's arraignment and agreed to meet with Brett and Annie in Brett's office. His handshake was firm. "I don't believe we've met, Frau Young-Perret, but my wife certainly expressed confidence in your ability to write about the company."

"I appreciate her confidence," Annie said. She doubted if she'd ever have gotten the assignment had a man been at the helm. Everything she'd discovered so far was that Petra's grandfather was certainly different from her great-grandmother. Creativity seemed to skip a generation and the women who ran the company were more forward-thinking than the by-the-numbers men. At the same time, Annie knew for any company to be successful, both skill sets were needed. Walter Ritzman looked to her more like a numbers man than a creative thinker.

Why she was included in this meeting she still wasn't sure. Maybe just to bolster Brett.

Herr Ritzman pointed to the coffee maker in the corner. "May I?"

Brett blushed. "I should have offered you some."

The banker smiled but only with his mouth. His eyes remained uninvolved. "These aren't ordinary times for any one of us. May I make a suggestion?"

Brett nodded.

"If the employees voted to have you take over, I think you should work out of Fritz's office. That shows authority but also leaves Petra's office free for her return."

"I'll move in the morning unless you think she'd mind."

"I'll brief her, but the move should be tonight." Without waiting, he picked up the folders on Brett's desk and started walking down the hall toward Fritz's office, which retained his name on the door.

As he passed Frau Küper's desk, he rested the folders on her desk. "How are you doing during these difficult times, Frau?"

Annie guessed he hadn't remembered the woman's name.

"As well as can be expected, Herr Ritzman," the secretary responded. She'd offered to stay late in case she might provide information for the meeting that Brett and Annie had not thought of in advance.

"I know it's difficult," Herr Ritzman said.

"Not as difficult as it is for you." A gray hair escaped from the bun at the back of her neck.

"Thank you, but we'll survive it." He picked up the folders. "Can you get the night janitor to move Herr Windsor's file cabinet to my brother-in-law's office and have his name taken off his office door? Herr Windsor will be using his office."

The move was completed within a half hour. Brett was an organized executive who kept everything filed, making the transition simple.

"Have your secretary moved tomorrow," Ritzman said. "It's not fair that she come in in the morning and see all her things transferred." There was no worry about Fritz's secretary. Fritz and Petra had shared Frau Küper, which made Annie wonder if the woman had the wisdom of Solomon to work through the family discord.

They settled into Fritz's office, which had many pictures of Fritz on the wall, mostly of him skiing, hiking, and shooting a crossbow. Two were with expensive cars.

No one sat at Fritz's desk, but rather at the table and chairs off to one side.

"I'm seeing Petra again tomorrow morning before her hearing," said Walter.

"I thought it was today," Brett replied.

"It was postponed. We expect she'll be granted bail on surrender of her passport," Walter said.

"I can't imagine she would be thought of as a flight risk. She's not apt to leave the kids and her company," Annie said.

"Exactly," Walter said. "However, and although I can't speak for her, I suspect that she will leave a majority of the work to you, Brett. She'll be so tied up in her defense that she'll need backup, which she never got from Fritz." He glanced at his watch. "I'm late."

He left.

"I hope he keeps us posted," Brett said.

"I can't imagine that he wouldn't," Annie said.

"Thanks for being there. I thought as an outsider, you might be able to back me up in case Herr Ritzman wanted both an insider and outsider opinion."

Annie wasn't sure that Herr Ritzman gave a damn either way. He hadn't questioned her presence. Maybe he just didn't care, but that wouldn't make any sense. The factory had to be a major part of the family income.

Long ago she had given up trying to figure out what made other couples work. Why should this be any different?

# CHAPTER 33
# 1965

## VALENTINE HEARTS

**Ingredients:**
1 1/4 cups all-purpose flour
3 tablespoons sugar
1/2 cup cold butter, cubed
1/2 cup maraschino cherries, patted dry and chopped
1 tablespoon cold water
1/4 teaspoon almond extract
1 cup semisweet chocolate chips, melted
1 tablespoon shortening

**Directions:**
Preheat oven to 325°F/162°C.

Mix flour and sugar.

Cut in butter.

Stir in the rest of the ingredients except the chocolate chips.

Make a ball from the dough.

Using a lightly floured surface, roll dough to 1/4-inch thickness.

Cut into heart shapes with a heart-shaped cookie cutter.

Put on ungreased baking sheet about 1 inch apart and bake for ten minutes or until slightly brown.

After cookies are baked, dip cookies into the melted chocolate chips so they are half coated.

Unlike the warm temperatures when they had left for the Columbus Day weekend in Maine, Jacqueline Fuller and Thomas Bircher returned to Boston in an early snowstorm. Although mild by local standards, the storm left just enough of a coating to make the drive from the New Hampshire border quite treacherous. The lightweight Spitfire did not have winter tires, and it was only Jacqueline's skill that had pulled the car out of several skids.

They found a parking place in front of Thomas's triple-decker.

"Why don't you stay with me tonight?" He wondered how he would ever get his case-study figures compiled, but he didn't want her driving across the city. At least at the end of the three-day holiday weekend, regular commuter traffic was far less, despite some companies staying open.

"Mummy and daddy have plans for tonight. I'm expected to be in attendance."

Thomas knew that often the Fuller parent plans involved introducing their daughter to a man deemed more suitable, but he also had learned that Jacqueline resented this interference. Thus, instead of trying to get her to change her mind, which was a challenge that made Gibraltar look like a pebble in comparison, he kissed her and said, "Call me when you get home."

She nodded. He watched the car inch its way down the slippery street.

His flat was on the ground floor. It had taken him a while to be comfortable that Americans called it the first floor. In Europe the first floor was the American's second. After almost a decade in the States, he had acclimatized himself to many of the differences, but the feeling of homesickness never had left.

Each time he went back for a holiday and his father had driven him to the Zurich airport, he had thought about begging to stay. He never did. His duty was to get the education to help him keep the family business profitable. Why his father thought that his son's exile was the only route, Thomas did not challenge.

The flat he'd rented was more or less empty. There were three bedrooms. Originally Thomas had considered renting them out to other students to reduce the rent, but after all the years of living in a dorm, living alone was, as Jacqueline would say, "spectacular," especially when she stayed overnight.

There were two faded beige corduroy chairs picked up from Goodwill and a TV in the living room. For the kitchen he'd found a table that someone had put in the trash and he had bought his pots, pans, and dishes from the Salvation Army.

The only thing new was his mattress, mounted on bricks and a board. His desk was a board on cut-down sawhorses. His books were stored in empty milk cartons he'd taken late at night from behind a local supermarket. His typewriter was a brand new Olivetti bought in Yverdon and carried with him on the plane over when he started at Phillips.

The place had come with paper shades and Thomas saw no need to add curtains. The shades sufficed to keep the neighbors, who were within hand-shaking distance, from seeing his every move.

There was little need to unpack: he'd taken so little on the trip. He dumped his dirty underwear in the washing machine that had come with the apartment. His shaving kit he put on the back of the toilet.

Playtime was over. He made a pot of coffee and went to the room he called his study. He'd been arranging and rearranging figures for almost an hour when his phone rang. A sense of relief that Jacqueline had crossed the city safely ran through him. "You made it, lovebug," he said.

"Thomas, *deiner Mutter hier.*"

Thomas was taken aback by the Swiss German. He'd lived in English so long that his native language was buried when he first stumbled on it. Even on trips home, it took him a few hours to switch languages. He did not consider himself gifted linguistically but prided himself on being aware of his strengths and weaknesses.

"*Mutti?*"

"There's no good way to tell you. Your father died this morning."

"I'll get the next plane home."

# CHAPTER 34

*Day 24, Wednesday*

Annie was happy with her progress on her assignment. Despite all the distractions, she was almost up to Petra's generation, which meant maybe one or two weeks more work. Her contract was up next week. However, there had been nothing in her contract about time lost due to the murder of one of the owners and the arrest of the other.

With Petra in jail, or about to be out of jail, she would have no chance to review Annie's work—thus Annie did not know if what she had done was acceptable or not. On most of her assignments her work was approved with only minor changes. This time, because she was writing in German first, she was slightly less sure of herself. She found writing in English, French, or Dutch easier, but that was because she'd spent only two years in the German school system. That she'd finally determined her working method was a relief.

Annie located old photographs and drawings of different family members as well as of the production line. When she'd told Petra, she'd said that she wanted to put some into the book, and Petra had given her a tentative okay. Her favorite was still the young girl in a long dress, apron, and cap rolling cookies off a contraption. "Contraption" was the best word for it. It looked like an oversized fire hydrant with a roller. On the roller was a sheet with cookie shapes imprinted with hearts. Baked cookies had been removed and were on a sheet next to the roller.

As she went through the company history, Annie tried not to overpraise the women. "I'm not writing a social case study," she said to herself as she fought with herself to give a fair balance.

"What did you say?"

Annie jumped and turned to look at Brett.

He apologized for startling her. "I'm so excited that I just had to share this with you. Maybe you have ideas of how to present it to Petra as soon as she can get back."

"Why me?"

"When you're a marketing department surrounded by lawyers and accountants, any creative mind in a storm."

Annie laughed. He wasn't dressed like an executive. Instead of a suit, he wore a Norwegian ski sweater, black jeans, and boots. "Shoot."

"Forget all my other ideas. They are nothing in comparison." He put the large sketchbook he'd been carrying next to her laptop. "Ignore my lack of artistic ability here."

Annie opened the pad. His artistic ability was not as bad as he claimed in creating what looked like a warm, old-fashioned cookie store.

"Petra has been thinking about how to market her gourmet cookies beyond Switzerland. We already have hotels and restaurants as clients, but only in the Swiss-German part."

Annie knew this. She wondered what had made him give up on his earlier ideas, but kept silent. She hadn't said to him that she thought playing with the Swiss stereotype of cows, chalets, and mountains wasn't that exciting. Workable yes: exciting no.

"Up until now things I've thought of didn't stand out."

Annie waited.

He started pacing the room, his hands waving. Outside the high window Annie could see that it was beginning to snow again. She brought her mind back to him.

"What if we were to become the gourmet leader of cookies? Franchise cookie shops only in upscale communities, top quality malls, tourist areas? I mean gourmet of gourmets?"

"It's a good idea. In fact, it is a great idea."

Annie and Brett turned to see Petra stroll in. She was dressed in her usual black and looked as if nothing had happened.

"You're here," Brett said, then quickly added, "Boy, was that a dumb thing to say."

"I was told I'd find you up here, Brett."

"It's good to see you," Brett said.

"It's good to be out on bail. My first stop was here, although I want to be home when the children come back from school." She turned to Annie. "I'm going to need all the help I can get from your husband. Where is he?"

"At home with Sophie."

"Ask him to come down here, ASAP. Sophie can go in the *Krippe* or you can have her up here if you want. I need him more than ever."

Brett shut the sketchbook. "This will have to wait," he mouthed to Annie.

# CHAPTER 35
# 1965

## BROWN SUGAR COOKIES

**Ingredients:**
1 cup softened butter
1/2 cup packed dark brown sugar
3/4 cup sugar
1 egg
1 teaspoon vanilla extract
2 cups flour
1/2 cup finely ground pecans
1 teaspoon salt
1/2 teaspoon baking soda

**Directions:**
Preheat oven to 350°F/176°C.

Cream the butter and sugars together.

Add egg and vanilla.

Combine everything else and add slowly to the butter, sugar, egg, and vanilla.

Cover and refrigerate for at least 20 minutes.

Shape into 1-inch balls and place a small amount of sugar on a plate and roll the cookie balls in it.

Put 2 inches apart on ungreased baking sheet.

Bake 10–12 minutes.

## Frosting:

1 cup packed dark brown sugar
1/2 cup half-and-half cream
1 cup confectioners' sugar

Combine all ingredients except the confectioners' sugar in a saucepan and bring to a boil.

Stir for 4 minutes.

Remove from heat and sift in confectioners' sugar.

Drizzle over cookies.

"No."

"No?"

Jacqueline Fuller and Thomas Bircher sat in the Blue Parrot in Harvard Square. They had had their first date there over three years ago and the restaurant was their special-occasion place. Not that the Blue Parrot was a luxury restaurant, but it had good food that students could afford.

He found her as adorable as ever. Her normally sparkly eyes had what he thought was a sadness as she held the small, black velvet box.

"It's a beautiful diamond. I wish I could say yes." She took the ring out and held it to the light before putting it back.

"Don't you love me? You always said you did."

When he'd called her after their Columbus Day weekend in Maine—one of those perfect weekends that included making love, walks in the woods, making love, reading to each other, making love, visiting the nearby village with its tourist shops, and their end-of-season-holiday-weekend sales, and making love—to say his father had died, she'd said she loved him.

"The no has nothing to do with the fact that I love you."

Thomas pushed his plate aside although he'd not eaten half of his taco salad, so excited had he been to give her the diamond. Her answer had shocked him.

Despite the sadness of losing his father, being back in Einsiedeln had been nourishing. His mother had been stronger than he thought she would be, so strong that he wondered if the marriage he had thought had been so perfect was as good as he had imagined. It was not a question he would ever ask her.

His twin sister, Mattie, had come back from Paris and left again right after the funeral. She'd said to him, "I suppose I should be angry that you outed me for sleeping with your friend—I can barely remember his name."

"Bob. I did it for your own good." He had outed her for sleeping with several of his friends, but Bob had been the one too many.

"God, Thomas, you're still a stuffed shirt. I swear you must have messed your diapers neatly."

He'd looked at his sister, who always felt like more of a stranger than a being who had shared a womb with him for nine months. Her hair was too long and she was dressed in black, perfect for a funeral, but he suspected that she always wore black to maintain her Parisian artistic persona. "I do my duty."

Mattie had stuck out her tongue, then gathered her things to catch the train to Zurich, which would be followed by another to Paris. "Darling brother, I'm leading the life I should live. I doubt if Papa hadn't brought me back, I'd probably have gotten pregnant. Instead, a year in the convent and I was off on my own."

He'd wanted to say she'd broken her father's heart, but he wasn't all that sure that hearts could break until the minute when Jacqueline had said she wouldn't be his wife.

The three weeks away from her while he put into motion

what he needed to take over the business before coming back to close out his apartment, to quit Harvard B-school, and to ask Jacqueline to marry him had seemed endless.

"I love you. But I have no intention of moving to Switzerland. If you want to stay here . . ."

Even if he did want to stay in Boston, that would be a dereliction of his duty to his family. It was enough to feel guilty at the happiness he felt at his release from more study. At least he wasn't happy that his father had died, although the man seemed more like a stranger to him in death than he had in life.

". . . I have my career."

"It's a job with a publishing house. They publish textbooks, for God's sake. It isn't like you're contributing to great literature." He knew instantly that he had said the wrong thing.

"Maybe that is another reason we shouldn't marry. You don't consider what is important to me important to you." She put the diamond back in the box and snapped it shut. "It's a beautiful ring. And I do love you, but not enough to sacrifice my life."

He took the box from her and slipped it into his jacket pocket. Before he could say anything, she stood although she hadn't finished eating. "Maybe it's better if I go." As she passed him she kissed his head.

He wasn't sure if he'd imagined her whispering "I'm so sorry" before she disappeared.

# CHAPTER 36

*Day 25, Thursday*
Roger and Annie sat in Petra's office. Sophie was in her portable car seat between their chairs. She was playing with the mobile suspended from the handlebar.

"I'm sorry, Petra, I don't have many leads. In fact, I don't have any," Roger said. He was sitting back in his chair, while Petra was leaning forward, her elbows resting on her desk. "The police certainly don't want a French ex-policeman interfering, which makes it hard talking to anyone."

"Have you gone through Fritz's house?" Petra was pale under her makeup. She had circles under her eyes.

"I haven't had access."

Annie knew her husband wasn't going to be doing any breaking and entering.

Petra stood. "I do. That's where we will go now. Are you bringing the baby or do you want to leave her in the *Krippe*?"

"Take her," Roger said.

"Leave her," Annie said at the same moment.

Roger picked up his daughter's carrier.

Fritz Bircher's home was above Einsiedeln. The construction was modern with floor-to-ceiling glass windows giving views of the village and the lake below. The living suite was soft gray leather with glass tabletops.

The artwork on the walls was also modern: single large flowers, geometric shapes, contorted bodies that were either obese or bulimic. From her auction-house work Annie recognized some of the painters as lesser-known Swiss-German artists. She looked closely at the geometric over the sofa and read the signature Klee.

On a stand was a sculpture of a man but with overlapping layers of clay. Walking over to it, she was not surprised to see the name Giacometti on the base.

"They are all original," Petra said. "Fritz only collected Swiss artists, some known, some he hoped would become known, although the Klee is a signed print. Fifty-five out of two hundred—you can see it on the left."

"Impressive."

"But none of this helps us much," Roger said as he removed Sophie's snowsuit. He put a pacifier in her mouth. She watched the adults as they moved around.

Petra pointed to three large cartons next to the door. "The police returned all the papers that seemed to have no relevance to the case."

"And . . ." Roger said.

"I want you to go through them and see if they missed anything."

"Good idea." Roger hoped Annie would help him with the German.

"Your wife, with her imagination, might be of some help," Petra said. She had not taken off her coat and now was reaching for the keys that she had dropped on the table at the entrance. "I'll leave you here and come back . . . ?" She glanced at her watch almost at the same time she shoved up the thermostat next to the front door. "Feel free to build a fire." She pointed to the wood next to the fireplace made of flat gray stones, which was almost large enough to walk into.

Annie glanced at her watch. It was 14:38. Sophie was due for a feeding at 17:00, but Roger had packed a bottle. At this point the baby ate whatever they ate, only processed down to glue consistency. Since she and Roger were here, she assumed that they would eat out later since no one was home to cook. "Around seventeen hundred?"

"You won't be finished," Petra said.

"Tomorrow is another day." Roger spoke in what Annie called his "I'm the boss" tone. It didn't usually work with her unless she wanted it to, but it did work with Petra, much to Annie's surprise. Usually order-givers made terrible order-takers.

"Seventeen hundred it is."

They could see Petra's car wind its way down the narrow road leading to the village.

"So?" Annie asked.

"Wild goose chase, probably. However, let's start."

Both were surprised that the police had returned Fritz's agenda. It was a combination of business and personal meetings. "I'm surprised he had a paper agenda," Annie said. "I'd have thought he'd use one online."

"Maybe he was afraid someone from the office would break into it." Roger used a paper agenda, a small one that he could keep in his back pocket. He wasn't afraid of a security break; he just felt the less time he was at the computer the better.

Roger sat on the couch thumbing through the agenda. "Who are York and James Capital?"

"The scumbags who want to buy the company. If you look them up, they are a private business based in the US. I didn't do all that much research on them. Why?"

He tossed the agenda to her. "Look at all the meetings, although some have a FTF, CC, or TP next to them and some have a place."

"Telephone meeting, conference call, or face-to-face is my guess?" Annie said.

"We could coordinate face-to-face with any travel details."

"Who is Tobias?"

"The lawyer who was the intermediary, I think. He spoke to the staff when the staff voted Brett in as acting head in Petra's absence."

Annie dug into the box and pulled out a packet of business cards held together by a thick elastic band. Shuffling through them she set a few aside for future examinations. "Here's another attorney, a Jason Anders, a Baltimore lawyer. He wasn't at the staff meeting."

Roger let out a long sigh. "Not surprising if he's in the States. I wish it were my investigation so I could talk to the company and that lawyer, the lawyer at the meeting, this lawyer, anyone. How many lawyers do you think were working on this thing?"

"I'm sure a bunch of lawyers." She wondered if you had a gaggle of geese or a herd of cows, what did you call a group of lawyers all working on the same project?

Expensive, she decided. Roger wouldn't appreciate her saying it. He had little sense of humor where his work was concerned.

The two worked silently, mostly picking up a paper, looking at, and then putting it aside in one of two piles: useful, not useful. The useful pile was small. She began to understand why the police returned the stuff.

"He had dates with lots of women, not just the two I talked to." Roger spoke softly to not wake Sophie, who'd fallen asleep in her carrier.

"He was good-looking; he was rich," Annie said. "Also extremely arrogant and uncaring of anyone but himself. Do they have contacts?"

"Usually only first names: Anna, Elizabeth, Marianne, Suzanne, Sonja, Maria, Anita. A few are initials only: Y, S, T, A, and G. No telephone numbers, addresses, etcetera. Maybe he had a, how do you call it, a little black book with more information?"

"Maybe he did but maybe the police kept it." Annie shrugged. "Or they made copies, more likely. I read somewhere to save storage space some departments scan documents."

Fritz's financial papers produced even less information. He had an accountant who paid all his bills and handed him a rather generous allowance. Money was set aside mainly for investments in art. Purchases were correlated to notes in his agenda for auctions or gallery visits. There were statements for each month going back several years.

"He spent lavishly, but he also saved and invested," Annie said. "Doesn't look like he had any financial problems."

"What about gambling?"

"So far nothing to indicate he'd spent time in Monaco, Las Vegas, or any other gambling mecca."

They came across a folder marked "Florida" that was about two inches thick. Because these were in English, Roger tackled them. It was filled with real estate listings and letters about the eventual purchase of a home in Palm Beach. Most were written last September and October when negotiations had started on the sale of the company, and most said he would not be ready to make a decision until sometime this spring but he wanted an idea of what was available.

It was almost dark when Walter Ritzman opened the door. "Petra asked me to come for you. She wanted time with the children."

"Do you think we could take these with us?" Roger indicated the papers that they hadn't read through. "We can work at home."

"I don't see why not," Walter said. He lifted one box and headed out the door as Roger dressed Sophie and Annie gathered their outerwear.

# CHAPTER 37

# 1979

## LEMON CINNAMON NUT COOKIES

**Ingredients:**
1/2 cup softened butter
1 1/2 cups sugar
2 eggs
1 teaspoon vanilla
1 teaspoon fresh-squeezed lemon juice
2 1/2 cups flour
1 teaspoon cream of tartar
1/2 teaspoon baking soda
1/4 teaspoon salt
1 cup cinnamon-flavored baking chips
1 teaspoon ground cinnamon
1 cup chopped pecans
2 tablespoons sugar

**Directions:**
Preheat oven to 375°F/190°C.

Mix butter, sugar, eggs, vanilla, and lemon juice until creamy.

Add flour, cream of tartar, baking soda, and salt.

Add cinnamon chips and pecans.

In small bowl, mix 2 tablespoons sugar and the cinnamon.

Shape dough into balls.

Roll in sugar-cinnamon mixture.

Place balls 3 inches apart on ungreased large cookie sheet.

Bake 13–17 minutes.

Petra Bircher loved the fact that she was born on the day man first walked on the moon. Although she knew she wasn't the only child born as Neil Armstrong stepped out of the space ship, it still made her feel as if the future belonged to her more than other people born on less historic days.

Cat Stevens had been born on her birthday, although not in the same year. She'd loved his songs, although singing was certainly not one of her talents. She was strong in mathematics and the sciences.

Although she was only ten, she knew that she wanted to run LK when she grew up. From the time she was little, she'd begged her father to take her to the plant. It wasn't the smell of baking cookies, or being able to con the workers out of giving her all the samples she wanted. She wanted to know how everything worked.

She would never tell her father that she didn't really like cookies all that much. Not that she disliked them, but she preferred things that were salty to things sweet.

Still she felt she could taste what was going to be a best seller. The woman who worked in the testing lab would send samples home for Fraulein Bircher to test.

"How are sales on the lemon nut cookie?" Petra would ask after saying she loved it when it was still in the testing phase. And she asked about the chocolate mint sales as well. She found most of the cookies didn't do justice to their names.

Lemon nut, okay it told what it was, but boring, boring, boring. Wouldn't something like Paradise Lemon and Nut be better? Or Lemony and Nutty?

Thomas Bircher found her interest amusing. Petra had heard him tell one of his friends that his daughter was a funny child, who took an interest in the company more like an adult.

"Check the sales figures," she once said to him when he was teasing her on a Saturday morning. "Do it now." Together they went to the factory.

"I owe you an apology," Thomas said. "The ones you liked are doing better."

Petra thought that the fact that her father could apologize was a good thing. She also knew it would not be a good idea to gloat, because her time in the factory wasn't encouraged, especially by her mother, who thought Petra should be playing with her friends, the same friends that Petra did not find all that interesting. They were into make-believe and dolls. She wanted to deal with reality.

What she loved most about being in the plant was to watch the machinery at work. A few of the workers, especially a man named Herr Handel, would explain what the machinery did and how. She'd been there one day when it had broken down and he had been sitting on the floor using his wrench to loosen something. One of the three-hundred-pound cylinder molds had been removed and was resting near the winch that was needed to lift it.

The machine had six cylinder molds, all different shapes. Herr Handel had explained it was less expensive to change the molds than buy the full machinery that held them. He'd explained not in the way that most adults talked down to a child but in exact detail, with the reason he was doing each turn and pull on the cookie press.

She'd wanted to stay and see the machine start working, but her father had to leave and it was over a week before she'd been allowed back. By then the machine was running as it should and Herr Handel only had time to wink at her as she walked through the factory.

Today her father had promised that she could go with him to the factory, but then he changed his mind, leaving her in her room. She'd moved from the nursery to this room only two years ago. Her mother had wanted them to go shopping for new furniture together, but Petra didn't really care what her soon-to-be-redecorated bedroom looked like. In the end she'd gone and pretended to be interested.

Petra loved her mother, but she didn't want to be like her. Staying home, worrying about the house, visiting with friends, just didn't seem all that interesting. Her mother had already begun putting away duvet covers and other household items for when Petra married.

Being married didn't seem all that awful if she could fit it around being the head of the company. Her mother told the cook and maid what to do. Petra thought she could do that in the morning before she left for work. She could hire a nanny just as her parents had for herself and her baby brother, Fritz.

Upstairs in the nursery she heard her brother throwing a tantrum, one of the many he staged each day. He wasn't quite a year, but he had mastered the art of getting attention. His nanny ignored him, but their father would give him what he wanted. As for their mother, she might chide her husband for being too lenient with their son, but Papa would wave his hand as if he were swatting a fly.

Petra tried to love her baby brother. She'd been taught in Sunday school that jealousy was bad, and she didn't want to be bad.

At night, when she'd been tucked into bed, always earlier than when she was sleepy, she would go over in her mind different events where it seemed her brother was—well—just awful.

There was dinner that night. She and Fritz ate with their

parents two nights a week. The rest of the time they ate in the nursery.

Dinner was a sausage and potatoes boiled with romaine lettuce. Fritz was in his high chair. She was sure when she was his age she ate much more neatly, using her fork. She'd been five before she'd been allowed to cut her own food, although she had begged for at least a year before that to be allowed to do so, because that was what grownups did, and she wanted to be grownup as soon as possible.

Her father had asked her about school, but before she could tell him about the good mark she'd received, Fritz started banging on his tray. Immediately both her parents turned to Fritz and ignored her.

As an experiment, when Fritz was acting as a good boy, she'd tried once again to say something about her good grade, but she was shushed in favor of her brother.

If her brother tried to get attention away from her, she was pushed aside. If she tried to get attention from her brother, she was pushed aside. Her resentment, she decided, wasn't jealousy; it was a realistic sense of injustice.

She knew that Fritz must be too little to gloat, but she could not ignore the look in his eye whenever he pulled his parents' attention to him, sometimes by being cute and if that didn't work by being bad.

As she turned out the light and snuggled under the covers, Petra promised herself she would try to love her brother more. She knew it was going to be hard work.

# CHAPTER 38

*Day 25, Thursday*

By the time Walter dropped Annie, Roger, and Sophie off at home, it was nearly nine. They immediately got into their own car and went to the restaurant across from the *Rathaus*. The waiters were clearing the tables and laying new place settings. Two couples lingered over coffee.

The owner now knew Annie, because she'd eaten there with both Brett and Petra. After cooing at Sophie and being rewarded with her smile and gurgle, he agreed to process green beans and mashed potatoes as well as warm a bottle for the baby.

Roger ordered a steak, but Annie went for *spätzle* and a salad, things the chef could prepare quickly. The baby seemed more than content to accept the "ohs" and "ahs" of the rest of the wait staff. She played to her audience with smiles. Then she fell asleep.

Once they were home and Sophie was settled, Annie took a shower, a long one, where hot water beat on her back, taking away the tiredness and the cold from the long day with its emotional roller coaster. Even if she wasn't directly involved and her future had no relationship to what was going on around her, it was like the emotions of those who were involved were sucking her own energy. She put on her thermal pajamas with the leopard print and climbed under the duvet with her laptop.

"I thought we were planning to go through Fritz's papers," Roger said, as he too headed into the shower. "You aren't playing computer games are you?"

"No games, but I think I want to learn more about the company that wanted to take over the bakery."

"York and James Capital?"

She nodded. "Somehow I remember some connection with a Peterson Group or maybe it was something, something toys, but I'm not sure why." She knew that she wasn't thorough enough last time and had just scanned the stuff for her own curiosity. She put the oversized pillows against the quilted headboard and pulled the duvet up to her waist, resting the laptop on her thighs.

Soon Roger emerged from the bathroom with a towel around his waist and his hair wet. The stapling after his heart surgery had left a fading scar resembling a zipper. Annie glanced up and a wave of gratitude that he was still alive swept through her. She mistyped "York and James Capital" as "Dork and James."

Wikipedia had no write-up on them, but a website that gave all American headquarters had them listed in Boston. "If I had to have guessed where York and James were located, I'd have said Delaware," she said.

Roger pulled on the sweats he'd slept in since coming to this "damned cold climate." He mumbled at least once daily about the warmer temperatures in the South of France. Each day he'd checked the weather site to see that Argelès was around ten to twelve degrees centigrade while in Schwyz it was several degrees below zero. "Why Delaware?"

"Good tax state for corporations," Annie said.

Roger climbed into bed next to her and looked at the laptop's screen, which had a news item from a Kansas City newspaper. "It says that they were sued by R. J. Toys two years ago."

"The employees tried to block the sale in court."

Annie brought up the court web page and typed in "R. J. Toys v. York and James." "The court dismissed the case, because they said that the employees were not owners."

"Makes sense."

Annie started searching the white pages to see if she could find a phone number for any of the plaintiffs. She didn't bother with the common names, but she had hopes for Paul Z. Jankowicz. "I doubt if the law firm would tell me much, but maybe this man can." She clicked on the laptop keys to use the inexpensive voice-over-the-internet service she subscribed to.

Annie had for a long time used a service where for ten euros a month she had ninety free days of calls all over the world. She dialed Jankowicz's phone number. It rang several times before a woman answered, who said she was his wife. She called her husband.

Annie explained what she was looking for.

"Whatever you do, stop any sale to them, if you can," the man said.

"What happened?" Annie asked.

"There's an echo."

"I'm on the computer," Annie said. "I hope you don't mind." She explained that the call was free.

"I understand free," Jankowicz said. "I can put up with the echo." He then went into detail about what had happened. Annie typed notes, trying to take down the words as fast as she could, not worrying about typos.

"York and James had investors and they brokered a deal . . . but set up a mgr . . . fired staff . . . cut benefits . . . threatened to move production ovrcs . . . quality not imprtant . . . bottom line only . . . resold company . . . new owners brght in people from ovrcs and we had to train . . . everythng shipped to Asia . . ."

"How many people lost their jobs?" Annie could hear Jankowicz sigh and she thought she might have heard ice tinkling against a glass, but she couldn't be sure.

"About one 50. York and James mde fortune on fees . . . never risked a cnt of their own . . . the investors mde a fortune . . . This is a smll town . . . take away that number of jobs . . ." Annie didn't need any more explanation of what happened.

"Judge said it was all legal . . . legal not moral."

Annie thanked Jankowicz.

"If you can do anything to get those bastards, I'd love to know about it."

Before the night was over Annie had made seven calls to people who had worked for different companies that York and James had destroyed.

"Same story, no matter who is telling it," Roger said. He'd been watching her as her fingers had flown over the letters.

"The problem is that I don't see how any of this fits into Fritz's murder."

Roger nodded. "If the sale failed, it was only a small, how do you say, droplet in their water bucket."

"Maybe the lawyer wanted the sale to fail."

"Doesn't make sense. The lawyer would lose whatever bonus he would get for the deal."

"He'd still be paid for his upfront work," Annie said. "Was anyone from York and James in Schwyz when Fritz was murdered?"

"I don't have the sources to check that." Roger took the laptop from Annie and shut it down. He rolled over and turned off the light. The deep kiss he gave her was at the same moment as Sophie cried.

They played rock, scissors, paper to see who would go to their daughter. Roger's paper covered Annie's rock.

# Chapter 39
# 1986

## Chocolate Turtle Cookies

**Ingredients:**

2/3 cup sugar
1/2 cup butter, softened
1 large egg
2 tablespoons milk
1 teaspoon vanilla
1 cup flour
1/3 cup cocoa
1/2 teaspoon salt
1 cup pecans (chopped well)
18 pecan halves lightly toasted

**Directions:**

Preheat oven to 350°F/176°C.

Mix butter and sugar until fluffy.

Separate egg, set the whites aside.

Beat egg yolk, milk, and vanilla into the butter and sugar.

Mix flour, cocoa, and salt.

Combine the wet and dry mixtures.

Cover and refrigerate dough.

After 1 hour shape into 1-inch balls.

Dip each ball in egg white and roll in the finely chopped pecans.

Place on greased baking sheets.

Make a deep indentation in the center of each ball with your thumb.

Bake 10–12 minutes or until set.

Press a toasted pecan half on top of each cookie.

Petra felt so proud of herself. She'd completed fifty-two pages in her report on the economic history of bakeries in the German part of Switzerland. Much of it had been original research. Typing it, especially fitting in the footnotes, had taken her almost the entire weekend.

She expected to get a top grade on it, but her real purpose was to convince her father that she would be capable of working for the company. She'd even mapped out a training program for herself after she finished her schooling.

She'd start on the factory floor, using the huge mixer to combine the ingredients, then worked her way through each department until she knew every floorboard in the plant and everything that happened on those floorboards. There wouldn't be a speck of dust that she would miss by the time she was ready to run the company.

She didn't mean to imply he should retire. Her father had kept saying Fritz would be the new head of the company, but Fritz had shown no interest at all in business. Granted, he was only eight, but at his age she'd begged her father to let her spend time with him at work. About half the time he had said no, but when he said yes, she had systematically worked her way through the production lines until she felt she understood what was going on.

Petra also talked to the workers every chance she could get. From them she learned things her father didn't know and didn't seem to want to know. Her father thought of the workers as a necessary evil, while she saw them as much a part of the company as the bricks in the building.

She sat back in her chair, her hands on top of her head, happy with herself. Behind her on the bed, she'd put her handwritten draft in various sections. Her note cards were in piles that were color-coded based on the subject and neatly stacked on her nightstand. Unlike many teenagers Petra's room was neat most of the time.

She looked at her watch: time for a shower and a shampoo. Petra was extremely proud of the long black hair that fell to her waist, but it did take care. After her shower she planned to tumble into bed, thus making it necessary to free it from the papers that were in piles.

Some students might have thrown the papers together. She carefully filed everything in folders for future reference.

In the bathroom she turned the water up as hot as it would go to steam the soreness from her shoulders. She had been hunched over the typewriter far too long, transferring the handwritten draft with its inserts and notes on notes.

With her hair wrapped in a towel and wearing her bathrobe, she returned to her room. She understood the phrase "bone tired." The problem with the length of her hair was the time it took to dry, but finally she was done. Normally, she prepared everything for the morning the night before, but she was just too tired. Instead she set her alarm for fifteen minutes earlier than normal.

As always before she went to sleep, she scanned the room to make sure everything was in its place. Even though it was late

May, the night temperature dropped enough so that being under the duvet felt good and cozy. She shut off the light and closed her eyes. As she lay there she felt something wasn't right.

She turned the light back on and stared at her desk. The report that had been in a neat pile to the left of her typewriter was gone. She flew over to her desk. Where could it be? Was she so tired that her mind was missing something? She hadn't put it in her backpack, had she? Of course not.

Bending over she looked into her wastepaper basket under her desk. It was full of paper scraps—her report, which had been torn into hundreds of shreds. For a moment she hoped she could tape them together, show them to her professor to show she'd done the work and beg him to either look at the mess or give her time to retype it all. Just the idea of spending another eighteen hours typing made her shudder, but what choice did she have? Dumping the wreck of her report onto her desk, she realized it was hopeless—most of the pieces were too small.

As she was working she had no doubt that her brother was responsible. Now that she knew she couldn't save the paper, she wanted revenge. She shot out of the room, up the stairs and into Fritz's room. He was pretending to be asleep. She could tell. He wasn't good at faking sleep.

"Why did you tear up my paper?"

Fritz opened his eyes and stretched. "Wha . . . ?"

"Stop pretending, you little shit."

He rubbed his eyes.

Nanny Marie came in. "Petra, what *are* you doing?"

"My brother tore up my paper."

"Why would he do that?"

"Because he's a miserable little bastard." Her voice was shaking.

"Watch your language." Nanny Marie grabbed Petra by the

shoulders and propelled her to the door. "Let him go back to sleep. Leave the room."

Petra removed Nanny Marie's hands.

"NOW!"

Petra debated fighting, but decided against it. She stomped back to her room, gathered all the report scraps and headed to her father's office. Her mother went to visit a friend every Sunday night while her father hid in his office and prepared for the week to come.

Petra didn't bother to knock.

Thomas was behind his desk costing out a new piece of equipment. He often said he could accomplish at home in an hour what would take him a day in the office. There were no interruptions. It was a rule he wasn't to be disturbed on Sunday nights unless the house was burning down, and then they should wait until the fire was just outside his door as long as there was a corridor left for him to escape.

Her father looked up frowning. "What do you want?"

She dumped the report scraps onto his desk.

Thomas stood, his hands on his desk, and leaned forward. "Clean this up immediately."

"This was my report. The one I worked all weekend to type. It's due tomorrow."

Thomas looked confused. "Why did you tear it up?"

"I didn't. Your son did."

"Why would Fritz do that?"

"Because he's a miserable child." She knew better than to use any nasty words when talking with her father.

"I'm sorry, but I can't believe he'd do such a thing."

"And do you think someone snuck into the house and did it? Or someone in the house? The cook? Nanny? *Mutti*? Or I'd do it?"

"I'll ask him in the morning."

"Ask him now."

"He needs his sleep."

Petra gathered up the scraps. "And I won't have any sleep while I retype this whole thing."

Petra's professor was in his early thirties. Every girl had a crush on him. He was married, happily, and talked glowingly of his wife and baby son. This only made him more desirable. Even if he was already taken, he was the kind of man they wanted for themselves.

He could have been a Spanish bullfighter with his almost-black hair, which he wore just long enough to graze his collar.

Petra waited for him outside his office door before classes started. She was pale with circles under her eyes.

"Fraulein Bircher?" He opened his office door and ushered her in. It was a room not much bigger than an oversized closet. It held a table that was only large enough for a typewriter with papers on one side and one book on the other. Book-filled shelves were floor to ceiling behind the table where a window should have been. With a wave of his hand he indicated she should sit.

Instead she emptied her backpack. She placed the pages she'd managed to type before she had to dress for school. "This is the report I typed all last night. I haven't been to bed."

He rubbed his hand across his stubbly chin. No matter how often he shaved, his beard grew, it seemed, within minutes. It added to the appearance that his female students found so sexy. "Perhaps you should have started earlier."

Petra produced a sack filled with her destroyed paper. "I did. I worked all weekend and my brother tore it up."

He picked up the three pieces that were large enough for him to read and make sense off. "Well, I've heard a lot of excuses as to why a student hadn't finished his or her work, but . . . "

"But I did finish." Petra reached in for her handwritten draft. "See."

He thumbed through the pages.

"I know you have a no-extension policy, but can't you make an exception?"

The professor leaned back and started reading the handwritten copy, comparing it to the pages Petra had completed. Sometimes he had to turn a page to see what she'd written on the back.

Petra found herself saying a prayer to a God she didn't believe in. Although she wanted to interrupt him, she didn't dare.

A clock between the books on his second shelf ticked. Each sound matched her heartbeat. Let him give me more time . . . let him give me more time.

When he'd read the completed pages and compared them to the handwritten, he put them on his desk and folded his hands. "I don't know what to say. I've never had a situation like this."

"I've done the work. If you can give me until tomorrow, I will stay up all night and finish it."

"Losing two nights' sleep? No. No, that won't do at all."

"But it will ruin my grade."

He held up his hand. "I suspect there are a few more typing errors because of your all-night vigil with your typewriter, but the little content I see here is really impressive. I do want to read the rest, but I can't in all conscience make you stay up a second night in a row." He leaned back in his chair.

Petra held her breath.

"I'm going to give you until next week to finish typing. Leave what you've done with me and I'll consider that you passed it in. Besides, I've so many others to correct, that I probably won't get to yours until next week anyway."

Tears ran down Petra's cheeks. She didn't want to cry in front of her professor because it made her seem childish, but she was so, so exhausted.

He reached into the drawer where he kept tissues for crying students as well as for his own spring allergies, which were in full force. "I would suggest you try to find out why your brother did this, although that is none of my business."

Petra took the tissue and blew her nose. Trying to regain some sense of dignity, which between what she felt had been groveling and her breaking down, she repacked the sack with the destroyed papers and took the draft from the point she'd stopped to get ready for school and stuffed it all into her backpack.

"I can't find words to thank you."

"If you make the rest of the paper as good as what I've scanned, the pleasure of reading it will be more than enough thanks," he said.

# CHAPTER 40

*Day 25, Thursday*

The last few nights when Brett Windsor arrived home, the house was dark. No good smells tickled his olfactory senses when he opened the door. It was left to him to build the fire in the fireplace in the living room that threw enough heat to warm the first floor, turn on the radiators in the bedrooms, and start dinner.

That was the price of Trudi's working: he had to admit it was nicer before she'd started her job to have his children rush downstairs and jump on him in greeting, unless, of course, they were engrossed in a DVD or game. However, her job was the price of being allowed to keep their mortgage. He was so tired of prices that weren't necessarily monetary, for things that he shouldn't have to pay.

On the kitchen counter, next to where he dropped the day's mail, was a note to put the casserole into the oven for fifty minutes at 210°C. Which casserole? When he opened the refrigerator there were two casserole dishes covered with tinfoil. If he chose the wrong one it would lead to a temper tantrum, something he certainly didn't want to face tonight when he had so much work to do.

He'd gone into overdrive to get the concept of the cookie stores from his head into a written plan. Petra had given him the go-ahead to work with an agency on the preliminaries. Instead of going to their usual one, he'd contacted a friend who owned a small agency in New Hampshire. Pete Welch was one of the most creative people he knew.

Normally, Petra wanted to use local people, but as much as Brett loved living in Switzerland, he did not think of them as a creative people, something he could never say. The company's own agency mostly placed their ads and developed his ideas. They could come up with demographics and trends, but creativity? No, he wanted something that would rock the cookie-loving world.

Once he had wanted his own agency, but Trudi would never have wanted to risk it, and even if he did, he was not sure that his ideas would be sellable to many of the local businesses. Safe, not sorry, was the operative phrase here.

One of the casseroles looked like lasagna. The other was more like a shepherd's pie. He knew his wife spent Sunday making the week's meals and complaining that it was much better to prepare things daily but she was just too tired after work.

He made an executive decision to go with the shepherd's pie, hoping the time and temperature were right. To compensate if he were wrong, he set the table, took salad out of the vegetable drawer, rinsed it, and spun it dry. He opened a bottle of red to breathe, hoping that the wine would mellow his wife's mood. That her mood would not need mellowing was so unlikely that he didn't consider alternatives.

Her transition into the workforce had not been a happy one. She complained as she left the house, and complained when she came home. She moaned about things not being done to keep the house clean, although she'd only been working a week.

Saturday, he'd made them all a pancake breakfast then ordered a cleaning morning. Trudi had objected that (1) the girls shouldn't be made to do housework and (2) the house wasn't as clean as it would be had she had the time to do it her way.

Only his whispered remarks that the girls were so proud of the job they'd done and that she shouldn't discourage them had stopped her tirade. He'd suggested a cleaning woman, which she also turned down, although most of her friends had them. Maybe in time she would come around on that one. He hoped so. However, he couldn't refute the logic that between the babysitter and a cleaning woman, there would be less money than if she weren't working and just relying on his salary.

He did a quick survey of the kitchen, dining room, and living room to make sure it was neat enough to meet Trudi's critical eye. Then he took the mail up to the room that he used as an office. This was the fourth bedroom in the house and the smallest, located under the eaves with a skylight occupying half the roof space. During the day it seemed open, but at night it was a bit claustrophobic, especially after he lowered the *Rolladen* covering the windows. Still it kept the heat in, and the heating bills down. During the day he shut off the radiators and closed the door.

Most of the mail was the usual bills: television tax, electricity, health insurance, and the girls' gymnastic lessons for the month. There was a letter from the post office where he held a savings account, still in his own name. The postal service bank had gone private a few months before. He read it.

"Shit!"

To keep his account opened they wanted five years of certified copies that he'd paid his FBAR, the form all ex-pat Americans had to fill out for the IRS listing their foreign bank accounts.

Hell!

His accounts weren't foreign. They were local. If he had an American bank account, that would be foreign for him.

Did they think he'd risk the hefty fines for not filling out the damn forms? The letter went on to say if he could not provide them, they would have no choice but to close his account.

Losing the postal savings account would leave him totally at Trudi's mercy. He would not be able to prove to a single person in Switzerland that the money in Trudi's account was really his. He worried regularly that she might decide to cancel his ATM card, leaving him virtually penniless despite his making a more than adequate salary.

As for her working, he still hadn't had the courage to tell her that everything she earned as his wife was also subject to IRS reporting. One crisis discussion at a time.

Granted it was a small account, but it was the one account in his name that was still open. Even though he had kept copies of the filed forms, he couldn't imagine that the IRS would respond to a request for certification.

The phone on his desk rang. He exchanged pleasantries with Jason Costello.

"Listen, do you have a postal account?" Jason asked.

"You got the letter too?"

"What the hell are we going to do?"

Brett didn't have an answer. None of the alternatives to bank like a normal person were available to them. Going back to the States would mean a divorce and losing his kids and that was even less acceptable. It was hard enough keeping his marriage together in Switzerland.

"I don't know."

"I know it's happening to other ex-pats in other countries."

"Doesn't help us."

"Have you talked to Heather and Jennifer? I bet our friends got letters, too."

Brett shook his head then realized that Jason couldn't see him. "Maybe because they don't work, it won't have the same effect."

"I know that Alexander has a mistress. She's putting pressure on him to leave Jennifer."

Brett hadn't realized that Jennifer's husband was cheating on her. He could only imagine that if Alexander did leave Jennifer, she would be left with nothing at all since the couple had already transferred everything into his name alone to keep their bank accounts open. He remembered the discussion they'd had about it. Jennifer had been almost crying when she told them, adding over and over, "I'm not a tax dodger. I don't earn any money in the US. I don't own anything there."

"And it costs us a couple of thousand Swiss francs for a specialized accountant to tell us we don't owe any American taxes," Alexander had growled.

At the time Brett had worried about the extra strain on Jennifer and Alexander's marriage but not as much as he was worried about the strain the situation had created in his own. That it was the same story with all the American ex-pats he knew didn't make him feel any better.

God, all he wanted to do was live a normal life and to be able to concentrate on work, which at present was making him feel more excited than he had about any project he'd done for years. And now this.

"I'm going to do a Scarlett O'Hara on you and think about it tomorrow," Brett said.

"What do you say if I make an appointment with the post office in Zurich? Round up other Americans to say it is impossible to meet this requirement," Jason said.

"Tell me when and where and I'll be there."

He heard a car pull into the driveway and three doors slam. A few seconds later he heard his daughters call, "Papa, Papa, where are you?"

# Chapter 41
## 1999

---

## Tea Cakes

**Ingredients:**
1 cup butter, room temperature
2 cups powdered sugar
2 teaspoons vanilla extract
2 cups all-purpose flour
1 cup pecans, toasted and very finely ground
1/8 teaspoon ground cinnamon

**Directions:**
Preheat oven to 350°F/176°C.

Beat butter until light and fluffy.

Add 1/2 cup powdered sugar and vanilla and beat until well blended.

Blend in flour.

Add pecans.

Divide dough into two equal balls.

Wrap separately in plastic.

Chill 30 minutes.

On a flat plate mix 1 1/2 cups powdered sugar and 1/8 teaspoon cinnamon.

Make chilled dough into 2 teaspoon bits and roll into balls.

Place balls on baking sheet 1/2 inch apart.

Bake 18 minutes or until golden brown.

When dough is cool, roll in sugar-cinnamon mixture.

Makes about 4 dozen.

Petra sat on the futon in her Aunt Mattie's Paris atelier. The sun streamed down through the skylight, warming the room without needing to put on the electric radiators.

Various-sized canvases, from miniatures to those that would occupy the good part of a wall, were stacked on the floor against one brick wall.

"I'm just not sure I want to marry Walter." Petra accepted a bowl of tea from her aunt, who was dressed in paint-splattered jeans and a T-shirt that matched the portrait she was working on. Mattie earned her living from portraits.

She painted abstracts for herself and sometimes she combined the two. Her success was measured by having enough—enough money to pay the rent, enough food, enough to host friends for her monthly salons.

She never touched her share of the family business income, a small amount earned by being a board member, a member who drove her twin brother, Thomas, Petra's father, to distraction in the best of times. In the worst, he muttered that he wished he'd driven her out of the womb.

"I'd have left the womb if I could have, which would have been better than staying that close to you," Mattie had replied. She smiled when she'd said it, although at the board meeting where the exchange was uttered, the other members—Jemma, Petra's mother; Herr Peter Ritzman, the father of Petra's fiancé;

Tobias Grunner, who doubled as the company's attorney; and Herr Arne Friedman, the union representative on the board— weren't sure whether to smile or pretend they hadn't heard.

Or at least that was how Mattie had told it. She loved telling the story to Petra every time her niece visited her. Petra loved hearing it.

"Then why marry him?"

Petra found her aunt never pussyfooted around an issue.

"I'm thirty. I want to have children. He's our banker's son. His father is on the board."

"Do you love him?"

"What's love?"

Mattie took the tea bowl from her niece. The bowl had been made by one of Mattie's friends, a potter and sometimes lover. "If you don't know, then you aren't in love."

"But I want to have children. He'll make a good father." Petra was wearing jeans and an oversized black sweater that she kept at Mattie's for her visits to Paris, which had started when she was a student at the University of Zurich, much to her father's disapproval.

The relationship between brother and sister would probably have disappeared entirely had not the terms of Theo's will placed Mattie on the board. Her removal would have disinherited Thomas. Family companies, family politics were the same thing, Theo had written.

Neither twin was willing to go to court. Mattie had taken as the will to mean that finally her father had accepted her for who she was, not whom he wanted her to be. Thomas didn't want to spend the money on a court case that would put the company in a bad public relations position. So they suffered with each other.

Mattie loved her niece as the child she never had and would never have. She'd mothered some of her lovers' children over the years, but Petra was her blood. To the degree that the aunt–niece relationship annoyed her brother was a small plus, but even if he'd encouraged it, she would have loved Petra the same.

"You don't have to be married these days to have babies."

"In our family we do."

Petra stood up and began to pace. The atelier was large enough that she could make a good circle.

"And Papa still is keeping me in minor roles. I am much better than Fritz. Do you know he caused almost five thousand Swiss francs' worth of damage? Carelessness."

Mattie shook her head. She didn't understand Thomas's attitude toward his children. Petra wanted to take over the company. She was competent and full of ideas. Perhaps when Fritz finished school and settled down he would be all right, but Petra had the business in her soul.

Perhaps it was unfair to compare a twenty-year-old male with a thirty-year-old woman, but Fritz, in her mind, had always been a spoiled brat.

"The men in our family never truly appreciate the women. *Opa* Theo never appreciated his mother. I'd have loved to have known Grandma Annabel."

"She would have adored you." Mattie didn't say that she also would have understood Petra far better than Thomas did.

# CHAPTER 42

*Day 25, Thursday*

Trudi slammed her keys against the kitchen counter and stomped over to the oven. "You put in the wrong casserole," she said to Brett, who had come downstairs to greet her.

"Does it really matter?"

"I'd been thinking how much I wanted to eat lasagna tonight."

"We could go to the Italian restaurant."

"The girls have homework."

"We'll get a sitter."

Trudi took off her coat and hung it up. She sat on the bench by the door and took off her boots, replacing them with the pair of house slippers kept on the shelf between the door and the bench. Outdoor shoes were never worn in the house. As she folded her arms across her chest she glared at Brett. "You don't get it, do you?"

He resisted saying "get what," because he didn't want to know what he didn't get.

"I hate working. I hate you for making me work." She pushed past him.

He wasn't sure how to respond to that.

"It isn't good for the girls not to be able to come home after school." At that, their daughter Hanneli pounded downstairs. "Look, Papa." The seven-year-old thrust out her wrist to show him a leather-braided bracelet.

"Did you make that at school, sweetheart?"

She shook her blond curls. Hanneli looked like her mother. Nine-year-old Gisela resembled him with her dark straight hair. It was as if each girl had received only one of their parents' genes and not the other.

"*Tante* Jennifer showed us how to do it. Tomorrow she says we'll blow bubbles outside and maybe they'll freeze and we can take photos with her phone if they do." She started back up the stairs. "I hope it will be cold enough. I'm going to look up the weather on the computer." With that she bounded back upstairs.

He knew that he would only stoke the argument when he said, "I can see how Hanneli is suffering by going to Jennifer's after school."

When Trudi was angry, she either went ballistic—a phrase she hated—or imitated igloos, where if she spoke at all her words were encased in icicles. This time she went the frigid route, speaking only to the girls during dinner. She refused help in cleaning up and told Brett she would take care of getting the girls to bed.

Although the girls could read themselves, no one wanted to give up the bedtime ritual of a story. Long ago the girls had decided that they wanted to share a bedroom and use the free bedroom as a playroom, although allocation of space for different activities often required the wisdom of a UN peacekeeper.

Brett sighed and went back to his office. With the time difference this would be an opportune hour to talk with Pete Welch and arrange for him to come to Switzerland. He placed the call.

Pete wanted to brainstorm so he would have something to present once he arrived.

"Art nouveau, art deco, old-fashioned," Pete said over Skype.

"What about a woman who looked modern in the 1920s but also was a good baker?" Brett threw in.

"Mannequins in period dress in each store?" Pete asked. "And you'll want store layouts?"

"Yes, and I'll need packaging, boxes, bags, adverts."

"Adverts?" Pete asked.

"Commercials. Advert is Brit for advertisement," Brett said. "Our current advertising agency speaks U.K. English."

"If you're going prestige, I'd start out with glossy ads."

"I agree, but we can't forget social media."

Brett thought Pete needed a bit more information. "Petra is having a history of the business being written. Maybe you can use that in some way."

"This will be fun." Pete sounded like he did at college, when he'd come up with some scheme. "Will you have a translator for me?"

"Petra speaks great English, only she doesn't like to."

After he hung up, Brett sat back in his chair. Strange, his work life was going better than it ever had been, but his home life was worse than it ever had been.

# Chapter 43
# 1999

## Strawberry Vanilla Cookies

**Ingredients:**
1 cup butter, room temperature
2 eggs
1/2 cup white sugar
3/4 cup tightly packed brown sugar
1 box of strawberry gelatin (2 ounces)
2 2/3 cups flour

**Directions:**
Preheat oven to 350°C/176°F.

Line a cookie sheet with parchment.

Sift dry ingredients together.

Cream butter until fluffy.

Add both sugars and gelatin powder.

Add eggs.

Add sifted ingredients into mixture and mix well.

Drop by spoonful onto baking sheet.

Bake a maximum 10 minutes.

★  ★  ★  ★  ★

Petra sat outside the conference room where her future was being decided. The board, made up of her mother, the company
lawyer, her father-in-law, her aunt, and the head of the union,
were deciding her future.

She deserved to be the CEO.

Deserved it.

She knew every board in the factory, every process, every
employee, every employee's strengths, weaknesses, and even
their spouses and children's names.

Fritz, what did he know? He worked there summers not
because he wanted to but because his father insisted. In theory,
Petra understood her father's reasoning. If Fritz were to take
over after his death, then he had to understand the operation.
What his father didn't take into consideration was that the new
head of the company needed to care about the company.

Now her father was dead from a heart attack. And Fritz at
twenty was nowhere near ready to take over.

She was.

Petra, when she looked over the family history, had decided
that all the men could qualify for the Male Chauvinist Pig of
the Year award, while Annabel Bircher, who was the one who
had made the company what it was, was a woman.

Petra was uncomfortable sitting in her current position. The
baby was beginning to tap dance on her bladder. As much as
she wanted this child, the timing was awful. In fact she hadn't
known it but she was probably three weeks pregnant when
they'd gone to the city hall to be married. Her mother also
wanted her to have a church wedding, but Petra refused. All
that fuss about dresses and flowers was, in her opinion, a waste
of time. Make the commitment and get it over with.

The lawyer didn't think women should be in positions of
authority at all. And mothers? They belonged at home with

their babies.

Her mother tended to agree with the lawyer on the baby part.

Her father-in-law agreed with them.

Mattie and the head of the union were on her side, or so Petra hoped.

When she couldn't stand it any longer, she whispered to the secretary that she was heading for the plant floor.

Outside the mixing room she put on the plastic head covering. The required throw-away white coat looked like a wispy raincoat. In another couple of weeks she wouldn't be able to button it over her stomach.

The folding chair next to the cabinet that held the hygienic clothing was not that stable, but it was something to hold on to so she could slip the blue plastic booties over her flats. One of the workers passed and said, "Be careful you don't slip." She thanked her, although she was tempted to say that she already knew those plastic booties could be lethal if someone tried to run. She'd searched for a product that was less slippery, but couldn't find one. At least once a year, and sometimes more often, an employee would injure themselves as they were walking hygienically but not safely shod.

Instead, she had posted signs warning employees of the danger, much to her father's disgust. She even had a contest for the employees to design new safety messages, with the prize a morning off, making her father even angrier. He had threatened to fire her.

Petra did not think that his anger contributed to his heart attack. He had been overweight, a heavy smoker, and had high blood pressure. He refused to change his habits, saying he wanted to live until he died, not have a living death.

The vats of dough for the vanilla-strawberry drop cookies were turning. The smell of the fruit, all fresh, wafted in the air.

They only used fresh strawberries, and now that they had convinced a farmer in the Canton of Grabünden to grow them in hothouses all year round, they could produce this best-seller cookie twelve months a year. Periodically Petra had gone to the farmer's place to check that the strawberries tasted just right.

She felt the baby move. Three more months, and she knew it would be a long three months.

Walter was delighted he was going to be a father, although he had said he wished that they'd waited until after his promotion to assistant vice president at the bank. He'd have more time then, or so he'd said. Petra didn't believe him. He barely took time off for their honeymoon. Other executives took their full six-week vacation time, but Walter felt not doing it gave him some advantage. He chafed under the legal requirement that every employee in the country take at least two weeks off consecutively.

He would be delighted if his wife were not made CEO. He'd said more than once that he hoped she would think more of the baby and the family and less about the company. She could have said the same thing: when he was home, be it nights or weekends, he usually was working.

She knew how driven he was when she married him. In him, she recognized herself, but he didn't see or wouldn't admit their similarities. His being devoted to his work was one of the reasons she had married him. It would leave her free for her own career.

Becoming a mother had been in her plans, just not so soon. Had she known her father would die, would she have considered an abortion? Probably not. She did want children and she wasn't getting any younger.

She followed an employee pushing a rack of cookies that were ready to be baked. The ovens looked like closets. The racks of cookies were pushed in and then circulated so they would cook evenly.

Petra had plenty of ideas about reorganizing the work flow. Her father had told her that her ideas would never work, but Petra had talked with a few members of the staff that she trusted. They had tweaked her ideas into a better plan. However, no matter how good her ideas were, unless she was given the power to implement them, they were useless.

How long would the board take?

She entered the packing room, where she was greeted with smiles. Before she could say anything, she heard her name paged, asking her to come to the executive suite.

As much as she wanted to rush, she was afraid of slipping. She moved slowly until she came to a chair where she could remove the blue plastic slippers.

The stairs were quicker than waiting for the elevator, but the baby made it harder for her to run up them. She still took them two at a time. Outside the executive area she paused and took several deep breaths. She smoothed her hair before turning the knob and walking slowly to where the secretary was sitting. "Did you page me?"

"They're ready for you." Before Petra could open the conference room door, the secretary whispered, "Good luck." There was no way that the woman knew what had happened. The lawyer was taking the minutes of the meeting. Even his assistant hadn't been invited.

Inside Jemma Bircher smiled at her daughter. The union leader smiled. The lawyer frowned.

She took his frown as a good sign. "May I sit down?" Petra asked pointing to the empty chair around the circular table that was made of a very fine oak.

The lawyer stood up and pulled the chair out just enough that Petra could sit, but not far enough that she could do it with any grace. Her stomach touched the table.

"We've reached a decision," the lawyer said.

Petra waited.

"You will be director of the company."

Petra's face broke into a smile.

"But," the lawyer said, "your brother is to be codirector."

Jemma Bircher reached over and took her daughter's hand.

It was all Petra could do not to snatch it away. Think, think, think! Don't react yet.

"You're not saying anything," the union leader said. He was in his fifties and had known Petra since she first came to the plant. At that time he was the employee who made sure all the machines were running perfectly. He would carry her on his shoulders at break time and buy her ice cream from the company cafeteria.

"I'm wondering how and why you reached that decision," Petra said. "I'm certainly competent to run the factory on my own." She wanted to add that Fritz had no interest in working at all, much less in running the factory. However, she didn't want to appear against him if they were to work together. "My brother hasn't finished university."

"We want him to transfer to Zurich and work part-time. You two will have to make joint decisions."

Petra wondered just how she would be able to get Fritz to concentrate long enough on any problem to get an answer from him.

"What if we can't come to a joint . . ."

The lawyer smiled. "You'll come to me. I'll confer with your mother, of course."

Jemma leaned into her daughter. "I know you aren't happy, but with the baby coming and all . . ."

"Many work with children." Petra wanted to scream, but she forced her voice to use the same cadence as if she were discussing a new dress, what to eat, or to suggest a movie.

"However, think of Hannah."

Petra wasn't sure what her mother was referring to.

"Hannah, after having her baby, decided she wanted to give up her job. It was too hard to leave the baby every day."

Hannah, Hannah, Hannah. Petra tried to place her. Then she remembered that she was the daughter of the pharmacist and worked in the pharmacy for her father. "But she had a job. I have a career."

"You will see that it will work out."

Petra wasn't sure how it would, but there wasn't much she could do. She needed to figure out how to work with Fritz and make sure that he caused the least damage possible.

"Thank you," she said.

She went back to her office.

After the meeting broke up, her aunt came and sat down. Mattie was wearing black, but the style was anything but mourning with the zigzag hemline. "You don't know the fight I had to get them to agree to you at all. I threatened everything I could think of."

"I can only imagine," Petra said. She didn't blame her aunt for having to compromise. She tried to be grateful that she'd won as much as she had.

# CHAPTER 44

*Day 27, Saturday*

The snow feathered its way to the ground outside the window of the house where Annie and her family were staying. Her parents, Susan and Dave Young, had come for the weekend to see Sophie more than Annie, who joked that once she'd produced a grandchild she had become a has-been in her parents' eyes. "Daddy calls the baby Kitten II," she complained. "Although I suppose I'm lucky that I'm his original Kitten."

In reality, she wasn't at all jealous. Watching how happy Susan was toting Sophie around on her hip and stopping at the window to watch the two German shepherds in the snow reminded her of how lucky she was to have her family, past and present, together and all of them healthy.

Roger's heart attack last year when they were in Ely had been a major lesson in appreciating the now, although she wasn't about to admit it.

"How's the project going?" Dave asked. "With the murder and all, were you distracted?" He rested his arms on the kitchen divider and watched his daughter trim the fat off the lamb chops they were having for lunch. "Leave some of the fat on. It's the best part."

Annie bit her tongue about fat and clogged hearts. "I'm a bit behind. All of last week was crazy."

"Will you finish on time?"

"You and your deadlines." Annie put a small amount of oil in the frying pan.

"It comes from years of running a business and trying to keep clients. Well?"

"I've emailed Sharon that I'll be able to finish it up when we get back in Argelès." Yesterday Petra had said she wanted to see all the English and German, which Annie had pretty much under control.

Annie found it amazing how the woman had been able to focus on the company with a murder trial in her future—or at least she faced a murder trial if Roger couldn't prove her innocence, something that he hadn't much luck in doing.

Annie's cell phone sounded in her pocketbook, but it stopped ringing before she could answer. Seconds after her cell stopped, the landline rang. After saying hello she covered the receiver and mouthed, "It's Sharon."

"Your agent?" Dave asked.

Annie picked up a pencil and wrote on the shopping list pad next to the phone, then showed it to her father: *She's also owner of this house.*

"I know," he mouthed.

Just as she hung up, Roger came in. After returning from Petra's he'd been sweeping off the sidewalk, despite Annie's admonishes to the contrary, but he had at least agreed not to shovel, only to use the broom.

"Sharon called. She's had an accident water skiing and is in traction. She won't be back for at least three more weeks. When she comes back, she'll be staying with her boyfriend for a couple of weeks, so she wanted us to stay here until then."

"And . . ."

"Also, Petra called her and wanted to extend my contract. She, Petra that is, figures I can help Brett with the marketing plans."

Roger looked out the window at the falling snow. "You realize how much warmer it is in Argelès?"

She did realize it. Sophie could be walked in her stroller wearing only a light coat. "You realize that I'm being paid one hundred CHF an hour? That's almost four thousand a week and I wouldn't have to work for the best part of a year."

"But you will if you find anything interesting." He hung up his coat.

Dave slipped off the stool and went to the living room, where he took Sophie from Susan. Roger took Dave's place on the stool.

Annie picked up the potato peeler and slashed at one of the potatoes she'd already washed. "I suspect part of it is that Petra wants you to keep working for her as well."

"It'll bring us almost into Christmas. Think of the cold."

"Think of the money," Annie said.

"Think of the fact that we've reached another dead end in the investigation," Roger said.

Annie knew that Roger was upset that they had found nothing so far in Fritz's papers that might be construed as close to a lead, although they did find some skullduggery in the deal. Roger loved the English word "skullduggery." He said it sounded less evil to him than the French *grenouillage* or the German *Schandtaten,* although Annie had assured him *Schandtaten* was evil enough.

"Petra told me today that she was thrilled that you discovered that Fritz would have received more money than she would have for turning over the company," Roger said as Annie kept attacking the potatoes. "Thrilled might not be the word. Furious. At him."

"When you talked to her earlier did she tell you she'd fired the lawyer who was drawing up the sale contract?" Annie asked. "He never thought she had any right to run the company and fought her on almost everything." Annie directed the second sentence to her parents.

"She did. She was sputtering that he had hidden language that would protect the current employees for only six months before the factory would be moved," Roger said.

"How can you hide language like that? Petra would have read every word," Annie said. Petra was usually so calm that Annie had difficulty imagining her sputtering, but if you thought of what she'd gone through what with her brother's murder and his treachery. She knew how upset she would be in Petra's situation. Imagine having as a brother not just a turncoat against the workers but against the family and their traditions covering parts of three centuries.

"Three copies of the contracts. The one with the six-month clause would be under the first contract. Fritz must have been taking it for granted that his sister would only read the top copy and sign all three. Then he would destroy the top copy. She wanted me to look at the contracts," Roger said.

Annie didn't point out that Roger couldn't read German. She had read and reread the contracts herself, when Petra had asked her to. She hadn't picked up any difference either. Only printed copies of the emails between the attorney and Fritz Bircher revealed it and in such veiled terms that probably the police themselves went over it without noticing.

"I had Frau Küper compare the two documents sentence by sentence. I had no idea when I found another contract in Fritz's papers that it would be different from the one on file."

"That's a fine *flic* instinct, your husband has," Dave said. Annie had almost forgotten he was in the room with them.

"In a way, having found that, I feel less guilty taking her money." Roger took the peeler from his wife and started on the last potato. "Before that I didn't think I was getting anyplace."

Annie cut the already-peeled potatoes into pieces and put them in a pot of water to boil. The meal would be lamb chops, mashed potatoes, green beans, and mint sauce made in the Welsh style.

How did I get so domesticated? flashed through her mind along with the question which she wouldn't ask: did it bother him that she was earning so much more than his pension brought in, although they had enough to live on without her working? The one way she could communicate with him on the issue was to point out that her mind loved challenges. Peeling potatoes wasn't enough of a challenge. "Does she still want you to find out if her husband is cheating?"

Roger sighed. "I never thought I'd come down to being a private eye checking on philandering mates. There I've also proven diddly squat."

Annie loved it when he used one of her slang expressions. She reached across the divider and brushed his hair out of his eyes. "At one point you were complaining you'd never work again. Now that you're working you're unhappy at what you're doing." She had to stand on tiptoe to kiss the tip of his nose.

If not a scrap of leftovers was an indication of the quality of a meal, then Annie's cooking was deemed a success. The two couples were at the table waiting for their caffeine-free coffee to perk. Sophie had fallen asleep halfway through the meal and had been carried to her cot. "Out for the night," Roger said. "Or at least I hope so."

"The baton has been passed to a new generation," Susan said. "You used to visit me and I cooked. Even when I visited you in Argelès, I cooked." She started to clear the table. "I remember the first Thanksgiving when my mother let me host the family."

"But you only did it one year, because we moved to Holland before the next Thanksgiving," Dave said.

"And if we went Stateside for either Thanksgiving or

Christmas we were always staying with your or my parents, which left me as sous chef," Susan said.

"Even when we were there in the summer, you seldom cooked and when you did it was more as helper." Annie turned to Roger. "I loved going because I was always treated like the visiting princess."

"And it's our turn to treat Sophie as a princess," Susan said. "Except we won't emphasize the princess or how pretty she is, although we'll tell her enough."

"Like you did with me." Annie turned to Roger. "Mom and Dad told me I was pretty, but looks are temporary. It's more important to be creative, intelligent, kind, considerate, and independent."

"You certainly believed their last goal," Roger said to Annie, who was now in the kitchen area making coffee. "I don't know whether to thank or curse your parents for your independent streak."

Annie brought the coffee to the table and filled the four demitasses. Only Susan took sugar, never having become totally accustomed to the strong European coffee.

Roger brought out a chocolate cake he had purchased at the local bakery.

"I see no sense in doing something that someone else can do better," Annie had said when she'd sent him into the center of town for something delicious, sweet and calorie-laden. She wasn't about to spend a weekend in the kitchen baking while her parents were visiting.

As they drank their coffee and ate the cake, Susan said, "Your father and I have made a decision about our banking problems."

Annie grabbed Roger's hand—not that holding it would stop the announcement she'd been dreading. They were going to move to Caleb's Landing, where her father had inherited a house and her mother was now part of a cooperative of artists that catered to the tourist trade in the Massachusetts seaside community.

"We're renouncing our American citizenship," Dave said. "It is probably the hardest thing we ever had to do, but we can't continue to live here, bank, and be Americans."

"It's a good thing we took Swiss nationality as soon as we could," Susan said. "Of course that means he's limited to how much time we can spend in Caleb's Landing as foreign nationals. That hurts too."

"You're only there summers anyway," Roger said.

"The other thing you need to know," Susan said, "is that we're selling the house."

No! Annie screamed inside her head. After moving from country to country and always living in rented apartments, she'd been so happy when her parents had bought a house. It made her feel as if there were something permanent in her life, a place she could always go back to.

She loved the house where she'd spent her high school years. It was in a small village on the outskirts of Geneva. She loved getting up early on a summer morning and walking five minutes for a dip in the lake. And her best friend across the street had a stable where they kept horses. They'd go riding through the vineyards. There were memories of sleepovers and her friends crashing there sometimes for weeks if they were having trouble with their parents. The Young household had always been a refuge for anyone who needed sheltering.

Dave reached out and touched Annie's cheek. "It's the only way, Kitten. I have to pay twenty-three percent of everything I own as a punishment for renouncing."

"Isn't there any alternative?" Roger said. "I heard some others talking about it, but it seems so drastic."

Dave explained the pressure the United States was putting on banks with threats of huge fines and being shut out of the

US market if they didn't turn over all the account information on every American account holder. The banks found it easier just to close the accounts of their American customers.

"Harry's doing the same thing. It's the only way we can keep the business going." Annie had never really liked her father's partner, another American, although she admired the success they had made of their consultancy after Digital had given them both very golden handshakes. "No bank account, no business."

"We'd thought about going to Caleb's Landing permanently, but with you and the baby here . . ." Susan left the thought uncompleted.

"But it is a Swiss house bought with money you earned in Switzerland," Roger said.

"Doesn't matter to the IRS. Sophie's not American, is she?"

"We haven't registered her yet."

"Don't," Dave said.

Roger frowned and tilted his head.

"Every cent she will earn, no matter where in the world she earns it, will be taxed, even if she never sets foot in the USA. And she may never be able to bank anywhere outside the US if she has American citizenship."

"We haven't had any trouble in France yet," Roger said.

"It's coming. France has signed on to follow the American demands. Annie, if you lose the right to a bank account, how do you feel about Roger having total control of your money?"

Not good, she thought. They still kept their finances separate at her insistence, throwing money into a communal pot for household expenses.

Susan stood up and picked up the empty coffee pot. "I'll make more. No one has touched much of their cake and you'll want coffee with it."

"Isn't there any other solution?" Roger asked.

"We've been over it every which way and if there's a better

241

alternative we missed it."

Annie didn't know how she would feel about renouncing her American nationality, even if she had only spent her first eight years there and her freshman year of university.

She didn't feel American. Nor did she feel Dutch, German, Swiss, or French. She felt she was hodgepodge, not even a third-culture kid. She loved windmills, bikes and dikes, *Würst*, oompah-pah music, fondue, and French baguettes. She loved double and triple cheek kisses and switching languages and feeling comfortable in Amsterdam, Stuttgart, Geneva, Paris, Argelès. Those things made her what she was, maybe a fifth-culture kid, which meant she was part of none of them completely.

What she was was Dave and Susan's daughter, Roger's wife, Sophie's mother, a multilingual tech writer and translator, and a sometimes author more by default than deliberately setting out to write anything.

# CHAPTER 45

*Day 29, Monday*

Roger pulled into a parking spot outside the building marked ZBFI. The logo was a stylistic crossbow, which seemed strange to Roger for a private bank. He wondered if they got money into the crosshairs and shot it to profit.

Petra had told him that the four-story office building was where her husband worked as a senior vice president. He also had an office downtown, which he used to meet with important clients, but this building held IT, marketing, and the nonvisible functions that he oversaw.

Roger knew nothing about private banking. He knew nothing about banking at all except it seemed to mess people up more than it helped and it was causing his in-laws all sorts of problems.

He'd done only a few stakeouts since leaving Paris over a decade ago. An advantage of being a chief was that he could assign others to the most boring part of police work.

Petra had given him the coordinates and recommended where to park to watch the front door leading to the parking lot.

He did a quick look-see for a security camera. It wouldn't do anybody any good for him to get arrested. Annie had fixed a thermos of hot chocolate for him, saying, and rightly so, that coffee would increase the pee desire while chocolate wouldn't.

The building was like the others in the industrial zone—four stories, plain stucco front—creating a cookie-cutter effect.

He'd dressed in thermal underwear, heavy flannel shirt, ski jacket with a hood, some things that he hadn't thrown out since his skiing days at least two decades before. He'd been tempted to discard them when he'd moved to the South of France, but he had hoped to ski sometime, somewhere. That he could still fit into them was a source of pride, although part of the reason was the weight he'd lost after his heart attack. At least he'd kept it off. He patted his flat stomach.

Along with his ski clothes, he'd put on a phony mustache and a black wig. When Annie had told him he looked adorable, he'd almost growled but instead admitted that he felt ridiculous.

At 12:37, he watched Walter Ritzman leave the building. He was with a young woman with long blond hair. She wore sharply creased trousers, but he could not see if she had on a suit jacket under her camel hair coat. A brown scarf was around her neck and it blew in the wind. She reached up to push her hair out of her eyes.

Ritzman opened the door of his gray Mercedes. His parking place said RITZMAN in oversized black letters. That had at least helped Roger know where to park so he could watch the car.

Petra's husband was neither a reckless nor careless driver as he managed to move onto the autobahn leading into Zurich. Roger was able to stay at least two cars behind, sometimes more. He suspected that Walter would be so intrigued with his passenger that he wouldn't notice that he was being followed. Besides, there was no reason for him to suspect that his wife had hired a private detective.

The words "private detective" would have stuck in his throat if he'd spoken them. PDs were the scum of the earth, their glorification on certain television shows and book series notwithstanding.

Not far from the train station Ritzman pulled into a garage.

Although unfamiliar with Zurich, Roger knew that the bank itself was on the opposite side of the business area from where Ritzman was parking. He let a minute go by before turning into the parking garage. No other cars were between them when Roger pulled his ticket. He could see the tail lights ahead of him.

Ritzman took the first parking place and Roger drove by. About six cars down another free space was available. The couple stayed in their car a good twenty minutes. Roger didn't want to walk by them. Instead he waited until they left the car. He moved fast but by the time he locked his car, Ritzman and the woman were far ahead of him. They stopped and kissed. Roger grabbed for his cell but he missed the photo opportunity. *Merde!*

The couple walked into the gourmet café of a major hotel. Black wooden chairs were against marble tables that matched the counter where pastries were laid out. Behind the counter, glasses were lined up and then a selection of good alcohols. A huge bucket with ice was filled with champagne bottles.

Roger glanced at his watch. It was now a little after twelve.

The couple took a seat as far from the window as possible. Roger sat close to the door. He took out his cell phone and pretended to text a message but angled the phone so he could snap their picture. It was pure luck that he did it at the same time Ritzman put the woman's hand to his lips. Gotcha, he thought. "Gotcha" was another word that he'd picked up from Annie.

When the waiter came over he only ordered coffee and paid for it at the same time the waiter placed the demitasse on the table, so he could leave quickly when the couple left.

Ritzman and his girlfriend were now holding hands. As he pretended to text, he snapped several photos. He wished he could get closer, but no private eye would go close to their targets and demand that they smile and say cheese, although the idea amused him.

Roger always kept a paperback in his pocket. He took it out and pretended to read as Walter leaned over to kiss the woman on the cheek.

Click.

The couple ordered salmon and as she ate, Walter talked, waving his fork in the air. She finished long before he did.

When they left, Roger followed them to the garage. Instead of driving to the headquarters in the suburbs, the man stopped and let the woman out. She strode down the street with her briefcase.

Walter Ritzman drove in the same direction that the woman was walking. He entered a parking garage near the main bank as she entered the bank itself, a building that must have been a few centuries old. Roger didn't follow him into the garage, but found a parking place where he could watch the entrance to the bank. The place where he stopped was only a thirty-minute parking zone.

It took another fifteen minutes before Ritzman appeared at the entrance. A doorman opened the door and Roger could see the lavish lobby as Ritzman chatted with the doorman.

Roger had enough to tell Petra. He still had no idea how to help her prove she hadn't killed her brother.

# CHAPTER 46

*Day 29, Monday*

Annie sat in Petra's office and still wondered how the woman could look so calm after having been charged with a murder. They were drinking the coffee and eating the cookies that accompanied every morning meeting.

"I'm really pleased with the material you've done so far," Petra said as she clicked through the screens on her computer. Annie had emailed her the manuscript.

Annie knew her work was good, but good work did not always satisfy the client. "Did you notice two things?"

Petra stopped with a cookie halfway to her mouth and looked at Annie.

"At the end is a separate cookbook of cookies. If you go with Brett's idea of high-end cookie stores, this could be sold along with illustrations. I did put two sample pages but that's just an idea. You'll want professional artists to illustrate the pages to extend the marketing concept."

"But if people could make the cookies, why buy ours?"

"Because Brett is suggesting having cookie-baking aromas in the stores and people won't want to wait." Annie never took credit for someone else's ideas. "Also, they may buy the books as a gift, or take them home. If you're in an airport they're traveling through, this may be the only time . . . "

" . . . they will ever be in my store."

That Petra referred to it as "her store" told Annie that she had accepted Brett's concept.

"Plus you can get book reviews and publicity on the cookbook. Brett has already checked, but you should talk more to him about that." Annie really wanted to get back to the reason she was there—the family history.

Annie stood up and went behind Petra then clicked to page seventy-five, which unlike the rest of the manuscript was in red type.

"Why the color?" Petra asked.

Annie had worried about how to handle this issue, but face-on was her decision. "Two things came up and you may not want them in a book . . . or you may."

Petra frowned.

"Your great-grandmother Annabel had an affair with her salesman. It was in her journal in code."

Petra sat back. "The old devil. My grandfather Theo really was frustrated by his mother. He was quite sedate and everything I know about *Oma* Annabel, was that she was one feisty lady."

Annie didn't say, "That's probably where you get it from."

"Then the other thing is your Aunt Mattie."

"Now what's she done?"

"She's still alive?"

"Living in Paris and still raising hell: the word 'rebel' was created for my aunt."

"I've a letter from your father to your grandfather saying she was sleeping with his friend when they were at boarding school in the States."

Petra laughed. "That sounds like Mattie. My father didn't want me to have anything to do with her, black sheep he called her, but when I was spending a year in Paris I looked her up. She was on her third husband and was . . . er . . . is a fairly successful artist. Successful can be defined as earning a living, even if limited. Mattie told me she had 'enough' money and more importantly 'enough' freedom to live as she wanted."

Annie felt warmer and warmer toward Petra. Her first impressions had been that the woman was a cold career woman, though capable, but considering what she'd gone through in the last couple of weeks, she was amazing both in her focus and her understanding. And when Annie first met Petra she hadn't realized her sense of responsibility toward her employees, something that she respected more than she would ever be able to express. "However, I suspect you don't want the letter your father wrote to your grandfather published."

Petra swung around in her chair so she was facing Annie, who returned to her chair on the other side of the desk. "I'm not so sure. I suspect it would be more interesting to show a skeleton or two. Make it, what is the American phrase, a page-turner."

Annie had seen so much corporate drivel that she liked the idea but before she could say anything Petra said, "What you've done is good and factual and I'm not criticizing, but do I think we should go ahead with the spicing it up versus showing the human side? I don't know about you, but I'm sick to death of the blah-blah corporate side." Then she added, "You know I want to extend the contract . . ."

"I do. Sharon called yesterday," Annie said.

"Annie, I'm convinced in your ability totally. And your ethics."

"It'll be fun." Annie didn't add she was worried about Petra's future if Roger couldn't find something to prove her innocence.

"I wouldn't be averse to having you on staff permanently."

Not if we have to live here, although it is beautiful, Annie thought. If it were only her, she just might think about it, but as a wife and mother her alternatives had to take in family considerations. Amazingly, it didn't bother her as much as it would have two years ago.

"Let's look at alternatives," she said.

# Chapter 47

When Annie left, Petra spun her chair around facing the blank wall. She'd done some of her best thinking looking at that wall. Some people would have looked out the window at the mountains, but the outside world was too pretty. It would distract her.

Annie Young-Perret was a strange woman—not abnormal, but like none of the other women in her life. Certainly not domestic and as far she could tell not all that maternal. She couldn't criticize her for that. Although she adored her son and two daughters, Petra knew early on she wasn't the stay-at-home, hover-over-my-babies type of mother that most of her childhood friends had become.

Yet Annie, who had handled the assignment faster and better than she'd dreamed possible, didn't seem devoted to her career as a career. What did seem to make her happy was rooting around in the company's papers.

She'd love to have Annie on her staff as they went ahead with Brett's ideas. She could see that Annie had reservations about staying, but maybe they could be overcome. She suspected money wouldn't be a good motivator, but she wasn't sure what would be. It would be worth it to try and find out.

For Petra, not thinking about the possibility of being tried for Fritz's murder was a necessity. Since she always had been able to focus on what was important, she needed that focus on the company and its future more than ever.

Not for the first time was she glad that Fritz was out of her way. She wished she could say she was sorry he'd died, but from the time he had been born he was at his very best an annoyance and at the worse—well—he'd almost destroyed the company she loved. With him gone she was able to develop the company as she wanted and that made her almost happy.

At least she'd be able to develop it if she could shake off that murder conviction. Damn, it had snuck into her mind again.

She couldn't imagine what her father would have thought had he lived to know that she was accused of murdering his precious son. He'd have believed the police and done everything in his power to see she was convicted. The knowledge hurt.

Sometimes she felt that the employees were fonder of her than her father, mother, husband, and children were. She didn't think that she was that unlovable. She was polite, and she tried to be considerate of others, thinking of things they would like and doing them.

On the other hand, she didn't compromise her own beliefs to earn a smile. The balance of being true to herself and caring for others could be achieved. Some people had a natural charisma, and if she wasn't one of them, that she could accept.

Petra gave a deep sigh that ran all the way to her toes or so it seemed.

Her mobile croaked. She'd set it to a singing bird sound that wasn't as disturbing as some if it went off during a meeting or if she was talking with someone. It was a French number. Roger.

She and Roger exchanged the normal pleasantries in English, although she had problems with his accent. He had to repeat some sentences three times.

"I can send the photos I took today if you really want to see them," Roger said.

Just from the way he phrased the sentence, she knew she

didn't want to see them, because they would prove what she didn't want to know. However, once she saw them she would know with what she was dealing, and avoidance was not her style.

She decided to bring the photos up on her laptop but not before she had her secretary bring her hot chocolate and several cookies—comfort food.

The photos were as she expected, Walter with another woman in a way that proved they were more than platonic friends. Platonic friends don't hold hands or kiss passionately in a garage.

What surprised her was the woman, a vice president at the bank, was also married. They had been entertained at their home in one of those have-to dinners, which she so hated but gave and attended as a dutiful wife must. Walter, on the other hand, did not return the courtesy when she had some social occasion related to the factory.

She would have to get Walter out of her life, but not before she had been acquitted of killing her brother. Having both of them gone would make her future smoother. However, she didn't want her husband, her soon-to-be ex-husband, dead as her brother was.

For a moment she thought of how her children would react. One thing she had no doubts about was that Walter would continue to be a good father.

The phone rang and Petra saw that it was her attorney. They needed to meet to go over her defense. That she had a motive was without any doubt. What she didn't have was an alibi, but they also did not have any evidence that showed she did kill Fritz. She answered the phone to set up a meeting within an hour.

She shut down her computer, put on her coat, and headed down to the parking lot.

Her car, which was five years old but still ran perfectly, was parked halfway to the far edge. She refused to have special parking privileges, although she did one time after she broke her foot skiing, but if any of her staff were hurt and were still able to work, they were given the same premier space by the door. When everyone was healthy, the same space had a visitor sign.

As always she had to turn the key halfway, wait a moment, then turn it the rest of the way. The car had been that way since she bought it and the garage's first explanation that it was the cold weather had worn thin when the same problem continued during the summer. Walter had thrown a wobbly about how she should insist on them fixing it or giving her a new car. After all, he pointed out, they bought their fleet of delivery trucks from the same dealer.

Petra knew on one level that he was right, but that took extra energy better spent on the children or on the business and whatever little personal life with her old friends was left. The car hummed to life for the drive to Zurich where her lawyer's offices were.

The trip was the last thing she wanted to do, especially in the snow—not that driving in slippery weather was anything new to her. The thing she wanted to do was concentrate on the business plan. Her mind was focusing on a marketing budget and she didn't immediately notice the stop sign nor the other car pulling out of the cross street.

Petra's reaction was swift. She slammed on the brakes and went into a skid, as did the other car. For what seemed like hours they were caught in an ice dance as their tires couldn't catch.

The two cars came to a halt *almost* touching, headlights to headlights as if they were about to kiss.

The man who was driving got out and screamed, "What the

hell did you think you were doing?"

Petra hoped it was nerves that caused his temper. Her hands shook so hard, she had trouble turning the wheel to pull out of the intersection.

The driver of the other car must have thought she was leaving because he pounded on her trunk.

Petra pulled over to the side of the road and parked. "I'm only parking so we don't cause a real accident," she called through the driver's open window. She didn't quite trust herself to stand.

The man stomped back to his car, but instead of parking it, he drove away.

She had no idea how long she sat there. Cars came by. A big yellow bus pulled in front of her and discharged a woman with a cane who walked by Petra's car.

I should have never slammed on my brakes. I should know better, she told herself.

Her cell phone rang and she could see on the screen that it was her attorney's number, only it wasn't the attorney. His secretary asked if she was on her way.

Petra wanted to curse, but too many years of resorting to much more effective ways of expressing disapproval blocked her. "Traffic," she said. "It's delayed me."

Before she started the car she glanced at the passenger's side. Her purse had slid off the seat. As she picked it up, there was an envelope on the floor beneath it—an envelope that had no addresses or stamp and no obvious reason to be there half under the seat.

Several pieces of paper were inside, done in a very neat printing, so neat that it almost looked typeset.

How had they gotten here?

She wasn't sure, but as she read them she thought this might be the information which would free her. Only after she was back on track for Zurich did she think she might have been stupid to touch them. Maybe she destroyed all the fingerprints.

# CHAPTER 48

*Day 29, Monday*

This was Trudi Windsor's time to do the front desk stint at the bank. She sat behind the fake-oak reception looking out the large glass window to the main street.

Her friend Claudia Schmitz walked by the large window with her straw shopping basket over her arm. Trudi saw carrots sticking out, their leafy green tops grazing the handle. She wondered why Claudia didn't use one of the reusable plastic bags with the pretty scenes that Migros and Co-op sold, instead of that ratty old basket.

She hoped Claudia didn't come into the bank and see her sitting like some minion waiting to serve others. Claudia was one of her nonworking friends who felt sorry for working women just as Trudi had before being railroaded into taking this job. Taking a deep breath she tried to calm herself.

Getting angry didn't help at all, but she was angry: angry at Brett for being American and putting them in this position, angry at herself for marrying Brett in the first place—although if she hadn't she wouldn't have had her two wonderful daughters. Mostly she was angry at Fritz for getting murdered.

He could have been her escape.

Claudia turned the corner without looking into the bank.

When Trudi wasn't feeling angry about having to work she felt ashamed that her friends would think that she selected a husband who wasn't smart enough to make enough money to provide the basics, which was not the case. For all the bad things she said about Brett, he brought home a more-than-healthy pay packet, allowing them a nice house and vacations. Of course, too many had to be to the States to visit Brett's brother and his wife.

In a way, it reinforced the girls' English. Most of the English they heard was from their father. She spoke Swiss German to them. At this point they were almost trilingual, having started French in school.

For so many months, when she was in the first flush of her love affair, she had fantasized her girls and herself with Fritz in his home, which made hers look like a pauper's hovel. Frowning, she granted that maybe "hovel" was a slight exaggeration. There were no hovels in Einsiedeln, and a four-bedroom, three-balcony, three-bathroom, two-story house with a lake view and an ultramodern kitchen would have made most people happy.

Her mother and father had chided her for not being satisfied with what she had. Of course, they didn't know that she was sleeping with a man who wasn't her husband. She never had been satisfied, they'd complained. From the day she could talk, she would accept a gift, a treat, or an event—then demand another. Trudi had to admit to herself that they spoke the truth. It wasn't that she was jealous of what other people had and she didn't. She just wanted what she wanted when she wanted it.

That year at Boston University when she saw Brett, she'd wanted him. He was good-looking, bright, and wasn't like the other boys she'd dated, probably because he'd spent enough time in Switzerland to lose some of that American edge and at the same time keeping enough of the Swiss characteristics to make him different from the Swiss boys whom she'd dated before she became an exchange student. With the normal ups and downs of courtship, she'd caught him.

The bank lobby was quiet. People came in mostly for appointments with loan officers or financial advisors. They pulled cash from the machines. Sitting doing nothing was boring, allowing her too much time to think back in time and wish she'd done things differently.

She had to admit that for a time she and Brett had been happy. Even when the girls were smaller, weekends were spent going for walks, swimming or skiing, depending on the season, or just staying at home playing games, reading, watching TV and DVDs.

Brett often put in extra hours at work, but because they lived so close, he wasn't wasting time commuting into Zurich as many of her friends' husbands did.

If someone had asked her when she fell out of love with her husband, she couldn't have told them. Fritz wasn't the reason, for her dissatisfaction had started long before the mortgage problem, but that crisis made the seed of her discontent flourish into a complete garden.

The door opened. A couple she had seen in the store or bakery from time to time came in. They were newcomers, Norwegians someone had said. She directed them to see the loan officer with whom they had an appointment.

She wished she could get up for a cup of coffee. Women on the reception desk were allowed neither food nor drinks.

Men didn't work the reception desk. Never had she been restricted in something as normal as putting something in her mouth. Even peeing at these times was frowned upon, but if she were desperate she could have called for relief. That didn't give her much comfort, although a couple of times she'd done it when she didn't have to pee, just to prove to herself she still had some control in her life.

Fritz was gone. The last few weeks before the murder, she had been worried he was losing interest in her. She knew he took out other women, and his explanation that it kept people from being suspicious of them was something she forced herself to believe.

It didn't matter now. He was dead by a gunshot and buried. As much as she'd loved him, she hoped he felt some pain when he died for his infidelity. No, she pushed that thought out of her mind. She couldn't accept that he was unfaithful to her.

Now all her hopes were dead along with Fritz. She was stuck not just with her husband, but working at a bank, for heaven's sake. Gone were the days to herself where she could spend time with her friends when she wasn't making her house a home, even a semiloveless one. There was love, but it was only there for the girls.

When she'd complained to her mother, she'd been told, "Don't you realize how many people in the world today would be delighted to have that job?"

She wasn't one of those "delighted people."

She glanced at her watch. Someone would relieve her in another twenty minutes. Then she could go back to the boring work of checking references of loan applicants, although looking at the personal data of people she knew had a certain benefit of letting her see into other people's lives.

Like the Deckers. She hadn't known that they had a rental property in the next village and that they were buying an apartment in the new complex for their recently married daughter, who was already sporting a bump three weeks after the wedding—not that marriage and babies went together anymore. Still, in a small town, there was a bit of tut-tutting with the less-traditional arrangements—or a better term would be "old-fashioned." Trudi thought of herself as old-fashioned, a woman destined to be a wife and mother, which was more than enough for any one person.

Had she left Brett for Fritz, her parents would have been furious. They were even more old-school than she was. Once married, you stayed married.

Their marriage had not been all that happy, she suspected. Like she and Brett, they didn't have screaming fights—more tight-lipped verbal exchanges and digs targeted to wound. She'd learned how to freeze out a person from her mother, not that her mother gave lessons. It was enough to observe and even if she hadn't, her father's oft-spoken statement all seasons of the year, "I need a coat in here," would have told her.

A woman came in to ask for a balance.

"You can find it on the ATM."

"I forgot my card."

Trudi asked for the account number. Computers annoyed her, but the information came up. The woman had three accounts. Trudi wrote the amounts of 25,382.66CHF, 85,103CHF, and 10,281.32CHF on a piece of paper and gave it to the customer.

Her new boss, Hans Fiedler, was standing in the doorway of his office. He had been transferred in the same week Trudi had started, replacing the manager who had been so lenient with them on the mortgage and who had also given her the job.

Fiedler was frowning but he usually frowned. He'd been two years ahead of her in school and even back then, no humor ever was allowed to show on his face. It was as if he'd taken a page from the "Boring, Uptight Banker" Manual and tried to adapt each stereotypical characteristic to his personality, most of which were already in place.

"Come see me when you're replaced," he said.

What now, Trudi wondered? Almost everything she did was wrong according to Herr Fiedler, which he insisted on being called at work. All the employees used *Herr* and *Frau* and all of them used *Sie* rather than *du* even when they were on a first-name and *du* basis outside of work. Herr Fiedler thought informality bred sloppiness.

261

Trudi herself liked formality, but two of her coworkers had shared her playpen and sandbox, and using *Frau* and *Sie* seemed unnatural. It hadn't bothered either of them, they told her when she'd asked if it did. They referred to work decorum being proper for the place.

Trudi tried not to think of Fritz talking about them living together in someplace warm and near an ocean with palm trees.

Frau Hirsch broke Trudi's concentration. "My turn," she said.

Trudi went to get a cup of coffee and carried it to Herr Fiedler's office.

"Close the door, please, and thank you for the coffee," he said as she entered. She'd meant the coffee to be for herself.

His office was the largest in the branch. He had several posters of different bank advertising campaigns framed on his wall. His in and out baskets were about equal, but all the paperwork was aligned. Trudi knew he had a wife and daughter, but there were no photos, although no bank regulation discouraged personal items.

She had little choice but to give him the cup. She hoped he didn't like it black as she did, but he picked it up and took a sip before telling her to close the door and sit down. She did.

"You don't like working here, do you, Frau Windsor?"

"It is different from being at home and caring for my family." She debated asking the next question, but then she didn't want to prolong the conversation. Maybe she could short-circuit this process. "Why do you ask?"

He picked up a pencil and leaned forward in his chair, then put his elbows on the desk. He held the pencil in both hands. Letting out a long sigh, he shook his head.

Trudi was aware that despite Herr Fiedler's body language, at some level he was enjoying himself. She'd watch him before, zooming in on her coworkers for some minor transgression although it was done in such a way that someone might think it pained him to bring up the matter. Trudi thought of Brett saying how a good manager praised in public and criticized in private. This had to be bad, she thought, if he'd closed the door.

"Because your work is substandard."

"How?"

"You just gave a balance to a woman without asking for identification, for one thing."

"But I knew her." Trudi had seen her in Migros a few times and once in a restaurant when they were both with husbands, making it a half-truth.

"That doesn't matter.

"And I've heard you asking for references. You don't ask all the required questions, but you completely fill out the forms."

Trudi leaned forward. What she wanted to do was to say, "I quit." That would mean they could lose the house or at least be forced to sell it and move into a rental house—or worse, a flat.

"I'm not sure which references you are referring to, but the people gave me the information before I asked for it."

He frowned.

"I ask if a person is employed at a place, and the person I'm talking to doesn't just say 'yes,' but 'yes, for the last ten years.' Then I can tick off the box for time of employment and add the years without having to ask." Let him concentrate on what he can't prove.

"Hmmm."

"Is that all?"

Fiedler nodded and waved his hand.

Trudi wished the old manager were back. She wished she wasn't working. She wished her husband and not Fritz were dead. His insurance would pay off the house and give her more than enough to live on with the girls. She'd never felt so trapped in her life.

# CHAPTER 49

*Day 29, Monday*

Trudi began the trudge home. Trudge was the way she thought of it. She was tired, just plain tired, and she still had to pick up the kids at Jennifer Gerber's. Granted, Jennifer was a friend, and she took the girls home for lunch, but she fed them things like sandwiches for God's sakes. Trudi made sure they had a good hot meal with plenty of vegetables and a piece of fruit for dessert, not some packaged cookies.

It wasn't that she didn't appreciate how Jennifer had offered to take over when her first child minder quit even before she started because her mother was ill and she had to go to Schaffhausen to take care of her. Jennifer was there when the call came the night before Trudi was due to start work. Had she not been there, Trudi might have avoided starting.

As Trudi passed the Migros, she decided she should buy some carrots and broccoli to make sure the girls had least one green and one yellow vegetable. That she could no longer guarantee that they had a balanced diet battled with her tiredness and the children's reluctance to eat their big meal at dinner. Both preferred something light.

She hoped Jennifer had checked their homework, although Jennifer had said that she never looked at her own children's. Her philosophy was that it was their responsibility and if they didn't do it, they could just as well suffer the consequences. Trudi suspected it was Jennifer's lack of fluency in German that made her reluctant to perform what Trudi considered just part of being a good mother.

Still the girls did enjoy being there, because Jennifer "makes everything fun" they'd told her. She refused to allow herself to admit she might be jealous of the girls' affection for Jennifer, not to mention her jealousy that Jennifer wasn't working. No matter that Jennifer couldn't work, because she didn't have a work permit.

The line at Migros was long. Trudi tried not to be impatient, tried not to think that before she had had to go to work at the bank she could shop during off hours and avoid high-traffic times.

Why had this happened to her? All her life the only thing she wanted to do was be a wife and mother as her own mother had been. Making a comfortable, inviting home was an art, her mother had said, and Trudi had thought of herself as a second-generation home artist.

At no time did she feel her university education was wasted. Part of being a good mother was reading good books to your children, introducing them to good music and art, talking about history, and explaining a bit of science here and there.

When she and Brett were first married, everything had been fine. She had had a part-time job working in a bookstore. She'd enjoyed that and it had given her enough time to make sure that a good meal was on the table when he came home. The first apartment that they had rented, she'd decorated, making her own drapes. They'd saved to buy each piece of furniture. Both she and Brett had a horror of taking on debt. At least they still agreed on that. However, buying a house did require a loan.

She'd thought that as an American he'd want credit card after credit card, but he'd told her that his father had gone bankrupt when he was younger and it was probably a factor in his parents' divorce and it wasn't going to happen to him. Since he didn't want to talk much about his family, although she'd met his parents and stepparents, she'd treasured that confidence.

Trying to combine their two cultures had been both difficult and fun. Despite Brett spending so many years as a kid in Zurich, he'd been sent to the International School with a mixture of nationalities, so he never really had had a truly Swiss environment.

They could laugh about how when you made a toast, the Swiss wanted to look into everyone's eyes as they held their glasses high. "It can take hours," Brett would say when they were at a large dinner.

On the other hand he'd found *Schumtzli*, the companion to Saint Nicholas who brought coal to bad children on December 6, horrible. He found the Swiss aversion to noise over the top and would ask enough times to annoy Trudi, "Why can't I shower after ten at night?" which was against the apartment house rules where they lived.

Once they had their own house, Brett would shower before he went to bed and after ten. At least one time out of five times, he'd say that was one of the pleasures of owning your own home.

Bit by bit, the differences began to grate on Trudi, although she didn't blame either Brett or herself. She did blame him for the amount of time he spent at work after hours or in his office when he was at home. She felt that he should have been with the three of them during those times.

Then the whole banking problem was like a catalyst that drove an even bigger wedge between them. She couldn't blame Fritz for that wedge. He had come into her life a couple of years before and had shown her so much attention.

He had understood that her free time was limited around her children's needs, which made those afternoons that they'd met at his place even more important. At least three times he'd stopped at her house after Brett had gone to work, but both of them had felt it was too risky even if the danger of being caught had been an aphrodisiac.

If Fritz had lived, she would have left Brett. She would have been generous with visitation rights, for the girls adored their father. Fritz, she knew, was not overly fond of the idea of her keeping the girls. They'd argued about it the day before he died. Their last words had been angry ones.

Before she could think any more about the what-ifs in her life, she'd arrived at Jennifer's. No one answered, although there were lights on in the house.

Trudi imagined that the entire family had been murdered until she heard laughter coming from the side of the house.

She walked around to see her girls, Jennifer's two sons, and Jennifer rolling up snow balls. A snow wolf stood in the middle of the garden; three snow bunnies and a snow chicken were in a half circle around the wolf.

Trudi imagined that their mittens were soaked. Their hands must be freezing.

Hanneli was the first to spy her mother. "*Mutti*, help us. We're building snow bunnies and chickens to attack the snow wolf and drive him back to the forest."

Trudi thought how the children would probably have nightmares of monster wolves. Dinner would take too long to prepare and the girls would be overtired by the time they would be ready for bed.

"Come on, Trudi," Jennifer said. Her face shone red from the cold in the floodlights that allowed them to see what they were doing. "Stay for supper. Call Brett and have him join us, too."

Trudi wasn't sure. Normally events like sharing a meal with others were planned in advance. She wondered if they would have a thawed frozen dinner.

"I've made a beef stew, my grandmother's recipe," said Jennifer. "And I baked some oatmeal bread, also from her recipe."

"Let's stay, can we *Mutti*, can we?" Gisela said. "We helped with the bread and I want to eat it."

"Don't whine," Trudi said as she surveyed the ten eyes looking at her.

Gisela looked down at the snowball in her hands.

Jealousy is not a good thing, Trudi thought, but she said, "All right. Let's call Papa."

The whoops of joy from the girls did nothing to make her feel better.

# CHAPTER 50

*Day 29, Monday*

"Annie, please come down quickly."

Annie was putting on her coat when Petra telephoned. She had been looking forward to getting home, taking a nice hot shower, and settling in for the evening. Something in Petra's voice, not to mention the word "quickly," made her gather up her hat, mittens, and purse. When she found the elevator in operation she rushed down the stairs.

As she entered the executive hallway, she saw Roger carrying Sophie in her travel seat. "Do you know what's up?" he asked.

"Not a clue."

"Petra said it was urgent."

Annie thought a lot of CEOs' ideas of urgent weren't the same as the rest of the world, but most CEOs weren't up on murder charges either. She assumed it had more to do with the murder than with the business or Roger wouldn't be there. She didn't say it to him, because he would tease her that as a detective she was able to guess the obvious.

"Coffee, tea, chocolate?" Petra asked. "I take that back, there's no one to make it, and I don't want to take the time."

Annie's first thought was "how rude," but she said nothing.

When everyone was disrobed of outer clothing, including Sophie, and they were all seated, Petra said, "I've come back from my attorney."

"And . . . ?" Roger prompted.

"I found a new piece of evidence. On the car floor, my car."
She handed Roger a sheet of paper.

"If it's evidence you shouldn't handle it, and it should be given to the police."

Petra frowned. "I'm not *that* stupid. This is a copy."

Roger took the letter. He glanced at it before handing it to Annie. "I don't know Swiss German."

She reached for her glasses so she could read the very small printing. Never had she seen so small and perfect lettering. It was almost as if it were done on a computer in eight-point type. Annie wished that she could write that well. She translated as she read it.

*I love you . . .*

*I know you love me, and the idea that we can start anew in Florida is both wonderful and frightening.*

*I'm writing because every time I try and discuss this, you change the subject, and this is the only way I can think of to make sure you know the single problem we face.*

*I won't leave Switzerland without my girls. As much as I love you, I can't do that to them. Leaving my husband will be easy. I'll pack up and we can all be on the plane.*

*I know you've said that you don't want children. I don't want any more.*

*As soon as the sale goes through, we can be together. I can promise the girls won't bother you.*

*You are my heart, my soul, my life.*

*T*

"Annie, can you translate it a second time?" Roger asked. "I need to absorb it a bit better."

She did.

"Where did you find it?" he asked.

"About three days before he died, Fritz borrowed my car. His was in the garage. *T,* whoever she is, must have dropped it. It was under the passenger's seat."

"And . . ." he prompted.

"When I went to Zurich, my purse fell off the driver's seat where I usually leave it. When I reached for it on the floor, I saw a corner of the envelope sticking out from under the seat." She gave a half smile. "I'm enough of a Swiss German that I want my car to not have any trash."

"Do you have any idea who *T* is?" Annie asked.

"Not a clue. It sounds like Fritz was cheating on the two women he was already cheating on."

"I could be wrong, but although I believe he planned to move to the US, I'm equally sure he wouldn't want to be tied down with any woman, much less one with children. Fritz barely could stand to be around mine."

"So we might have a person with a motive," Annie said.

"Find a married woman with two children whose name starts with *T.*"

"From this area, also," Petra said. "My brother didn't borrow my car long enough to have gone very far."

"Assuming the woman hadn't driven here from anywhere distant to meet him," Annie said.

Sophie, who had been quiet playing with the mobile dangling from the bar of her carry cot, decided now was the time to insist on some attention. It wasn't so much of a cry as a noise that would notify her family that being ignored much longer wasn't an option.

Annie scooped her up. "Talk about needles and haystacks," she said.

# CHAPTER 51

*Day 29, Monday*

Petra was nervous as she pulled into her driveway. The day had been harrowing. Finding the letter from $T$ was wonderful because she thought it might be someone who the police would consider. Her lawyer told her not to be too optimistic, because once the police thought they had the murderer they usually didn't want to consider other clues.

Her lawyer had cursed her, politely, for touching it. He used tweezers to make the copies he gave to her, and put the original in a plastic bag to hand over to the police.

Fritz had never mentioned a $T$ to her, but then if his lover was married, he probably wouldn't. Even shits have some standards, she thought.

Her mind ran through her own friends. Tanya was single so she wasn't possible. Theresa didn't have girls but three sons. Tricia, who was English, wouldn't be able to write Swiss German that well. In fact, she couldn't write any kind of German at all.

So what about his own friends? The two women he was dating were out, both because of their names and lack of offspring.

Roger had said that it would be hard looking for a woman whose name started with $T$ and had daughters. He was right, of course.

Walter's car wasn't in the garage. He was probably still in Zurich with his girlfriend. Had this been the first time he'd cheated on her, she would have been more upset, but after the seventh time when she'd discovered there was yet another woman, she'd stopped loving him. Had it not been for the children she'd have divorced him long ago, although the family tradition seemed to be stay married and do your own thing. That was then and this was now.

And after this now was over and she was cleared of Fritz's murder, she would sort out her marriage problems. With every passing day, divorce seemed like the answer.

The house was quiet when she entered. She went through to the kitchen where the cook was preparing a soup and salad, which she had requested in the morning. The cook told her that the children were in their rooms and the nanny was in hers.

The two oldest at eleven and thirteen really didn't need a nanny any longer. Even her youngest, who was just starting school, could have done without one, but with the nanny in the house, Petra never had to worry about leaving the children alone when Walter was traveling and she worked late at the office.

In her experience with her friends' children it was the boys who were closer to their mothers and daughters to their fathers, but in her family it was just the opposite. The family Ritzman ponied up along gender lines. Alice was still her baby, affectionate and sharing. Perhaps that would end sometime during the teenage years when Alice went through what seemed like the obligatory revolt.

Amelie, named for a maiden aunt of Walter's in the hope she'd leave her money to him—she hadn't—was the most studious of the three. She was also the child who seemed to have the same interest in the business as her mother.

All the children had *A* names. Walter wanted them to be at the beginning of the alphabet, having been at the end of the lists most of his life when first names were used. Ritzman wasn't all that much better.

She walked up the mahogany staircase. One of the bars holding the runner in place looked loose. She thought she must remember to have the housekeeper fix it.

Sometimes she felt guilty about having a household staff of three, but it allowed her the freedom to work and be a mother without the daily drudge chores that most working mothers had to accomplish to keep their households running.

The first door on the left of the upper floor was Alice's room. It had been her own room when she was little and it had the best light. Her daughter was sitting on the bed cross-legged with a large sketch pad in her lap. She said she wanted to be an artist, like her great Aunt Mathilde. Alice had met Mattie when they'd visited Paris and the child was entranced with the studio, the canvases.

"Don't you love the smell of her paint, *Mutti*?" Alice had asked to Mattie's laughter.

Mattie had taken Alice to a museum and showed her works from the Pointillists and the Impressionists. The child had spent the next few months using her crayons and making specks of color to create her drawings.

She would support her children in whatever they wanted to be. As she'd read through Annie's work, she realized that it seemed too many members of her family either had been forced into roles they didn't want or had to fight for what they'd wanted to do.

Walter was against Alice being an artist. He thought girls should get a university education and quoted, "When you educate a girl, you educate a family," and Petra didn't disagree. Except for a minor glitch here or there, their problems overall weren't about how to raise the children.

Alice jumped up and hugged her mother. As much as Petra had wanted to keep the problems away from her kids, she couldn't. The town was too small. Alice had been chided at school about her mother being a killer. So had Adrian, but his method of dealing with it was to beat up the boy who taunted him.

Even if the town hadn't been whispering about the events, Petra and Walter had decided not to shelter the kids. Better that they deal with the facts than let their imaginations run wild. Except for his women, that was the way Walter and Petra ran their marriage.

When Petra asked Alice how she'd dealt with it, when she was first released from jail, Alice admitted half sheepishly and half proudly that she'd taken some of her allowance and paid Albert, the toughest boy in her class, to protect her. Petra felt that no matter what happened in life, Alice would find a way to deal with it.

As for Amelie, she did what she always did when something wasn't to her liking. She ignored it.

"Most of the time it goes away, *Mutti*," she'd said when Petra had tried to point out how the habit could create more problems in the future.

"Not all the time," Petra had said.

"I'll just have to decide when to pay attention and when not." Amelie left the room whenever anything to do with Fritz's murder was being discussed.

"*Mutti*, I asked you three times. What happened with the lawyer?" Alice asked.

Petra told her, adding, "I don't want to raise your hopes too high, but finding that letter is a good thing, and even if the police do nothing we have the detective working on it."

Please, please, please find something Roger, she thought as she watched Alice pick up the sketch pad.

# CHAPTER 52

*Day 31, Wednesday*

The receptionist called Brett, who was meeting with Annie in preparation for the advertising guy coming from New Hampshire early next week. Although it certainly wasn't what she had been hired to do, Annie wasn't complaining. She was having fun.

Brett answered the buzz from the receptionist. "Your husband and daughter are here," he said. "Is it okay if they come down here?"

"Fine with me, if it's okay with you."

Roger appeared holding Sophie on his hip. She reached for her mother with a gurgle. Annie took her and gave Roger a single kiss on his stubbly cheek. Since leaving the *gendarmes* he'd gone with the slightly-needing-a-shave look and was debating growing a beard. Annie was encouraging it, not just because she thought he'd look even more handsome but because it would get rid of the stubble. Sometimes she wondered if men having to shave matched women's monthly periods: probably not. "We have a bit more to do here," Annie said.

Brett motioned for her to go along. "I can finish up." He looked at his watch. "I do have to pick things up at Migros before it closes."

"We've got to pick up some milk and eggs," Roger said. "Give me a list and we can drop it off at your place on our way by."

"I couldn't ask you to do that."

"Why not?" Annie removed a pencil from Sophie's mouth. The baby had grabbed it from behind her mother's ear. "Unless it's hundreds of things."

"Maybe half a dozen," Brett said. He reached into three pockets before he found the list and handed it to Annie, who frowned when she looked at it, and then gave it to Roger, holding it by the corner.

Roger cocked his head as Annie opened her eyes, sending him a silent message.

"Who wrote the list?" Roger had taken it by the same corner that Annie had used.

Brett had turned his attention back to his work. "My wife. Why?" He added another photo to the pile he was gathering.

"It's just the most perfect printing, and tiny," Roger said. "Mine is next to impossible to read." He sent a signal to Annie.

"Mine, too," she said.

As soon as the Young-Perrets were out of the building and in the car, Roger said, "I'm ninety-eight percent sure that is the same writing as in the letter to Fritz."

Annie, who was fastening the baby in the car seat, said, "Me, too. What do we do now?"

"Tell the police, but first we make a copy."

Sophie was getting cranky as Annie and Roger pulled into the police station parking lot. It was their last stop for the day.

They had bought tweezers to handle the list, rather than add more prints. Then they had done the shopping, used the copy machine at the Migros, put the list in a plastic bag, and dropped the groceries off at the Windsors, although neither of the couple had been home. The kitchen door was unlocked, which wasn't all that unusual in the neighborhood. They'd left the purchases on the counter.

The police station could have been located in any of a

hundred cities in a hundred countries: dull walls, many desks crammed together behind a reception desk that was glassed off.

Annie had to be the one to talk. "May we see Feldweibel Nagel, *bitte*?"

"What's it about?" The person behind the desk was a woman probably in her early thirties and quite pretty. She looked too dainty to be a cop, but Annie had learned that sometimes the smaller they were, the stronger.

"The Bircher murder. We think we have some more evidence."

"The case is closed."

"Maybe we should give Feldweibel Nagel the choice."

The receptionist sighed and picked up her telephone.

Sophie was getting fussier and Roger took her and jiggled her up and down. Annie reached into the pack he carried and pulled out a bottle with apple juice, which appeased the baby slightly. Roger sat on the bench outside reception. The baby was losing a fight to keep her eyes open.

A long ten minutes went by before Nagel came out. "I was about to go home."

"We won't take long."

Nagel made no move to let them behind the reception area. "Petra Ritzman found a letter from one of her brother's lovers. She gave it to you."

"How do you know?" Nagel asked.

"She told us. She has a copy and she showed us before giving it to you."

"She's trying to throw suspicion on someone else. We've got the right person." Nagel started back inside then turned. "Besides, trying to find a woman whose name starts with T, who cheats on her husband and has two daughters, would be like looking for that needle in haystack."

"More like trying to find a certain piece of hay in the haystack," Annie said.

278

Nagel almost smiled but seemed to catch himself in time.

Lord knows you wouldn't want a smiling *Feldweibel,* Annie thought. The entire police force would break up. "Look at this, it is almost identical. I imagine if you put a handwriting analyst on it, they'd say it was the same person."

Nagel barely glanced at it. "I can't remember what the other writing looked like, although I seem to recall it was neat."

"That letter was written by a woman who signed herself *T* and has two daughters. This grocery list is written by someone named Trudi, who has two daughters."

"Leave it with me," Nagel said. "Thank you."

He was gone into the bowels of the station before either Roger or Annie could say anything else.

"Do you think he'll do anything?" Annie asked.

"I would, if it were my investigation," Roger said.

"You're not him. Let's go home. Maybe we can do something."

"I don't want you doing anything stupid," Roger said as they left the station.

# CHAPTER 53

Her assignment should have been over by now and the extension time was unclear. In a way she was glad. She would have hated to leave before the murder had been resolved, although she could always find out what happened from Argelès just by checking the Swiss papers online.

Annie pulled one hundred Swiss francs from her French account, using the ATM machine closest to the factory. She no longer had a Swiss account, which had been closed because of her American nationality, but to date her French bank had not decided to close her account. She didn't know any other Americans in Argelès to ask them if they had been threatened with denial of banking service.

Roger had said he had no problem with her having access to an account in his name only, but it niggled at her sense of independence. And if he died, she would be totally without funds at her disposal. This wasn't the current problem.

She needed money to buy laundry detergent. With Sophie in cloth diapers they went through laundry liquid like never before, but she had decided it was cheaper and better for the environment. What she wanted most was for this phase of Sophie's life to finish. That didn't mean she wanted to potty-train her too early, just looking forward to the day that diapers were not a part of daily life.

Roger still called them nappies—but he'd learned English-

English. Nappies or diapers, at least it was temporary.

Her diaper musings came to a standstill when she looked in the bank's window to see Trudi Windsor behind the receptionist's desk. Knowing Roger would disapprove didn't stop Annie from going inside.

"Frau Windsor?"

She noticed Trudi's eyes looked frozen.

"Annie Young-Perret . . . from your party . . . I work with your husband."

"Excuse me." Trudi's face relaxed. "A different context makes it difficult sometimes to put people in their proper place."

"I've the same problem, often." Annie looked at her watch. "It's lunch time. Do you get a break? Maybe we could have a bite together?"

Trudi smiled. "That would be nice. Today?"

"Why not? We're both here. When do you get off for lunch, Frau Windsor?"

"In about ten minutes, if you can wait. And please, call me Trudi. After all, we did spend that evening together."

"I'm never sure, so I err on the side of formality. I'll wait."

They went to the restaurant across from the Abbey. At this point the wait staff knew Annie and asked about the baby.

The restaurant tables were only about half occupied because the lunch hour was winding down.

Annie knew Roger would be furious about what she was planning to do. While they ordered and ate, their conversation was limited to women's topics: the baby, Trudi's girls, juggling work and motherhood.

Annie then switched the topic deliberately. "It's a pleasure working with your husband. He's so creative."

Trudi picked up her fork and poked at her *Apfeltorte*.

Not appreciative of her husband, Annie thought. "It's hard

though for the family when a man spends so much time at work."

Trudi nodded. "It's hard on the girls."

"I've seen it in the marriages of my friends." Annie let out a deliberate sigh. "In a way I wish I had that problem. My husband had a heart attack and had to retire. He acts as a househusband, when I'm working, but when I'm not, he's underfoot. Or maybe he thinks I'm underfoot."

Trudi's nonreaction caused Annie to veer off onto another tack. "It was terrible about Fritz Bircher."

This did provoke a reaction from Trudi. She put down her fork and sighed.

"Did you know him well?"

"Not that well."

"I suppose the police have questioned you recently?"

Trudi picked up her purse and lifted out her wallet. She placed two twenty-franc notes on the table, but instead of leaving she asked, "Why would they do that?"

"I heard they were looking at women whose name started with *T* who had two daughters."

"I don't understand."

Annie could almost hear Roger roaring at her to stop. Good thing he was at home with Sophie. "They found a letter from someone who was obviously his lover. I have no idea what it said."

Trudi sighed. "From what I heard, Fritz had lots of lovers, a real playboy." She looked at her watch. "I have to get back. We peons are watched like hawks for the least infraction and being late is considered a major sin."

"I'll take care of the bill." Annie handed her the money Trudi had placed on the table. "You run back. I'm not on the clock."

"You're lucky." Trudi put the twenties back in her wallet.

★ ★ ★ ★ ★

"You did what?" Roger said.

Annie had waited until they were in bed to tell him. "If the police won't talk to her, someone should."

He stared at her. "*Merde,* Annie. You spoiled what I was going to try."

"And that was?"

"I'm not going to tell you, because you'll probably ruin it."

The couple battled for the next half hour before each rolled over so they were back to back, instead of their traditional spooning position. They stayed that way until morning.

# CHAPTER 54

*Day 32, Thursday*

Trudi's hands were shaking as she pulled off her gloves and unbuttoned her coat.

"Are you all right?" Annick, Trudi's coworker, asked.

Trudi shared an office with Annick, although usually they weren't in it at the same time. One was on the receptionist desk or filing, while the other was involved in the grunt work of verification of loan documents.

Trudi didn't particularly like the woman, although she felt sorry for her. She was a widow with a teenage son who had a learning disability. What Trudi couldn't understand was why Annick was so happy all the time.

She'd come into the office humming a tune and smiling. She'd bring in cookies or a *Torte* she'd made for all to share.

The hardest thing for Trudi to understand was that Annick liked her job. Why? Didn't she find it boring? Tiring? How did Annick manage to handle all the responsibilities of home and her work? Alone?

Although she no longer loved Brett, or even really liked him, he did do the things that a husband should do: maintain the yard, help with the girls, handle all the paperwork. He would have helped with the housework, too, except she'd have to redo it to her satisfaction.

Thinking of Brett brought her back mentally to the letter. Which letter? She'd written many love letters to Fritz. There was the last one when she had gone to his house during the day that he had picked her up at the shopping center. She'd forgotten about it because she hadn't given it to him.

Could it have fallen out in Petra's car?

How could she have been so careless? Precautions had become second nature. Always she wore dark glasses and a coat, a special coat that she put on only when she was to meet Fritz. She kept it in the trunk in a plastic bag. If Brett asked she could say she was giving it to the charity shop. She had a hat in the trunk, too, whose rim hid her face.

When they went to his house, he would drive into his garage so even his distant neighbor couldn't recognize her—guarding against the rare chance she might be there and the even rarer chance she would be peeking out the window. Not that the neighbor had ever met her.

They never had much time because she always had to be back for the girls, but that made the time with Fritz even more special. She knew he had other lovers. In the bathroom would be a lipstick that wasn't her color and once she found a pair of panties.

"I need someone to go out with," Fritz would say when she confronted him with the items. As time went on there were no traces of other women. Maybe he just did a better cleanup. Trudi knew that he still dated, because she'd seen him with a woman when the family went out to eat one Sunday last September, about a week before the cold snap that started the leaves turning color.

Brett had gone to the table to speak to him, but she had ushered the girls to their table and started them on making their decisions from the menu.

It was after that time he started talking about her leaving Brett and the two of them moving to Florida. Only at Christmas did she realize he had not included the girls in his plans, but she didn't deal with the issue for the next few months.

How many love letters had she written? Nine? Ten? Twelve?

Most she had given him to read after they made love and were still under the covers.

To leave one around his house was too dangerous, so after he'd read them she would rip them in shreds even though it made her feel as if she were tearing a piece of herself with each new scrap.

Even the bits of paper she disposed of before going home. Brett almost never looked in her purse, but there was the day he went into it looking for the extra house key that she kept in the internal pocket just in case. That "just in case" could have been a nightmare.

At one point she thought Brett knew what she was doing. She thought she had seen him when Fritz had dropped her off at the shopping center.

What a bad day that had been all around. She and Fritz had argued about the girls being a part of their future, but before they left each other they'd kissed. That she would never again feel Fritz's lips on hers, his hand on her breast and her body coming to climax with his thrusts, made her want to cry.

She couldn't cry in front of Annick, who was still staring at her.

"Lunch may not have agreed with me." It wasn't a lie. What Frau Young-Perret had said hadn't agreed with her.

"I'll go get you an antacid from the medicine cabinet. And a cup of tea." Annick was gone before Trudi could protest, yet she welcomed the time alone.

Better to concentrate on work. Turning on the computer she brought up the loan application for a couple who wanted to buy a flat two streets from where Trudi was living. She'd watched the building go up.

What had Frau Young-Perret said to her about the letter?

She knew she signed all the letters with a *T,* only a *T.* Her fingerprints weren't on file anywhere.

The employer of the woman on the loan application had only an email. Annick would probably look up the address and get the phone number, but Trudi preferred to use email. That way she didn't have to talk to anyone. The bank preferred phone interviews but information was information.

Her mind went over everything to do with the letter again. It had to be, just had to be, the last letter she'd written. They had been in Petra's car. The fight they'd had was the worst. He'd said he would break it off with her if she insisted on the girls being part of their future, and she'd ended up begging him to continue. At the end, they'd agreed to meet the following evening when Brett had a late meeting scheduled and the girls were going to be staying with friends for dinner.

If the police had the letter and guessed who she was, they should have questioned her by now. But there must be lots of *T*'s with two daughters in the area. As far as Trudi knew and from what Brett had told her, Petra was the only one being considered as the killer.

As long as they stayed away from her, she'd be safe.

Annick returned with the tea and the antacid. She'd put the tea in one of the good cups that were usually only used for bank clients. "I hope this helps."

All Trudi could say was "Thank you." Tea and antacids could not solve her problem.

# CHAPTER 55

*Day 33, Friday*

Annie knocked on Petra's door with her free hand. In the other hand she held a printed-out draft of the project. Petra had made it clear she found it easier to read on paper rather than on the computer screen.

Once the woman approved the complete draft, Annie would make final corrections and the last tiny parts of the project would be over except for the translations into French and English, which would be done from home.

Brett would be the one who would have the final book designed. Like the end of any project, Annie felt both sadness and relief.

This assignment had been different. As her work progressed, she'd begun to feel as if she knew the Bircher ancestors personally. The men hadn't impressed her all that much, but she loved the feistiness and imagination of the women. Annabel was the type of person with whom Annie would have loved to share a cup of tea. Her story would make a good novel, but Annie had no idea how she would write fiction. Nonfiction was easy.

"I thought I'd told you, I wasn't to be disturbed," Petra said. "Oh, Annie, it's you."

Roger was sitting at the small, round meeting table in the corner of the room. Two sheets of paper were on the table top. Annie knew without being told it was the letter *T* had written to Fritz and Trudi's shopping list.

"I'm sorry," Annie said. "Where's Sophie?"

"I dropped her off at the *Krippe*," he said.

That he hadn't told Annie his plans to meet with Petra annoyed her. At breakfast he'd been cool, still upset at her conversation with Trudi the day before. They hadn't fought, but their conversation was of the pass-the-butter-thank-you-where's-the-jam type without any of the usual banter.

Annie only nodded. "I'll come back when—"

As she turned to go she bumped into Brett.

"You wanted to see me?" he asked Petra.

"Please sit down," Petra said. "Annie, you might as well stay."

Brett sat next to Roger, who had the letter and list in front of him. Petra was on the other side of Roger. Annie took the remaining chair. She saw that Brett's eyes went to the shopping list and the letter.

"I think you should read this." Petra pushed the letter toward Brett, who picked it up.

The letter took only a few seconds for him to read and absorb. "I don't understand."

"It's your wife's printing?" Roger said.

"It looks like it, yes." Brett drew out each word. He dropped the paper as if it were too hot to hold.

"Roger has been trying to prove my innocence. When I found the letter in my car, I thought Trudi might have a motive."

"This is ridiculous," Brett said. "Trudi? A killer?"

When Petra opened her mouth to say something, Roger held up his hand, then took over. "We didn't say that. All we are saying is that she might have . . . "

"Frau Ritzman, this isn't part of my job description to have my personal life examined. When you're ready to discuss work-related topics, let me know." Brett got up and walked out.

The three of them stared at the door Brett had closed behind him. He hadn't slammed it, but shut it so there was a click.

"What do you think?" Petra asked.

"I think he just discovered his wife has been unfaithful and he was in danger of losing her and his daughters," Annie said. "He needed space."

Roger nodded.

Before Annie could stop herself she blurted out, "I think he killed your brother."

"Don't be ridiculous," Roger said. "Where's the proof?"

"I don't have any."

Roger never accepted it when Annie went on instinct. She didn't claim to have a sixth sense, maybe a five-point-five one. So many times in her life, she'd had a feeling about this or that, and her percentages of being right were in the high ninetieth percentile. "Annie, this is another of your crazy feelings."

Annoyance flashed through her. As a French *flic*, he'd often said legwork combined with instinct was what made a good cop, but he didn't ever credit *her* instinct. If she pointed out what he had believed about the instinct-legwork connection, he would tell her she only had the instinct part of the equation. Even more annoying, he'd be right.

"So what do we do next?" Petra asked.

"Wait," Roger said, "at least until tomorrow."

# CHAPTER 56

*Day 33, Friday*

When Brett left Petra's office, he stopped outside the door that he'd just shut and took a deep breath.

Petra's secretary, Frau Küper, looked up from her computer. "Are you all right, Herr Windsor?"

"A bit of headache, that's all," he said.

She reached into the cabinet next to her desk, pulled out a small medical kit, and produced two aspirins, which she handed him.

"Thank you." He wished he had gone directly to his office and not stopped, so that this woman, who never smiled, wouldn't have noticed that he was upset, but he took the aspirin and waited while she poured a glass of water, which he gulped down with the tablets.

From inside Petra's office he could hear chairs moving. He had to get away before anyone came out. He took the few steps to his office and brushed past his own secretary, who hid a computer game as he passed. Under different conditions he would have told her to be more circumspect. Once inside he stayed just long enough to pick up his coat, neither shutting down his computer nor loading his briefcase.

"Will you be gone long?" This time his secretary noticed him. Her screen showed an Excel spreadsheet. He didn't care.

What was it with secretaries? They noticed every damn thing. "I'm going home. Tell Petra if she asks that I've a headache."

The fresh air was almost a slap in the face as he left the factory. The smell of baking cookies always stayed on his clothes.

Although his car was in the parking lot, he walked home.

Idea after idea on his next move tumbled around in his brain. When he arrived at his house, it was empty. Why shouldn't it be? The girls were in school. Trudi was at work.

He knew he couldn't let the girls come home. He called Jennifer and asked if she could keep them for the night and that he and Trudi were . . . He stopped because he didn't know what excuse to give Jennifer.

"You don't have to explain. They'll love having a sleepover in the middle of the week," Jennifer said. "Work out whatever it is and none of it is my business."

It might be none of her business, he thought, but damn it, he must have set off her curiosity. That Jennifer would say anything to his wife or anyone was unlikely. She was one of those rare women who knew everything, but according to her husband, waterboarding wouldn't get her to reveal other people's secrets.

He walked through each room of the house, his house no longer, his wife's house, the bank's house. Once it had been a happy place. They'd moved in between the birth of the two girls.

Technically Trudi had been a perfect wife, keeping a perfect home. He wasn't sure where it had gone wrong; maybe when he started working longer hours. His job had become his primary focus, something Trudi complained about. The more she complained, the less likely he'd been to come home . . . a circle.

He walked upstairs and into his daughters' bedroom. The girls' bedroom wasn't all that large. It held two small armoires, a bunk bed, a shelf with toys, mostly games and stuffed animals. Both girls had their own narrow desks and laptops.

The beds were made.

Brett sank onto his younger daughter's bed. The duvet cover and pillow case had violets on a white background. Both he and Trudi agreed that the children were not to have commercial characters in their bedroom décor. At least the girls had been one area where they were almost always in sync.

He picked up the teddy bear that was always left in the middle of the pillow. Freddie was its name. He never knew why.

If he could change anything in his life, it would not be his daughters.

He wondered how much time he had.

The house had a wall safe in the bedroom behind a painting from a Zurich gallery they had bought when they were first married. It showed a Japanese theater scene with the orchestra and stage performers in almost cartoon forms. The perspective was from the audience's point of view and the actors on the stage were light colored compared to the dark reds and blues of the curtains.

They had taken almost a year to pay for it. As he lifted it from its hanger, he had to think a moment to remember the combination. He knew he'd written it down on his laptop, the same one he'd left in the office. All his PINs were in his address book as phone numbers.

On the third try the door clicked. Inside was Trudi's sapphire necklace, a wedding present from her father, who'd given it as a peace offering after fighting her marriage to "that American," always spoken with a sneer. Only shortly before the old man's death had he told his daughter that Brett made a far better husband and provider than he ever thought possible.

If only Trudi had appreciated him that much. Brett refused to think that his wife wanted to be in opposition to her father no matter what. He was no shrink.

Their important papers were there: family book, marriage and birth certificates, life insurance policies. Only about a thousand Swiss francs were in the safe, emergency money in case of a computer failure at the bank.

In the back of the safe was a pistol and bullets. It wasn't legal. Trudi hated the gun, accused him of being a crazy American. Maybe she was right in that. He'd felt if he had to defend his family from an intruder, he would have a chance, but he also recognized it as typical American gun-culture thinking. She did point out that by the time he got out of bed, removed the painting, and opened the safe the intruder could have removed half their possessions.

That Fritz's murder was the first in over a decade in the town made no difference. Most of the time he forgot it was there.

He pulled out the gun, loaded it, and set it down next to Freddie Teddy. Maybe that was why his daughter named the bear that. She loved rhyming sounds.

He took out the insurance policies. The house insurance he put back immediately. He kept the life insurance policy and started reading it, cursing the legalese. It would have been bad enough to read them in his mother tongue, but the German was worse.

Brett had never been religious. All his life things had fallen his way, although he had never been afraid of hard work. All through school, he'd gotten good grades. He wasn't the football captain, his senior year, but the vice-captain, which didn't bother him. He'd gotten into the second college he wanted.

The timeline of their problems was unfathomable. No incident, no date marked their transformation from a fairly contented couple into an unhappy pair. He knew that the discontent had escalated when the bank problems started. None of the solutions were reasonable, but the least terrible was to put everything they owned in her name. At that point he'd realized that he had to do everything possible to make her happy.

If she left him, he'd have nothing.

Maybe it was a passing thing. Many couples had flings. He'd been unfaithful a couple of times, one-night stands during marketing conferences. His wife was not the one-night stand type.

As bad as the bank situation had been, and even if the situation had been under-wonderful, Brett could accept that.

What he couldn't stand was seeing Trudi that day in the parking lot with Fritz Bircher. He'd had some art supplies to pick up. That day he'd walked to work. His secretary was originally going to go, but she was in the middle of pulling the monthly sales figures together and she offered him her car.

That his wife was unfaithful was a shock in itself. That she was making out with Fritz Bircher, someone he neither liked nor respected, was worse.

Rather than jump to conclusions, Brett started investigating. First he searched Fritz's office. The man kept some things locked up, probably to do with the proposed buyout. Brett had no trouble hacking into Fritz's email.

He read that Fritz wanted to move to Florida. He read love messages from at least two women. From the tone, he couldn't be certain that Trudi was the one he would take with him, but she could have believed it.

The last time Brett went into Fritz's email with the intention of printing things out, all the messages were deleted. He had had no exact plans of what to do with them, but he still wanted them for whatever came up.

There were new emails where Fritz also had expressed to another friend that he was dropping two of the women because he'd found the one he wanted but she was encumbered. Fritz was sure he could convince her that this would be surmountable.

After that whenever he could and when Fritz left the office,

Brett followed him. Twice Fritz went home. Twice Trudi's car pulled into his driveway and disappeared into the garage. Trudi's affair was no longer deniable.

One by one, he loaded the bullets into the gun.

"What are you doing?"

Brett looked up to see his wife standing in the doorway. "What does it look like I'm doing?" Brett put the last bullet in the gun.

# CHAPTER 57

*Day 33, Friday*

"Annie, stop it," Roger lifted Sophie from the car. "We're going in and have a nice quiet dinner, put the baby to bed, and watch a DVD—not even a detective show. We can watch one of your girlie things."

Annie unlocked the door. Had Roger not been holding the baby, she would have slammed the door in his face. "Girlie?"

"I'm sorry. I just meant something that would please you more than me."

The two German shepherds came up to greet both of them. The dogs were well trained, but their head butts nearly knocked Annie over. She did the acceptable level of welcome recognition before letting the animals into the garden. Walks would have to wait.

"Why should I stop it? I think we should go over and talk to Brett and Trudi. Brett's my friend."

Shedding his outdoor clothes, he began preparing dinner without consulting Annie. "And in the car you said you thought he was the murderer."

"I could be wrong."

"And if you're not, he could be dangerous. Where's the peeler?"

"Dishwasher." Annie busied herself with freeing Sophie from her snowsuit. Maybe because the baby sensed the tension between her parents, she started to cry. Annie resisted saying

"See what you've done?" because it would only escalate the situation.

"We can't leave her alone." Roger began to take dishes from the pantry and put them on the table.

"Could we drop her at Jennifer's? You've become friendly with her."

Roger set the table then concentrated on peeling carrots.

"Could we leave it to chance? If Jennifer says yes, then we go. If no, we won't." Annie had learned a long time ago that giving Roger choices that involved his saving face created a more positive result. It worked.

Jennifer said she'd love to take Sophie. She still had the Windsor girls as well as her own girls.

"We'll be right over," she said.

"But I'm hungry." Roger's tone was almost a whine.

"Better to get it over with." Annie put on her coat and started to dress Sophie. A meal might make Roger change his mind. "Let's take the dogs; they need a walk anyway."

Roger stopped chopping lettuce.

After dropping off the baby they walked around the corner to where Brett and Trudi lived. The walk did not go as fast as Annie wanted, because the dogs were too busy checking canine messages at each tree, then responding in kind.

When they did arrive at the Windsor house it was dark except for one light on the second floor. They shut the gate so that the dogs were in the yard.

When Roger started to ring, Annie grabbed his hand then tried the front door, which was unlocked.

"Brett, Trudi, anyone home?"

At that moment Annie had another one of her insights. This one said how stupid she was and that they should both get the hell out of there. Before she could back away, she saw Brett at the top of the stairs with Trudi in front of him.

"Sorry to disturb you, we were out for a walk and . . ." It was then Annie noticed how Brett was holding his wife.

"I'm sorry, Annie, Roger. You came at a very bad moment," Brett said.

When Annie read a book where the heroine went toward danger, she didn't believe anyone could be that stupid. Her normal instinct was not to put herself in danger. She wouldn't even go on a scary carnival ride. She'd misjudged Brett—that was her mistake. He'd seemed too kind to be violent, but as Roger often said about seemingly kind, gentle people, "So was Ted Bundy." Annie often regretted ever telling Roger about the American serial killer.

But until that moment, she hadn't thought that Brett represented a danger to anyone. Probably one of her stupider moments, justified only in part by her belief in Brett as a decent human. She'd hoped that her flash that he might be the murderer was wrong and that it was Trudi. Either way, they shouldn't have come.

A small part of her refused to admit that she pushed it because of Roger's resistance. She made a vow that if they got out of this, she would try to be more adult about rebellion for rebellion's sake.

"Brett, put the gun down." Roger's voice was a combination of soft and authoritarian. He moved his hand in Annie's direction as if to say, "Don't say a word."

She wouldn't have spoken. What would happen to Sophie if they died?

"I'm not going to hurt you," Brett said.

Annie didn't have a great deal of confidence in this, but then things happened so fast that it was hard for her to believe what she'd seen.

Brett shot Trudi and as she sank to the floor he turned the gun on himself and crumpled over his wife's body.

*Day 38, Wednesday*

"I will never be able to thank you enough," Petra said.

Annie had emailed the last of the corrections on her project the night before. Now she, Roger, and the baby were in the office to say good-bye. Tomorrow they would go to the airport and pick Sharon up, and then they would return the house and dog to their rightful owner. They would leave the day after for Geneva to visit Annie's parents and then on to Argelès.

The last few days had been a flurry of work in between questions by the police, who withdrew their charges against Petra.

When the news reached the public, people whom she'd just begun to know at the plant kept cornering her, wanting to know how she was and what had happened to make Brett snap. He had been thoroughly liked by everyone. A cacophony of comments had swept the company but they all were a variation on the same theme.

"He didn't seem like a man who would kill anyone."

"He was so gentle."

"He was so fair."

"Something must have made him snap."

Annie, Roger, and the police knew what made him snap. If Trudi had left him, he would have nothing, literally not a centime, because everything had been put in her name so they could have a bank account and keep their mortgage.

When he felt she'd take the girls, too, it was more than he

could handle; that was what the police concluded. None of this did she share with those who asked. Her sympathies were with Brett, but not her approval. Even if Fritz was a scumbag, he didn't deserve to be murdered. Scumbagdom wasn't a capital offense, and even if it were, she was against the death penalty.

They finished the last cup of hot chocolate and biscuits that they were ever to eat in the office, because Annie had definitely turned down Petra's offer to take over Brett's post.

As they were about to leave, Petra said, "I know you're wondering what I'm doing about my marriage."

Annie didn't say, "Of course I am," much as she wanted to.

"My lawyer is drawing up divorce papers." Petra's tone had the same emotion as if she had said she had decided to have a cup of coffee.

"I'm sorry," Roger said.

"Don't be. I should have done it a long time ago. The important thing is that he and I will do all we can not to make the children take sides."

Annie swept Petra into her arms in a hug that would have done Susan Young proud. At first the Swiss-German woman stiffened, than she sank into the hug and finally she hugged back. It was Annie who broke the hug, taking Petra by both shoulders and looking her in the eye. "You'll be fine."

"I know I will. The kids are great. The business will stay in the family."

"And Brett's ideas are good. The man he knew from the States . . . "

"Since you won't take the job, I'm hoping he'll join our staff."

Annie didn't point out that if the man moved to Switzerland he probably would not be able to open a bank account, but that would be his and Petra's problem.

Once outside Roger asked, "How much more packing?"

"Not much."

They said little to each other on the short drive back to the house.

"Annie, can we stay home for a while, please?"

"Well, I do have someone who is interested in a project in Edinburgh. And we could stay with a friend who has just lost her husband—a hit and run."

Roger pulled over and turned toward his wife. "Could you sit this one out?"

"I love Edinburgh."

"Can we sit one out?"

Annie didn't think this was the time to mention the Amsterdam, Malta, Montreal, or Stuttgart projects that were possible. Then again, maybe a little time off wouldn't be all that bad.

# ABOUT THE AUTHOR

**D-L Nelson,** is a third-culture adult, raised in the United States but living in Switzerland and Southern France. She is the author of ten Five Star novels, five of which are about Annie and her adventures. Visit her website at www.donnalanenelson.com and read her blog daily at http://theexpatwriter.blogspot.com. She welcomes comments at dlnelson7@hotmail.com.